Earth Legacy
SURVIVAL

LAURIE RYAN

www.laurieryanauthor.com

EARTH LEGACY SERIES

Survival
Enlightenment
Birthright

LAURIE RYAN

DEDICATION

To Candis and Maradel,
who inspire me to make this world a better place
by their tireless efforts fighting
for a healthier planet
and a sustainable future for all.

PROLOGUE

100 Years AGMW (After the Great Magic War)

Wind whistled through the many holes in the weather-worn walls of the small, thatched-roof hut where they'd found shelter for the night. Rianth Royan's father knelt on one knee and splayed his hand flat on the dirt floor. With his long, blond hair untethered and a crazed expression in his eye, he had the look of a wild man, made worse by the fact that he hadn't bathed in days. None of them had. They'd been too busy running.

"They're coming."

The small fire, lit for warmth and to dispel the night's darkness, did not keep Rianth from shivering at the fear she heard in her father's voice. It also did not disguise the changes in him. Damian Royan's shoulders held no sign of the regal bearing she'd known. The man who'd been her rock of strength for all of her ten years looked beaten. That alone terrified Rianth, compounded by a pounding in her head that beat out the wind's screech. The sonorous vibrations grew in intensity. Sounds she couldn't hear swelled to crushing levels. Something or someone drew closer and closer. Doom would visit them this night. She knew it in her soul, felt it, like her racing heart.

Her father stood, taking the small bag he'd always worn from around his neck and settling it around Rianth's. His hands, heavier somehow, clutched her shoulders. "It's up to you now. I'll hold them off as long as I can."

"Hold who off? I don't understand, Father." Her voice, not more than a whisper, shook. How had they gone from peaceful wanderers to a family being hunted by some unknown enemy?

Unknown to her, at least.

"There's no time to explain." He glanced at eight-year-old Uja, who gripped their mother's hand while she writhed on the floor. "Get you and your brother to safety. I know you can do this. You have the power within you."

"What about you? And Mother and the babe?"

Valena Royan screamed, and both Rianth and her father knelt at her side. In the final stages of childbirth, she contorted in obvious pain. Father leaned in to kiss her mother's temple, then whispered unfamiliar words. Her mother's brow soothed and she loosened her grip on Uja's hand.

Boom! The building shook under the shock wave. Another explosion quickly followed. Damian stood, pulling Rianth up with him.

"Your mother cannot travel. And it may be too late

for the babe already. Help as long as you can. But when I tell you to go, do not hesitate. Grab Uja and run. As fast and as hard as you can. Head east. Find the village of New Hope. Find Bhren. He will help you."

"No. I don't want to run. Not without you. I can help you. We can fight together." Rianth pulled the wooden sword from her belt, the one she'd made so her father would teach her to fight. "We can beat them," she said, bravado barely concealing the tremor in her voice.

Her father smoothed her hair with his hand and kissed her forehead. "I'm sorry, my dear. You are too young for this war. Besides, you must save yourself and your brother now. That is your fight."

She dipped her head to keep her father from seeing the tears. He tipped her head up to wipe her cheek with his thumb, breaking her heart with the tender gesture.

"You are the hope of the future, daughter. Do not be afraid to find your destiny." With a last glance at his family, Damian drew his sword and disappeared through the rough-hewn door.

Tears streamed down Rianth's face, sorrow struggling against fear, both overpowering her.

"Daughter—" Her mother's weak voice drew her attention.

Rianth dropped back to her side. "What do I do?"

"Hold the babe as he's birthed. Cut the cord that has nurtured him all these months. Wrap him in my cloak." She gasped. "Feed him goat's milk."

"No. You'll feed him. You'll be here."

"No, daughter. My strength is gone. I will soon pass from this life. And you must run." Her mother's weakened voice held a finality that Rianth did not want to accept. She clutched Uja's and Rianth's hands. "I love you both dearly. And this little one, too." She bit her lip as her entire body tightened. "It's time. Push on my belly, Son. We must finish this now, before all is lost."

Rianth supported the babe's head, her vision blurry as the increasing clash of swords and the escalating booms from outside pulsed through her bones.

Now.

Father? How could she hear him? He was outside, yet it seemed his words filled her mind.

Run.

Yes. She knew her father's voice, even if unspoken. But her mother needed her.

One more push and the babe birthed. Her mother had been right. It was a boy. Rianth sliced the cord with her knife, wrapped the unusually quiet babe in her mother's cloak, and stood.

Run, now. Her father's urgent voice roared through Rianth's head.

"She's not breathing," Uja cried.

Panic consumed Rianth as she turned one way, then back. She couldn't do this. It was too much.

You can. You must. Go. Run. Now. Save—

His frantic words were barely a whisper in her mind now, and infused with emotion. Then, a roar of pain made her shrink back. Uja jumped up and stared at the door. He'd heard it too.

Tears obliterated Rianth's view of her still mother and an emptiness she'd never known before made the agony in her heart hurt even more. She edged to the window, pulled back a piece of the cloth covering it, and almost cried out. Her father lay on the ground, his sword still in his slack hand. Tall, ethereal shapes, barely discernible in the darkness, surrounded him. One stood near, his sword red with blood. Another, taller than the others, leaned over her father.

"I have found you at last. You cannot run from me this time." Even though the shadow did not speak to Rianth, the voice—throaty and low—entranced her, beguiling her to come closer. A calmness settled over her and she reached for the door's handle.

"Ri," Uja whispered. "What are you doing?"

Rianth turned to her brother, saw her mother's body on the floor, the babe in her own arms staring up at her. *What am I doing? What is happening?* She gasped, trying to will the strange enthrallment to leave her, the spell broken by a sharp shake of her head.

"Where is it?" the tall one said. For the first time, Rianth heard the jagged edge of intense anger. "Where is the talisman?" A bony hand grasped Damian by his tunic, yanking him off the ground.

"You will—" Damian gasped. "Never—find—"

His body began to glow, as if heating up. Brighter and brighter he burned, until it hurt for Rianth to watch. When the light dimmed, nothing remained of her father except dust settling to the ground.

The voice that had enthralled her let out a soul-curdling scream of frustration and hatred. So much hatred it hit Rianth like hot coals from a fire, burning hot and forcing her back. She brought her free hand up in an attempt to ward off the wave of emotion. Turning away, she almost cried out when her mother's body started to glow with the same heat as her father's just had. In moments, only the ashes of a life snuffed too soon lingered.

Rianth swiped at her tears with one hand and stared at the babe in her arms. It was up to her now to keep her brothers safe. She glanced outside, saw the shrouded shadows moving toward the hut. Saw golden eyes no longer defined by skin that chilled her to the bone. She knew she must leave with her brothers now, before the fate of her parents befell them.

Stifling the terror of what she'd witnessed and the crushing grief that pulsed in her heart, Rianth held tight to her new baby brother, grabbed Uja's hand, slipped out the back of the hut, and ran.

~~~

Cloaked in robes the color of night, the men walked in a solemn, unwavering line. The cave, large and round, was lit by an eerie glow that emanated from a central, circular stone altar and smelled dank and rotten. Shadows hugged the walls, shrouded figures that swayed to and fro with an unnatural fluidity. The novices approached the altar, forming a semi-circle around it.

No fear emanated from any of the candidates, only the eager focus of the enthralled. Taegar, taller than any person or shadow in the grotto, drank their fervor in, her power swelling as their devotion poured into her. Her euphoria was only temporary. She knew that only the *awen*, Earth's magic, could sustain her for the eternity she coveted. Soon, she would have everything she needed. Soon she would be the most powerful druid and magician of all time.

Soon all would bend to her will.

Damian and the rest of his weak circle thought she hadn't known about the talisman and its ability to bind the right person to the *awen* forever. She'd waited all these desolate years for it to resurface. Taegar's bony hands clenched into fists with a subtle crunch. She'd had it within her grasp when she'd caught Damian Royan.
~~~

Yet the means to harness total control over Earth's power had once again slipped through her fingers.

Damian had surprised her by not having the talisman. He'd hidden himself well since the war, using the druid's sleep as a shield. She'd sensed his awakening several years ago, though attempts to find him had frustrated her at every turn. She knew nothing about his life to aid in her search. Only a tip from one of her disciples sent out in search of him had led her to the empty-handed Damian.

Inside the nearby hut where she'd finally found her old nemesis, Taegar had found only ash. Damian had not been alone, though. A scent wafted in the air, a tinge of fear. Someone else had been there. Someone who may very well hold the key Taegar must control.

Earth's magic imbued light, emanating from the center of the altar, had become tinted with the orange of anger. Taegar slowed her breathing, calmed herself and reached out with her mind. The light dimmed, fighting her until she suppressed its will, forcing the *awen* to blaze with the purity of white that fed the darkness in her soul. She moved forward to the altar and reached into the glowing light, the direct contact permeating her with its potency. She consumed it and the fire consumed her in return.

Taegar raised her head, showing all the golden power in her eyes. One by one, she directed her gaze to the men in front of her. Light shot from her into each of their souls, infusing them with a limited magic. In debt to her by the endowment, they would do anything she asked of them. Little did they know their power was both finite and infinitesimal.

Only she must have unlimited power. For that to

happen, she must find the talisman and bond with Earth's magic. Then, all would be hers. Forever.

Taegar gripped the altar. The time had come to send more of her soldiers out in search. As the light dimmed, she gave each acolyte a silent directive, then watched as they filed out of the cave, knowing they would do her bidding or die in the attempt.

Only when they all left did she slump over, giving in to the weakness that ravaged her each time she tapped into Earth's *awen*. It worsened with each use and now she couldn't even leave this cavern, which held the only stream of magic she'd found. She must find the talisman or she'd be remanded to the druid's sleep by necessity, not choice. That must not happen. She had to find it. She would find it.

Soon…

TRUE-NAMING

CHAPTER ONE

New Hope Village, Seven Years Later

"No! No!" The sounds of battle crashed headlong into Rianth's soul as her father's sword clashed with dark, nameless, shrouded forms. Rianth's mother, with one final moan, pushed the babe out of her body.

"No. Not again. Please, noooo." Rianth watched in horror as her father fell. His death scream filled her anguished mind while she swaddled her baby brother in the cloak her mother would never again need. Deep sorrow dripped in salty tears onto the babe's cheek.

Run. Now. Save—

Again, she wanted to help her father, to save him. Again, she saw piercing golden eyes turn toward her hiding place while a voice laced with venomous honey beckoned. She would not give in. She could not. She must protect Uja and baby Tevy. Though it took all her strength to do so, Rianth turned from the shrouded figure, clutched the babe, grabbed her brother's hand, and fled.

Strong arms held her tight. Rianth struggled, fought, had to get away.

"Shh, shh, shh. You're all right. It's the dream again. You're all right. Listen to my voice. You're all right."

The low whisper filtered through and soothed her like ripples spreading out in the water. "Ri, it's me. Come on. It's just another nightmare. You're safe. It's time to wake up." Something brushed along her hair, over and over again. Slow, methodical, relaxing her and helping the memories to fade.

Rianth opened her eyes slowly, not easily able to let go of the last dredges of panic and fear from the nightly invasions that left a dark chasm of pain in her heart and fresh wounds each time she relived them. One final stab of pain rushed through her before she managed to snuff it. Rianth wilted into the bedding and so did the arms that held her, at least enough that she turned to stare into the sympathetic green eyes of her best friend, Kaiden Darcy.

Her brother's crude wooden toy boat, built with pride and Kaiden's help, lay on the table by her bed, comforting her as much as the arms that held her snug. She was in her own room.

She was safe.

She could breathe again.

"Same bad dream?"

"Same bad dream," she answered, thumping her fist lightly on his chest as she tucked her head under his chin to ward off the chill in the air. The memory was bad. The nightmares made it so much worse. If Kaiden weren't here... If he hadn't started sneaking in all those months ago when she'd first told him about the nightmares, she'd be waking up day after day in a very dark place.

Every night he joined her, and they talked until she could no longer stay awake. He held her tight through each horror that possessed her sleep. At nineteen, the years spent honing battle skills had given him a lean, muscled body and a quick wit, something he rarely showed except with her. She'd hinted more than once that she thought of them as more than friends. He hadn't noticed. Or worse. He'd chosen not to.

She glanced up to see Kaiden staring at her. His eyes were the deep green of the lake they fished, out in the middle in its deepest spot.

He leaned toward her and Rianth held her breath. She could almost feel his lips touching hers. Was now the moment? Would he kiss her? Should she tell him how her feelings were changing, growing? The words were right there on the tip of her tongue. The earth stood still as his breath brushed her cheek, then her world started turning again with jarring reality when he planted a chaste kiss on her forehead and pulled back, his eyes now clouded over.

Rianth's hammering heart plummeted. Before her world righted, Kaiden was off the bed and through the window. He stuck his head back in. "Don't be late for weapon work. You know how testy your instructor gets when you're late." He grinned.

Holding back a smile wasn't easy when Kaiden's grin lit up the room. Once he disappeared, so did her joy. It was hard to let go of the rush and fall of hope in her heart. When would he see her as she was now instead of the ragged little girl who'd fallen into his arms in complete exhaustion all those years ago?

Those days had been dark and full of danger. She and her brothers had survived only because of her sense for danger and Uja's uncanny ability to find herbs and edible plants. Always running, looking over their shoulders, waiting for golden eyes to find them. Waiting for the same fate as their parents.

Seven years they'd been in New Hope and still Rianth wondered when the danger would return. Deep inside she knew the respite could not last. Pulling Kaiden's pillow over her face, Rianth searched for comfort in his pine scent. She caught a hint of lavender and laughed. He must have grabbed the girls' soap by mistake again.

The faint sound of swords clashing drifted into the room, reminding her she was about to be late for practice, again. She leapt out of bed, threw on yesterday's clothes, and rushed out of the small hut she shared with her brothers, strapping her sword and scabbard on as she ran. She left her cloak on its hook. She didn't need it to ward off the winter chill. The sweat of a hard workout managed that just fine.

~~~

The harsh clash of swords grew louder as Rianth hurried to the training field, her breath huffing in the cool air, her unsheathed sword ready to join the battle. Rounding the last building, she sensed the whoosh of the sword before she heard it.

Clang!

Sword met sword as she stopped her opponent's downward cut. Adrenaline pumped through her veins with rabid intensity as she stared into deep green eyes, their heads close enough that their breathy fog mingled.

"As expected, you're late," Kaiden said.

Rianth tried desperately to slow her breathing so he wouldn't know she'd run all the way. To distract him, she
~~~

leaned in further and sniffed. "And you smell like a girl."

"You are going to pay for that," he said.

And she did.

In a village mostly sequestered from the world, where the only hunting was the necessity for food, there wasn't much call for weapons. Yet Bhren, druid and village elder, required everyone to learn a battle skill. Most grumbled about the required training. Rianth welcomed it. Never again did she want to feel helpless.

Today, the field that had been cleared of trees years ago was full, and swords and sweat flew in every direction in spite of the winter's cool temperature. Rianth knew the others were there without seeing them, knew they weren't a threat. None of them mattered. Only Kaiden, whose attack came from all corners.

Up, down, wide sweeping arcs, direct thrusts.

Rianth parried, dodged, and met each swing of his sword with her own. Minutes ticked by uncounted as they fought, Rianth patiently searching for the hole in Kaiden's armor. In all the years she'd been sparring with him, she'd never once seen a flaw in his technique or a weakening in his ability. It was uncanny. Add in the power he'd come into since his True-Naming, and no one ever bested him on the training field.

That didn't mean she wouldn't try every moment, and with every swing of her sword. Rianth's arms burned and sweat stung her eyes, yet Kaiden looked as fresh as when they'd begun. Her muscles were close to giving out when she finally saw it. His sword dipped. A flaw?

Rianth didn't strike. *Bide your time*, he'd told her over and over again. Wait for the perfect instant to attack.

They continued, moving back and forth across the field. Two more times he dipped his sword. The next time it happened she took full advantage of his error and struck, only to have her legs swiped out from underneath her.

"Oomph." Rianth hit the ground hard, the wind knocked from her. A cloud of dry, dusty soil settled around her as she heaved deeply to regain her breath. She opened her eyes when cold steel touched the skin of her neck.

She'd been played.

Kaiden stood over her, grinning. "Never assume that a flaw in fighting is a true weakness. It can as easily be a ruse meant to draw you in, as I've so aptly displayed."

Respect and admiration for his ability and knowledge welled up in Rianth, but she'd be damned if she'd give him the satisfaction of saying it. Instead, she glared at him.

"Say it," Kaiden ordered.

Rianth tightened her lips.

The flat side of the sword pressed deeper into her neck.

"Say it."

"No."

Kaiden leaned closer, his eyes fierce with joy as he spoke for only her ears. "Say it, or I'll tell them"—he nodded his head toward the group of trainees who'd stopped their own sparring and stood watching—"that you snore like a boar in heat."

"I do not!"

"Trust me, Ri. You do. I know."

Kaiden had sworn her to secrecy about their nightly ritual. It frustrated Rianth that he didn't want others to know. He said it would confuse things. She stared at him. "You won't tell them. You don't want them to know how you know that."

The flicker in his eyes told her she'd found the defect in his demand, but the reaction quickly disappeared. He turned to the others. "Did you know that Rianth—"

"Fine," she ground out, unwilling to chance it because Kaiden could bluff better than anyone.

Kaiden grinned and stood. "Say it."

Rianth bit out the words. "You are, as always, the supreme, most dangerous of all fighters, almighty Kaiden." She said it loud enough to be heard by the others. He'd make her say it again if she didn't.

"Don't you forget it," he said, pulling back his sword and helping her up.

"Arrogant—"

"What?"

Someone nearby chuckled and Rianth glared in their direction, sending half the group scurrying away. Kaiden called them back. "Let's work on some team attacks."

Back-to-back, they made short work of their opponents. As a foe, Kaiden drove her to, and sometimes beyond, her limits. Yet, when they fought for the same side, he never let her get far away and always had her back. Rianth knew she could count on Kaiden in a fight. He was strong and principled. Too principled by her reckoning.

Rianth glanced around when they'd finished for the morning. Her brother Uja once again hadn't joined them on the training field. All students were expected to learn either swordsmanship or bow and arrow skills in addition to Studies and apprentice work. Uja hated both. More than likely he sat in the midst of the growing fields, a place everyone knew as his favorite and where, she had to admit, his skills excelled.

Tevy was here, though. The seven-year-old raced full speed, crashing headlong into Rianth. Only her quick reflexes kept them both from tumbling to the ground, and she laughed at his enthusiasm.

"You were great, Ri!"

"Thanks, little brother," she said, trying to maintain a straight face as she tightened his cloak around him. "You know the rules, though. No entering the training field until all swords are sheathed." She slipped her own sword into its scabbard.

Tevy's enthusiasm was not to be diminished. He stabbed and sliced the air with his own wooden sword. The very same sword Rianth had made to spar with her father. That and a small knife had been her only weapon in those terrifying first weeks after her parents' deaths. She loved that her baby brother, who'd never known his father, now got to use it.

"You held him off right to the end in that fight," Tevy said, still grinning like a dog waiting for a treat.

And then I fell for his trickery. She should have known better. Kaiden would do whatever he had to when it came to making sure she was ready for any possible event. He worked tirelessly to keep New Hope prepared as well. Duty meant everything to Kaiden. She wanted the same safety for her home, but knew there also had to be more. Maybe he just didn't believe in anything beyond duty. Rianth stifled a shudder. That seed of doubt never really strayed far from her mind. Or her heart.

"You tricked me," she said.

Kaiden nodded. "And I will again. Never make assumptions. Where your safety is concerned, you *must* prepare for all possibilities."

Safety. One of Kaiden's favorite words. Safety and

duty. Nothing else.

"What are you doing on the field, Tevy?" Kaiden said, ruffling her baby brother's blond hair.

"Kaiden, you were mag…mag…mag…"

"—nificent!" Kaiden finished, laughing.

Rianth rolled her eyes as they walked off the field with an animated Tevy between them. Tevy. Angel. Her mother had mentioned that name months before his birth, so she'd honored the memory. The stab of losing both her mother and father still ran deep, especially with her dreams as a constant reminder. She'd give almost anything for a night's tranquility, for dreams not filled with horror and pain.

So much had changed in these peaceful few years. Those first weeks running from golden eyes, too young herself, Rianth had carried and tugged both her brothers across terrain seasoned veterans rarely traveled. They ate plants and winter berries for breakfast, lunch, and dinner, and sometimes a rabbit if they were lucky, giving them much needed protein. Something or someone had looked out for them during that time, because each day, a milk-laden goat had appeared to provide sustenance for baby Tevy. Somehow, following weeks of travel and on the brink of exhaustion, they'd fallen into New Hope, and Bhren.

After being the leader of their little trio for so long, Rianth had fought anyone who tried to help them at first.

"I know you're used to being the boss, Ri," Kaiden had said. "But you're home now. You're safe. Don't ignore the wisdom of those who have more experience."

Over and over again, he'd reminded her of that. It had taken a long time to meld her role as pseudo-parent to Uja and Tevy with the village's perception that she was only a child herself. Even now, Rianth knew she could stubbornly overlook what she was told to do in favor of what she thought she should be doing.

Maybe that was because she didn't know where she fit in. Everyone knew what they were meant to do, except her. The only thing she'd ever done was to keep her brothers safe. When Bhren had accepted her as his apprentice, the turmoil inside her had finally begun to settle down. To some degree, at least. Rianth still wasn't much for conformity. But now she had a purpose to her days. And she had a reason to exist other than to care for Uja and Tevy.

She shivered, missing her cloak, and looked at the gray sky to gauge the time, realizing she would be late for one of those routines. "I've got to get to Studies."

"And I've a meeting with Bhren," Kaiden said. Any laughter disappeared as his eyes turned somber. At his True-Naming, Kaiden had been named *thurisaz*, protector, which meant he now met with Master Bhren regularly. Rianth assumed that was to keep track of how things were proceeding with the students, the village, and, well, everything, since the druid oversaw most decisions and choices for New Hope.

Why would meeting with the master worry Kaiden?

"Tevy, go help your brother. He's probably in the growing field," Rianth said.

After her brother ran off, Rianth stopped Kaiden with a hand to his arm. "What's wrong?"

"Nothing that I know of," he said with a glance at the druid's two-story tower. He smiled, but it did not reach his eyes, and his shoulders remained rounded.

Something worried Kaiden. History reminded Rianth that getting Kaiden to talk when he didn't want to was nearly impossible. Duty bound his tongue more and more often lately and she did not like the wedge it created between them.

Warmth from the morning's workout had dissipated. Rianth hugged her tunic tighter. The chill of winter seemed permanently embedded in the grayness around them. She didn't remember a time when it had been cold for this long. There'd been no snow, yet it seemed like the world had put the sunshine to bed and gone to sleep. Was this some sort of omen?

The village bell tolled the Studies hour, giving Rianth no choice but to leave thoughts about the weather and other mysteries to another time and pick up the pace. Convincing Kaiden to talk would have to wait for a quiet moment later. She was about to be late for the second time this morning.

CHAPTER TWO

Bhren untied the leather strap that held his long, white hair while he looked out on New Hope from the second floor tower window of his keep. He had searched the lands for anyone with an ability to touch what Earth magic still remained, brought them together, and helped them create this place of *wunjo*, a place of harmonious existence where they all worked toward finding a better life for all. The weight of New Hope's subsistence lay heavily on his shoulders. The whole world, really. In his travels he'd seen the proof. This depression had left an indelible mark on every corner of life. He did not know how to make things better for them. Or for the world they shared. Dark days were encroaching, getting nearer and nearer as Earth weakened further. Soon nothing would help.

No, that wasn't true. Bhren toyed with the signet ring on his forefinger, running his thumb over the oak tree embossed in the metal, remembering when the ring had been designed to denote his druid circle. He knew there would be a catalyst to change things. He simply didn't know the when, or the who.

He heard the few students in Studies reciting passages in the building next door. She sat among them—Rianth Royan. He'd known she would find him. The runes had foretold this. And he knew her heritage, which was why he'd forbidden her or her brothers to mention their family name to anyone. He'd hoped these past seven years that she might be the conduit that would again release the *awen*. Yet extensive one-on-one training had yielded no sign of any ability. Kaiden, the strongest of anyone in the village, had shown an aptitude and strengthened ability to protect before his True-Naming. Afterward, his power had grown more. Not enough to give Bhren hope, but enough to know he must continue to seek the answer.

He'd prayed that search had ended; however, magic, and how to bring it forth, eluded Rianth, and Bhren had not been able to determine the reason. Now, instinct told him they were running out of time.

After the Great Magic War, he'd gone into the druid's sleep to recover strength wiped out by battle. He'd awoken prematurely more than four score years ago, sensing trouble. Bhren had tried to free Earth's *awen* himself to no avail. His own ability remained almost depleted. To prepare for the inevitable fight ahead of them, he'd traveled extensively, gathering together anyone with any talent for touching what little was left of Earth's magic. The state of humankind had shocked him. Very few had survived the war. Only pockets of small villages remained in a world that had once teemed with life, and the struggle to live continued to be a daily battle, even in the smallest hamlet. If the prophecy did not fulfill itself soon, it would be too late. There would be no one left to save.

Bhren moved to the fireplace and warmed his hands, indecisive on what action to take. After staring into the fire for too long, he reached for his rune bag, hefted it, and felt the solid weight that normally reassured him. An uneasiness had settled deep in his belly. The belief that something was close, something dark and dangerous. A familiar something, with the flavor of…no. He shook his head. It couldn't be them. They'd been sent to the final sleep all those years ago. He and the other Guardian druids had seen to it personally. The price had been steep. Only a few Guardian druids had survived to guard Earth and humanity. Now, he was the only one left.

An uneasiness grew in him each day. Things were changing. He sensed it. The weather struggled. Earth's equilibrium had worsened. A storm brewed, one he might not be able to guard against. The deep sleep had not been able to stop him from becoming an old man.

Enough. It was time to determine what must be done, how he could help mankind forge a better life working in concert with the ravaged planet so all might thrive.

Bhren ignored the manuscripts that were shelved on every wall and lay in open piles on almost every surface. He spread a white cloth over the dirt circle that took up most of the round central table in the room. He then emptied the bag of runes into his palm and tossed them onto the cloth, intoning the words of foresight as he had so many times before.

He stared at the stones for a long while, leaning heavily on the table and barely breathing as the reality of this foretelling sank in. Things were clearly coming to a crossroads and danger lurked much closer than he'd thought.

When Bhren stirred, he returned to the window, gazing toward the room Rianth sat inside of. Her life was about to change in a very big way and he did not know how to guide her on this journey. He wasn't certain, after what he must do, that she would even let him try.

Kaiden crossed the commons, New Hope's central area, on his way to their daily meeting. Bhren gathered his runes and tucked the bag into his tunic. His life was about to transform also. All Bhren could do is hope that both Kaiden and the girl came through their ordeals stronger, ready to take on the danger that approached much too quickly.

~~~

Kaiden stared toward the Studies room long after Rianth had disappeared inside the door, wishing there were a way to give her some of the honesty she deserved. Something was wrong. He knew it, but had nothing to back that up. Rianth wouldn't stop at that, not until her curiosity was satisfied, and there lay the problem. He'd known she was strong-willed when she first stumbled into New Hope and into his arms. Literally. He remembered the day like it had happened yesterday. Bhren had called him to the druid's tower…

"Someone comes," Bhren said.

"Who?" At twelve years old, Aiden, the name he'd gone by before his True-Naming, found himself easily confused by the old druid. The man was enigmatic and secretive. Aiden didn't understand a lot of what the man spoke of and got answers less than half the time he asked.
~~~

Bhren tied his long, white hair, a contrast to his dark skin, with a leather string as he hurried down the steps with Aiden following.

"We must find them. We need supplies."

Again, Aiden did not understand the urgency or who it was they must find. He would follow Bhren, though. The druid had convinced New Hope to take Aiden in when he'd been orphaned, and the druid leader seemed to have taken a personal interest in him. Aiden hoped to become his apprentice, and he trusted him.

Bhren slipped a baby bottle full of goat's milk into his pack as they stocked provisions. Just how detailed were these instincts of his?

They strode out of New Hope within the hour, heading north, deeper into the hill country, Bhren resolute on their direction. It took them half a day of hard walking with Aiden fighting to keep up with the long-legged druid.

A plaintive, quick wolf howl stopped Bhren in his tracks. He held up a hand. "They are close."

Aiden didn't have to listen very hard to agree. Whoever Bhren searched for, they were definitely close. He could hear the ragged breathing and stuttered footsteps of someone beyond exhaustion. Where were they? The sound seemed to come from everywhere. Aiden had not yet learned to track effectively. He closed his eyes and took a deep breath, then another. He reached out with his senses.

"There." He pointed west. "They are coming from that direction."

He ran, Bhren's urgency mingling with his own concern that someone was in trouble. Stealth wasn't important. He must find them. Aiden stopped to get his bearings. Suddenly, from behind the tree he stood near, a form lunged at him. He could do nothing but sink to the ground as it fell into his arms.

"A girl," he whispered. At least, he thought it was a girl. The dark, matted hair and dirt streaked face made it hard to tell. Amber eyes pleaded with him, then gave up and closed. Aiden clutched her to him. Something deep inside him stirred, warning him that he must protect her at all costs. Nothing else mattered. He didn't know why, but he'd done well so far trusting his instincts. Now was not the time for questions.

Rubbing her arms as well as he could, he tried to warm her from the chill of winter. The bundle she carried moved, surprising him. Aiden pulled the cloth aside. "A babe!"

"Hold them," Bhren said. "I'll start a fire. We must warm them and get some food and water into them."

Aiden nodded, trying to will his own body heat to warm the girl and the babe. It took a bit for him to hear the whimper. It didn't come from her. He looked around, and finally saw the small hand holding tight to the tree.

"Come here," he said. "I won't hurt you. We want to help."

A boy, not much younger than the girl, stepped around the tree.

"It's all right." Aiden soothed. "Come, warm yourself."

It took only a moment for the boy to decide, then he launched himself headlong at Aiden, almost bowling them all over. Aiden opened his cloak further, wrapping it around the rail-thin boy. The four of them sat huddled together, Aiden doing everything he could to warm them, to help them survive. They must survive.

"I've got water," Bhren said, holding out a cup.

The boy grabbed it and gulped the liquid down.

"Slow down," Bhren said quietly, refilling it and handing it back to the boy. "Sip it or it will make you sick."

"Do you…have any food?" the boy asked.

"Yes. Momentarily. Let me see to the others."

After the boy sipped the cup dry, Bhren filled it a third time and handed it to Aiden. "Dribble this into her mouth."

"Will she wake up?"

Bhren put his hand on the girl's forehead and bowed his head. "Yes," he said when he raised back up. "She will. They all will. If we act quickly." The fire's heat spread out, and Bhren took the babe from the girl's slack arms. He put the bottle to its mouth and the babe latched on hungrily.

Wolves began to howl all around them. Aiden didn't sense danger. Rather, they seemed to be grateful, even content. Wolf sounds formed a perimeter around Aiden and the others.

Nothing will harm you this night, the wind whispered.

Aiden shook his head, unsure of what he'd heard. He must be more tired than he thought. Still, the thought reassured him. He looked down again at the girl. Her eyes fluttered open and a smile touched her face as her hand reached up to touch his cheek.

He saw the moment reality crashed back into her conscious mind. Wide eyes filled with terror as she pushed against him, stronger than he'd expected. She leaped up and backed a few feet away with surprising strength, her hand pulling a knife out from inside her tunic. She waved the knife back and forth between Bhren and Aiden.

"Who are you? What do you want with us?"

Her voice, barely more than a frog's croak, held steel in it. Aiden respected that even as he held his hands up. "We will not hurt you. We"—he waved a hand between Bhren and himself—"only want to help. Look at the babe," Aiden said, pointing to the nearly drained bottle.

Bhren nodded for him to continue.

"We have food. Water. Warmth. That's all. Please." He held out his hand. "Let us help."

The knife wavered. She stared at the babe and the bottle, then pointed at Bhren with her knife. "Who are you?"

"I am Bhren."

Her eyes widened. "Bhren?" she whispered. The knife dropped and her shoulders drooped. "I've found you. Finally." She wavered, her body shifting back and forth. Her legs gave out and she collapsed to the ground, saying "we found you" over and over again.

Aiden helped her nearer the fire and put a cup of water in her hands. "Sip," he said, echoing what Bhren had told the boy. "Small sips, then we'll get you some food."

That had been seven years ago and Kaiden had never wavered in his need to keep them safe. To keep her safe. Now, as she disappeared inside for Studies, he turned to the druid's tower and saw Bhren in the second floor window, a deep frown on his face. Something was definitely changing. He walked slowly up the stairs, certain he wasn't going to like what he heard this day.

"Is the girl pressing you for information?" Bhren

said without preamble when Kaiden entered.

He nodded. "Yes." No sense in denying it. Everyone knew Relentless Rianth, especially when she wanted to understand something.

"What did you tell her?"

"Nothing." How could he? He didn't know anything, except some vague premonition that peril was coming and she was somehow involved. Bhren's interest in her proved that. As True-Named protector, Kaiden worked closely with Bhren. Still, because of his youth, he did not often speak his frustration and generally deferred to the druid's wisdom. Today, he could not keep quiet. Not where Rianth's safety was concerned. "I can't protect her if I don't understand the danger."

"I know." Bhren left the window and sank to a chair beside the biggest piece of furniture in the room, a round table with an inner circle full of dirt. This, in itself, was a breach of norm. Kaiden had never seen Bhren sit down except to eat in the hall. Unsure of what to do, Kaiden stood still and waited.

Bhren bent over, his loose, white hair hiding his face, his hands clutched tight, tapping his forefingers together. He stared at his hands for a long time, mumbling to himself. "What is the right thing to do? I cannot see a clear path." The old druid's ramblings turned to a silence that filled the room.

When Bhren jumped up from the chair, he startled Kaiden.

He waved his hands at the bookcases surrounding them. "I have all these books. I have gathered them all these years, studied tactics, science, the dark religions. I am a scholar, as much as one can be in this age. Yet I cannot determine what to do."

Kaiden leaned his hands on the table. "It seems simple to me. We do what must be done to protect New Hope." *And Rianth.*

"It is never simple. My life's work has been to bring the *awen* back, and I have not succeeded. In fact, the one time I tried, it drove the magic deeper into hiding. This"—he nodded out the window—"life of ours is my fault."

"How can our existence be your fault? My understanding is that life has been meager at best for a hundred years or more." Kaiden sat, running his fingers through the dirt in the middle of the table, more confused than ever. "How could the magic be hiding? It was destroyed at the end of the Great Magic War. It's gone, or mostly gone."

"Do you know how old I am?"

Kaiden didn't know how to answer. He'd heard the rumors. He wasn't sure if he believed them. Bhren had always asked for the truth from him, so he kept it simple. "Old."

Bhren laughed, the sound harsh and anything but happy. "Yes. Old. Very old. Old enough to see that things are worsening. The soil is less capable of nurturing life now than even a few years ago. " He kept nodding, speaking more to himself than to Kaiden. "Old enough to know things are changing. The war that we thought ended it all perhaps didn't."

"We?"

Bhren held out his hand for Kaiden to see. "This ring, this oak tree, is the symbol of the Guardian druids."

"*You* were a Guardian druid?"

"I still am. The last one. I am *tiwaz*—rune mage, protector, seer. And possibly the only one who can hold off what's coming. We chose the best way back then. At least, we thought it was best. Now, I can only hope we chose right. Only the future can judge that. I must focus on what I perceive is happening and pray that it isn't."

Kaiden raked both hands through his hair, perhaps more confused now than when he'd entered the room. "Master, if you are telling me this, you must need my help. I do not understand what you are talking about."

"I know. I know."

Kaiden pulled his chair closer and waited.

Bhren hung his head, drawing a deep breath before raising it. "I cannot explain everything, but I can tell you this. When the *awen* first appeared, some humans grew angry that they could not manipulate it. Some were able to, some weren't. One of the ungifted subverted one of our circle, convinced this druid that the magic should be used for a more…focused purpose." Bhren shook his head. "Our circle was devastated. The ensuing war went beyond anything we imagined and almost depleted our own abilities. Earth magic all but disappeared, and we had to make certain, until it returned, that no one else could access it and turn that power to their own uses. The prophecy was created and safeguarded, imbued with the powers of the Guardian Circle. If any of us tampers too much with how this unfolds, the *awen* will be gone forever."

Bhren stood and paced the floor for a long while before continuing. "So you see, Kaiden, you must not tell her anything. You can't tell anyone, or what little is left of the magic will disappear."

Shock stilled Kaiden's voice. He tried to make sense of what Bhren had told him. The Guardian Circle had used their magic to make sure no one else could manipulate the power when it returned? It was hard to believe anyone ever harnessed enough power to do that. More importantly, this seemed very close to meddling with the future. Hadn't Bhren said doing that would have dire consequences? "Why did you tell me this?"

"I see things, can foretell certain things, but it's as if a fog overshadows it all. I believe change is coming. I do not know whether that change is good or bad, and I cannot watch for it on my own. I am old. My magic is almost depleted. I need your eyes, your ears, and your loyalty until this is seen through."

Barely a year past his True-Naming, Kaiden was not ready for the weight of this burden. At nineteen, he had plans. Dreams. Yet, he'd been born to do this. His heart—his entire body—told him this was his life quest.

Rianth would not easily tolerate him keeping more secrets from her. Would the relationship he'd hoped might blossom survive? Kaiden doubted it. Quicksand swallowed the future he'd planned for until nothing was left. There was no hope at all if he could not keep Rianth safe. That was the only thing that mattered. To do that, he must set himself apart.

A new purpose helped the deep sadness within him ebb and Kaiden straightened. He'd been named *thurisaz* for a reason. He must live up to that name.

Kaiden nodded to Bhren. "You have it. My eyes, my ears, and my loyalty." *But not my heart...that will forever belong to someone else.*

Bhren nodded, accepting Kaiden's pledge. "Good. Because there is more I must tell you."

CHAPTER THREE

Studies began the exact same way, with a recitation of the One Prophecy. Day after day, week after week, year after year.

Shattered by darkness the magic vanished.
It lays in wait for one who's banished.
Hidden power will blossom anew.
Only by passing the darkness through.

Rianth knew these words well. All the students did. Looking around the small mud and stucco building that served as the Studies room, she saw the usual boredom on the faces of the others. Senseless Anniah flicked her straight, black hair and stared out the doorway. A year younger than Rianth, she seemed more interested in following Kaiden around like some simpering puppy than being stuck in this room. Like he would even look at those teardrop brown eyes of hers in that way. Would he?

He'd better not. Rianth turned away, unwilling to even entertain the idea.

The blank stare and small smile on Mokie's face meant he was planning yet another joke on his next victim. How he managed to do that, Rianth did not know. He, too, was younger than Rianth. And he'd not had his True-Naming. Yet he had an uncanny knack for stealth. How could anyone surprise people with that flaming red hair? Was it magical ability?

While the room baked because of the usual too hot fire their teacher kept going, the others in the room recited the prophecy words by rote.

New Hope had survived for all these years not by searching for some long gone magic, but by the hard work of its people. Tilling soil that did not easily nurture, hunting animals too sparse to sustain them comfortably, seeing sunshine more clouded than bright and a sun that looked more like a watery reflection of itself than a smooth, round orb. Every part of life here was a constant struggle and took the time and effort of everyone. Rianth understood why the others did not want to be here day after day. After Studies, each went to their assigned jobs and it would be after the dinner hour was complete before they could indulge in choices of their own.

Life hadn't always been this way. Bhren had taught her some of the history, both before and after the Great Magic War. Humankind had thrived in great cities beforehand, with all sorts of wonders to make their lives easier, as well as so much food that they threw away the excess. Machines carried them from one place to another. There were large animals, like cows that gave milk, and horses that were ridden and raced. Those had been the first to succumb to the destruction. Nowadays, it seemed the wasting planet fought their will to live at every turn. Plants withered instead of growing, natural springs dried up. It all made no sense, since the teachings drilled into Rianth over and over again said that the magic had come to heal the earth, and the druids had become focal in facilitating that. The Great Magic War had not only wiped out most of humanity, it had done major damage to man's relationship with Earth. At least, that's what Bhren said. The prior winter had been their harshest to date, causing Rianth to wonder if Earth and mankind would ever be able to get along again.

For now, they must each do anything and everything to help the village survive. Rianth suffered an extra layer of responsibility. Bhren had chosen her to take private studies with him. Kaiden had been the only other apprentice who worked directly with Bhren, until a couple years ago when Rianth had told Kaiden what her father had said, thinking he might understand it better.

You are the hope of the future, Daughter. Do not be afraid to find your destiny.

Kaiden had told Bhren, who'd since taken an interest in Rianth, his ageless, obsidian eyes always on her. Always searching for the seed that would bring the magic again and heal the earth. She was destined for greatness, apparently. Why else would Master Bhren spend so much time with her? All that extra attention had to mean something, right? It had to mean she had power within her just waiting to burst forth. Maybe even *the* power. The thought had exhilarated her until reality brought her crashing back to the ground. She had no special talent. Each person in the village seemed to have some magical ability. Kaiden had strength and cunning in battle, even more since his own True-Naming last year. His adoptive mother's ability to speed healing must be magic enhanced. Mokie could hide just about anything, which lent credence to his practical jokes.

Not her. If she'd had even an iota of power, she would have done more to save her parents. That slice of pain still cut deep. Rianth missed them each and every day and wished so much that they were here to guide her. To see Uja's flourishing gardens, and Tevy's extraordinary happiness.

Everything Rianth tried, except maybe sword fighting, she seemed to do badly. In the privacy of her own mind and heart, Rianth dreamed of finding her place in this world, of maybe even being the one who could unlock the magic, heal the earth, and give her people a better life.

Logic always crushed that hope. The prophecy had nothing to do with her. No one had ever banished her.

Run. Now. The brightness of her world dimmed as the words crashed through her. To this day, the thought of her father's words brought the sting of tears to her eyes. The memories always hit her out of the blue and always bit deep into the unhealed hole in her heart.

"Student." A stick rapped a quick staccato on the back of her chair.

Rianth snapped to attention.

"Repeat."

With no clue what passage their teacher had dug into today, Rianth could only shake her head. She was in for it now. "I am unable to, Master Deakon." He was the only one in the village who required them to add a rank to his name, except for Bhren.

The disapproving frown aged his angular face. Master Deakon seemed older than his dark, brittle, over-washed hair evidenced. At times, Rianth and her friends had wondered if he'd found some alchemist way of keeping it from graying. The amount of time the man spent in the showers had been a constant source of humor to them all. However, as a rule, they all avoided him whenever possible, mostly because of his inquisitive questions and disapproving demeanor. The man seemed bent on knowing everything about the people of New Hope, even as he held himself above them.

"Since student Rianth does not see fit to focus in class, we will all start at the beginning and will stay until we've completed this lesson."

Rianth bit her lip. The collective groan that rippled through the other ten students promised retribution at some later time. Master Deakon began again.

"On the edge of death, the earth awakened."

Ah, the Great Magic War saga. She should have known. It was Master Deakon's favorite passage.

"Magic loosed to heal the soil."

She still found it hard to believe the earth could heal itself. There had been no sign since the war, over one hundred years ago, that the earth had any magic left. If it did, wouldn't things be better by now? Yet these stories, handed down by recitation from druid to apprentice all these years, bespoke of a great awakening.

"Mankind's selfish struggle for power…"

Rianth knew more than this story told. Master Bhren had spoken to her at length about the war and man's arrogant belief that they could harness this newly formed power. The struggle to own the magic had been humankind's undoing and the point when the magic had all but disappeared.

"Meant that we must for generations toil."

So because of those who chose power over everything else, humanity had been reduced to a pittance of what it had been. Master Bhren had told her stories of dense towns with tall buildings, full of people and even moving machines called cars and buses and trucks. She'd seen remnants of some in her hunts, rusted hulks left to be slowly reclaimed by the earth. Rianth would have liked to see them in action.

"Repeat."

This time, she was ready. "Until the One Prophecy comes to pass."

The teacher nodded and moved on to the next passage, which spoke of the True-Naming ceremony. Rianth's ears perked up. She was so close to her own True-Naming. Only a week away, on her eighteenth birthday. She'd had two very important jobs since arriving at New Hope. Taking care of her brothers and preparing for this day.

Every time a True-Naming occurred, the village as a whole waited anxiously, hoping that the one meant to fulfill the prophecy finally unlocked the magic.

A day of awakening each passes through,
To learn our strength and find our power.
The druid's runes will tell the tale,
As you enter a child into the tower.
Once the ritual is complete,
You'll assume the duty you were born to do.
You'll know your vocation and unlock your power,
And help awaken the magic anew.

Rianth had waited forever for this. As scared as she was about what her calling would be, her True-Naming was supposed to be her time to shine, to finally find her place in New Hope, and to truly belong. Exactly what had happened to Kaiden at his a year ago. Rianth remembered it like it happened yesterday.

He'd stood before the entire village, a child in their eyes, then entered the druid's tower. It seemed like he'd been in there for hours, but only minutes had passed before he returned, his skin pale next to the ebony-skinned Bhren. Kaiden's stance proud, he'd proclaimed his purpose to all.

"I entered the tower as Aidan, a child. I stand before you now as Kaiden, *thiurisaz*." *Protector druid!* Kaiden had explained to her that the name change denoted that the child should now be considered an adult. Each person's vocation was different, and they were expected to take up that vocation upon completion of the ceremony. In Kaiden's life, only three other True-Namings had occurred. None of them had been named protector. He was the only one.

Celebrations had continued well into the night after Kaiden's True-Naming. If Bhren had seemed a little sad, Rianth chalked it up to a druid's disposition. Maybe Kaiden's magic hadn't been what Bhren had hoped for, but his ability did strengthen with his True-Naming, as he proved every day on the training fields. Rianth knew he held back with her and everyone else. She didn't think anyone could best Kaiden with a sword. That had to be good. Kaiden was proud of his vocation, and rightfully so. Only one vocation held more respect than his—that of one who could call the magic at will—*tiwaz*. Mage. And only Master Bhren held that title.

Rianth had realized that day Kaiden was more than just a friend in her heart. She prayed that, in one week's time, he'd be as proud of her as she was of him.

~~~

Studies ended late and those in attendance glared at Rianth as they rushed to their other chores. She shivered at the cold and walked quickly toward the keep where Master Bhren lived, unwilling to take on his ire at her delay also. Kaiden walked out of the keep and toward the woods.

"Kaiden!"

He didn't seem to hear her. He strode off with his head down and his shoulders bowed.

"Kaiden!" Rianth tried again, yet he continued to move away as if he hadn't even heard her.

What had happened that he was so glum? Ready to follow him, Rianth realized she was about to be late for the third time that day. Torn, she clenched and unclenched her hands, then continued toward the tower. She'd have to find Kaiden later to find out what had turned his mood.

Pausing as she always did, Rianth fingered the carving in the rock beside the tower door. A circle. Inside lay three lines emanating from three small spheres, like rays from triple suns. She'd never questioned the meaning of this. One of these days she'd ask. Not today, though. She was officially late.

Racing up the steps, Rianth stopped short when she saw Bhren. Tall even by men's standards, he towered a full foot length above her. His hair, a stark white against his dark skin, was long, yet the top of his head was bald. He chose to wear robes over the more traditional pants, shirt, and tunic that most wore. And his dark eyes saw everything. Right now, though, Bhren stared almost unseeing at the fireplace, as glum as Kaiden had seemed.
~~~

"Master?" She approached him slowly. "Is everything all right?"

Bhren turned to her, his eyes glassy with visions invisible to her. And something else. Something that chilled Rianth more than the cold of this winter. Fear. Then he shook his head, dispelling whatever held him away from the present.

"Everything is as it should be," he said in the monotone she'd known all these years. If a hint of worry lay embedded in his words, Rianth knew she wouldn't pry the reason from him. Neither would she unbend Kaiden, who'd learned to keep his own council from Bhren himself. Still, it can't be coincidence that both Bhren and Kaiden were in troubled moods. Something was afoot and she needed to get to the bottom of it. Eventually.

Bhren gestured to the table. "Let us begin."

Frustrated beyond belief, Rianth rubbed her hands to warm them and sat down, ready for another dull history session. The dirt in front of her was the same as it had been every other day. She dragged her fingers through the soil. A jolt of emotions—fear, pain, anguish—hit her like a strike of lightning, yanking her breath from her as every nerve ending burned from the fire that rushed through her. Rianth yanked her hand back.

Bhren was right there when she gasped. "What happened?" he asked. "What did you see?"

"I…I didn't see anything." She took a couple deep breaths, trying to calm her racing heart. See? In dirt? What was he talking about?

Bhren grasped her by the shoulders. "You touched the soil. You reacted to something. What, girl? What happened?" His voice was urgent, almost excited.

"I didn't *see* anything. It was…what I felt."

"What? Tell me now."

"I felt fear. Overwhelming fear. And…a danger. Beyond anything I've known. Worse than…" Worse than when her parents had died. Rianth jerked her head back. Nothing had ever equaled that pain. The fact that she'd compared this to that horror meant there must be a world of trouble coming.

"What else?" Bhren urged.

"Pain." Rianth whispered the word, afraid to give it voice. "Intense pain. And also…" She had trouble putting it into words. As the sensations faded and her breathing steadied, she frowned, focusing on what had broadcast through the soil to her. "An underlying grief, I think. And a sense of urgency." She stared at the dirt on the table. "How could I get feelings like this from dirt?" she asked, looking up at the druid whose eyes focused so intently on her. "What just happened? What's happening today? First, Kaiden and you both acting strangely. Then, this…" She waved at the table.

Bhren sat across from her, running his fingers through the dirt with only a small hesitation. "Do you know what this is?"

"You told me it's the dirt you do your foretelling in."

Bhren nodded. "This dirt is ancient. There is a tube that runs all the way down the center of this tower to the soils of the earth. We are tied to the very core of the earth through this soil. To its *awen*. And it can sometimes enhance what I see." He stared at Rianth intently. "On rare occasions, others have shown a sensitivity to this magic."

"Why hasn't this happened before?"

The druid shrugged. "I do not know. Maybe you had

to reach a certain age. Your True-Naming is next week. Maybe the proximity to that has awoken something in you." His voice lifted with hope.

Rianth bit her lip. Could this be her calling? Her vocation? Did she have the ability somewhere deep inside her to become…a seer? A mage? No. She wiggled her fingers. Not an iota of magic had passed through them up to this point. Nothing Bhren had tried had brought out any ability, innate or otherwise. She glanced at the dirt, unable to refute that something had happened.

Bhren stared at her with a bemused look on his face. "You know your history. That a magic manifested itself to heal the depleted soils of the earth. And that some were able access this power."

"Does that mean…? Do you think…?" She couldn't put a voice to the question.

Bhren cocked his head. He gripped the table with white-knuckled hands that belied the calm in his voice. "I have always believed something lay inside you. Something special."

Rianth shook her head. "There can't be. I've tried. You've tried to teach me. I…if there had been, it would have manifested itself earlier." Her voice dropped to a whisper. "I should have saved them. My parents."

"It was not your time yet. You were meant for something different," Bhren said.

His dismissal did not assuage her grief. Or change her belief that she was not the person he thought. This was not her destiny. It couldn't be. She had no magic within her.

"I suggest we not try to interpret what has happened here," Bhren continued. "Not without more tests."

Which meant she must try to recreate what had

happened. Rianth recoiled, not wanting that wave of emotions again, and certainly not wanting that intensity.

"It might help us determine if this was a fluke or shows a talent awakening within you."

Torn between wanting to know if she'd be able to repeat what had happened and never wanting those feelings coursing through her again, Rianth shook her head and stood, backing away from the table. "I don't think I can."

"It won't be easy," Bhren said, following her, an insistence in his voice she'd never heard before. "You might sense nothing, or you might repeat what happened, or worse." He backed off, turning away in a futile attempt to show indifference. "It's your choice. If you want to know, this is what you must do."

Worse? Rianth shook her head, shrinking into the wall. *Terror, agony, ashes in her mouth.* It was too much to ask.

Bhren walked to the window and looked outside. Grateful for the time to make her own decision, Rianth stared at the table. In the end, it would bother her if she left without knowing. She'd be able to think of nothing else. With slow movements, Rianth moved closer to the table, staring at the innocuous circle of dirt waiting there.

"Focus on the soil," Bhren said. "Let everything else go. There is nothing except you and the earth, bonded by threads no one can see but you. See the soil. See through it."

Rianth sat down, working hard to let go of the fear and do as Bhren said. It wasn't easy. She still shook with the emotional remnants from before. Not at all sure she wanted to do this, she focused on the dirt. Began to see the granules of grays and browns and beiges. After a bit, a slow, silent throb emanated from it, getting stronger the longer she stared.

"What do you feel?" His whisper seemed to come from a great distance.

She never took her eyes off the soil as she answered him. "It's almost as if the earth is calling to me."

"A good sign. Are you ready to connect fully?"

She didn't know, and wouldn't until she touched it. Rianth reached out, tapping the soil with the tip of a finger. Nothing happened. Emboldened, she slid her hand into the soil and let it sift through her fingers.

"It's gone," she said. "I don't sense anything."

Sensation bit into her like the slice of a sword, this time with visions to match. *Substanceless shapes mumbling evil words. Darkness broken only by a weak funnel of light emanating out of a circular altar, breaking off into many smaller streams of light. One for each shape.*

A bony finger reached toward her. "Who are you?" a disembodied voice said. "How are you here?"

Instinct froze Rianth's mind. She could not, would not, answer.

The caped shadow moved toward her and malevolent golden eyes floating in nothingness glared.

Rianth gasped. The eyes of her worst nightmares.

"Who are you?" The voice changed to a softer lilt, calling to Rianth. It took every bit of strength to keep from reaching out. Yet still no answer came.

"You must come to me."

No. Rianth shuddered. No matter how beguiling the voice, she would never again be lulled into believing there was anything this apparition held for her except contempt.

"I will find you. Soon. Very soon. You cannot run from me. You will join with me. Until then, remember this." Light flared from the finger.

Intense and overwhelming pain hit Rianth. She tried to break away, to pull her hands from the soil. Something held her captive, unable to move. To run. Anything. Deep, stabbing agony engulfed her body and soul. Fire burned her skin. Knives of ice sliced at her insides. She couldn't take anymore. She would die from the pain.

Something hit Rianth, knocking her away. When she fell back, the vision disappeared. She found herself on the floor without knowing how she got here. Rianth lay there, chest heaving, unaware of time as the pain slowly ebbed. Shock stole her strength, making movement impossible. Then the shaking started. Uncontrollable and rattling her inside and out.

"Tell me what happened," Bhren asked, releasing her.

Rianth dusted her hands off. Even this simple task was difficult, as if all the energy in her body had been drained. She tried not to think about those golden eyes and what they had done to her. Bhren seemed more concerned with what had happened than with her welfare.

"I'm all right, thank you," she ground out, glaring at him.

Bhren paused, staring at her, then went for a chair and helped Rianth into it, settling a blanket around her shoulders. "Better? Good," he said without waiting for her response. "Now, did you see anything or just sensation again? Tell me. I must know."

"There was much more than before." Rianth hugged the blanket tight. Several long moments passed before the shaking subsided and she finally drew a deep breath.

Memories assailed her, bringing remnants of the pain with them. "I think…I had some sort of vision."

Bhren's excitement showed as he began to pace. Rianth had to stifle her response to his lack of concern for her, something not easily done. She took a few deeper breaths, calming herself, trying to understand his focus.

"A vision," he mumbled. "A vision," he said again, louder this time. He turned to her. "What kind of vision?"

"I didn't understand it. I was in a cave, of sorts. There were shapes, black, ugly shapes, moving as if by the wind. And a…light in the center. It came out of a raised round stone slab like lightning and spread out to each of the shapes."

Bhren stood behind the other chair. Even across the table, Rianth saw his grip go white-knuckled. "Lightning from an altar?"

"Yes. Then…then, one of the shapes, taller than the others, turned toward me."

"Tell me, quickly. What happened next?"

"I saw the eyes from my nightmares. Disembodied golden eyes stared at me."

Bhren started, his eyes large and intense with worry. Did he know those eyes?

"I heard words in my head," Rianth continued. "'I will come for you. You will join me.'" Rianth shuddered. "What does this mean? Is someone, something, coming for me? Who? Why?"

He paced away from her. "I'm not certain," he said. His voice told a completely different story. Her vision had struck a chord with him. The way he stared off into space, his deeply furrowed brow…he knew much more than he was telling her. He began to mumble, low and quiet. Rianth couldn't hear any of it except for one word she didn't recognize. Yet she knew, deep down inside, that this was a name that would change the course of her future.

Taegar.

When he turned back to her, a blank mask had replaced the worry on his face. "We'll determine what happened here eventually. For now, though…" He strode over to a chest and opened it, pulling out a pair of black gloves. "Wear these. Until we have a better idea of what is happening here, refrain from touching ground soil in any way, unless you are with me. No part of your skin should touch dirt. Is that understood?"

He was withholding something. If he had information that might explain what Rianth had just gone through, he should tell her. She wanted to drag it out of him, but Bhren was too enigmatic for that to work. She must bide her time, waiting for the bits and pieces that would fill in the puzzle of the day's happenings. But only for a little while.

Still, his advice was well heeded. Rianth tugged on the gloves, not even a little tempted to take a chance on another vision coming to her if she touched dirt.

"Today," Bhren said, solidly back in his teacher persona, "we will talk about what caused the strife that both started and ended the Great Magic War."

The swift subject change was hard for Rianth to adapt to. Bhren spoke of the Guardian druids who had awoken because of Earth's release of the *awen*, sensing an evolution about to occur. They'd tried to guide man's foray into this new existence, tried to help those who the magic had touched learn to use it for good, to speed healing of man, animal, and plant.

Those who did not have the gift and could not tap

into this new power became jealous and fearful. At the same time, a small group of druids split from the Guardian Circle, choosing to use the magic for their own devices, to bend it to their will. They teamed up with willing ungifted who wanted to turn the *awen* to their own purposes. Thus began a war that lasted much too long. Druid against druid, with mankind caught in the middle. Cities burned, becoming unnatural funeral pyres for the dead. Great swaths of land were destroyed and lay darkened to this day.

In the end, the Guardian druids defeated these Dark druids, but not without great cost. No one was left to help rekindle the magic. The earth lay decimated, the *awen* depleted, used up in battle.

Electrical grids failed. Technology followed. Rianth had heard of electricity. Lights that turned on with the flip of a switch. Containers that kept food cold. A web that could solve any riddle. None of that had returned after the war. Cities had crumbled as what remained of man and animal spread out in search of food, gathering in small, rural communities like New Hope. They worked tirelessly with the soil, nurturing it until it grew food. Humanity survived, although in the one hundred years since the Great Magic War, the soil barely grew enough food to sustain them.

Such was life for New Hope, and for other communities across the world, from what the rare travelers would say. All efforts went toward food, shelter, water—the basic needs. No one returned to cities that could not sustain them.

Rianth sat quietly, letting the horror of those days wash over her as Bhren talked of war and the ensuing struggles. It all made sense, yet something bothered her.

When he gave indications their time for today was about at an end, she finally figured it out.

"Bhren?"

"Hmmm?" He'd turned away, having dismissed her.

"You talk as if you were there, but how can that be? Even if you were able to live this long, I thought all the druids were destroyed in the war."

He stilled, his face a cross between admiration and consternation. "I am a student of the druid way of life. For now, that is all you need to know."

Tired of secrets, Rianth glared at the druid master. The way Bhren stared back at her, daring her to challenge him, she knew once again she would not get answers.

"Thank you for your wisdom." She ground the words out, the same leaving ritual as yesterday, and every day before that. Today, it did not seem like enough. It would have to be. For now.

"Remember to wear your gloves, Rianth. I will work on finding an explanation for what happened here today."

As Rianth left to get her cloak and then track down Kaiden, she knew in her heart that Bhren had just lied to her, yet again.

CHAPTER FOUR

Kaiden had disappeared. Rianth couldn't find him in any of his usual haunts and it frustrated her to no end. Giving up, she walked through town to see what mischief Tevy had gotten up to while she'd been in class.

When they'd arrived in New Hope, a bedraggled trio of siblings, Rianth had refused to be separated from her brothers. Because of that, they'd been given a small two-room hut to sleep in and she'd happily continued to act as both mother and father to Uja and Tevy. These days, fifteen-year-old Uja's head was in the growing fields and his alchemist studies. He was a good kid, but his thoughts were too focused and Rianth quite often had to track him down to make sure he ate. Only a couple years separated them, but he'd accepted her role in his life. Mostly.

Tevy was another matter altogether. The entire village had adopted her baby brother, and everything he could see or climb had become his playground.

It took quite a bit of searching to find him. He was snuggled up with a brood of wolf pups and their mother in the hay barn. He had a way with animals, and with these pups especially. Watching him and the way the pups stared at him, then jumped around, it was like they were having some private conversation.

She'd heard that some people understood animals, but had thought that to be rumors only. Could Tevy tap the *awen*? The day's events hit her again and Rianth shuddered. If she had a magical ability, she'd rather be able to talk to animals than have visions like the one today.

"Come closer, Ri," Tevy said.

"I didn't think you knew I was here."

"I knew. Come slow, so you don't upset Sarsa, the mother."

Rianth slid carefully to Tevy's side in the pungent, tangy hay, surprised at the cozy warmth compared to the cold outside. The hay must act as a shield against the chill. She pulled off her gloves and picked up a pup whose eyes seemed to be turning different colors, one blue and one brown. This one stared at her for a bit, then reached out with her soft tongue and placed a tender kiss on Rianth's cheek. "How old are they?"

"Two weeks." He paused, smiling. "Taschia likes your touch."

Rianth continued to run her hand along the soft fur. "Taschia?"

"Yes. That's her name."

"You've named them all?"

"No, silly. They told me their names." He held up one with white streaks through his gray fur. "This is Hark, the oldest. That one over there is Marin, and the greedy one still nursing is Grog. And that's Joek over there sleeping."

"Can you understand the animals, Tevy?"

"Sure," he said. "Can't everyone?"

"No. I can't."

"Well, that's okay. I can inter…" He paused.

"Interpret?"

"Yeah."

Yet one more revelation for Rianth in a day that had been filled with newness. She'd had about all she could handle for now. "Come on," she said, setting the pup down and pulling Tevy up. "Time to go help in the kitchen."

"I want to stay here. Sarsa says I can if I'm careful."

She wrapped his cloak around him. "You know we all have to do our part. If you can't eat, you won't have the energy to play. And in order to eat, we have to help prepare the meal."

"Ah, I know. I just don't wanna. Not right now."

Ignoring his protests, she led him out of the barn while they talked. By the time they reached the communal kitchen, he'd changed subjects about four times and had temporarily set aside all thoughts of sleeping with puppies.

With any food shared by all, New Hope had one main kitchen—a large wood-braced, mud-roofed longhouse that served as kitchen and dining house for all two hundred or so villagers. One end housed clay fireplaces for cooking and warmth, counters, and in-ground coolers, all designed cooperatively by the talented people who lived here. Handmade or civilization foraged pots, pans, dishes, and eating tools sat stacked on shelves along the far wall.

Each time Rianth walked through the doors or even got close, the nostalgia almost overwhelmed her. Her mother had loved to cook, and especially loved finding unusual herbs to use for spicing.

After all this time, her heart could still catch at the recollection. There were so few years of happy memories, and even those seemed to be fading with time. Rianth didn't want to forget. Ever.

Tevy squirmed to get out from under her hand, which rested on his shoulder.

"Go help Anniah with the salads," she said.

"'Kay," he hollered over his shoulder as he sprinted off. "Ann-i-ah!!!"

Rianth smiled. Tevy had a perennially happy disposition. He got into more than his share of mischief, but no one stayed mad at little Tevy, especially when he flashed that infectious grin of his.

He could be happy. He had no memories of those dark days after his birth, or of their parents. It saddened her that he never knew of their regal father or their loving mother. He knew they'd died, but Rianth had chosen not to tell him about the trials of searching for New Hope. Tevy believed he'd been born in this village, and no one wanted to dispel that belief. It took a village to raise Tevy Royan, and each and every person in New Hope had gladly signed on for the task.

Uja walked in, his arms full of produce from the growing hut. Carrots, parsnips, greens. It looked like today was a good day for vegetables and they'd eat well tonight. Some nights their plates looked more empty than full.

The slap to the back of her head came out of nowhere. Rianth whirled around. "Mokie!"

The short, wiry boy grinned. "Dishes are yours tonight."

"Because of class today?"

"Yep. We all decided."

Rianth sighed. "I figured."

"And don't forget to feed the goats the leftovers," Mokie hollered as he sped off. His laughter trailed behind him.

Rianth had known she'd pay for her inattention today. Dishes, though, were a cruel punishment. She prayed someone would take pity on her and help.

Later, with her arms deep in a cleaning barrel for about the hundredth time, Rianth swore she'd never again lose focus in Studies. She set the last plate on the stack and dried her hands as Tevy tumbled into the kitchen. "I'm gonna take Anniah to see the puppies!"

Rianth steadied him. "All right, but don't be long. Have you seen Uja?"

"You know him. He dropped stuff off and went right back out to the fields."

Tevy struggled in her arms until she laughed and let go. In seconds, he'd left the building and she was certain she'd find him sound asleep tucked in with those wolves again tonight.

Grabbing a spoon and the bowl of beans she'd set aside earlier, Rianth headed for the growing fields. At the edge of the village, smoke and light from the glow pots dissipated, giving way to the encroaching darkness. Rianth could find her way anywhere in and around New Hope in the dark without misstep. A nice benefit from living in one place for seven years and something she'd never had before.

When she got to the fields, Rianth stopped and

searched for her brother underneath the long canopies rolled over the rows designed to keep any warmth near the ground through the cold months. It didn't take long. She heard him mumbling to the plants, his words incoherent. Uja spent his days, and half his nights, coaxing growth out of each leaf and vine. When she got nearer, it surprised her to see a faint glow surrounding him, as if the sun had left a bit of its light in Uja's care for the night. The plant his hand encircled seemed to grow as she watched. Was this magic? It seemed her brothers had more ability than she did. Uja had already shown an uncanny ability with crops, more than she had shown with anything. Uja had his plants, Tevy his wolves. Rianth was happy for them. A part of her, a big part, wanted to know what her contribution would be. No. She shouldn't go there. Anything good for the village was good for her and that was that.

Uja moved his hand away with gentle care, letting a leaf settle into its slumber. "You may join me, Sister."

Rianth chuckled. Always formal, her brother. Always serious. And rail thin. She smoothed his dark hair that always seemed to stick out in awkward directions and pulled his cloak higher to warm his neck. "Have you eaten today?"

Straightening, he stretched shoulders more than likely hunched over plants all day. "Bits here and there," he said.

"And not enough. I saw you bring greens and tubers for dinner. I bet you didn't keep a one for yourself." She held out the bowl and spoon. "Here. I saved you some beans. You need the protein."

He hesitated.

"Uja, you are no good to any of us if you don't keep

up your own strength."

Nodding, he took the bowl, bowing his head as he thanked her.

Rianth sat between the rows of future food, careful not to touch the dirt with any bare skin, and watched the glow leave Uja while his eyelids drooped with tiredness. At fifteen, he had way too much responsibility on his shoulders. They all did. Life hadn't always been like this. The Great Magic War had changed everything.

"How are the plants doing?" she asked.

"It's too soon to tell. We shouldn't have moved them to the fields, but there is not much winter produce left in the growing house and they need as much sunshine as they can get."

The growing house was a long hut near the kitchens, with table upon table of dirt for starting plants. Smudge pots kept the newlings warm through the cold season, and the whole place stank thanks to some alchemy that also helped fertilize the soil. For that reason alone, Rianth chose not to go inside unless absolutely necessary.

"I don't know how you can spend so much time in that stinky place."

"It's not bad once you get used to it. And besides, I have to. Just like you have to hunt."

Uja was right. They all needed to do their part, both for survival and for magic's sake. Uja and Tevy, at least, seemed to have some ability to help. Unlike her.

"I'd better go tear Tevy from his beloved puppies and get him to bed."

Uja stood and held out a hand to help Rianth up. "He likes the animals."

"And you like the fields."

"For you, it's weapons, right?"

Rianth nodded as they walked home. "I guess." She loved training with her sword. Even hunting. That was when she felt most alive. "Do you think that will be my vocation?"

"At your True-Naming next week? I dunno. Maybe."

"Protector druid. I'd like that." *Thurisaz*, like Kaiden. "Or *tiwaz*."

"Setting your sights pretty high, aren't you?"

"Not me."

"Bhren? What's he saying?"

Rianth held out a hand to stop Uja, then stepped over a log in the path, pointing to it so he wouldn't trip. "He says nothing. Nothing at all."

"You seem worried. Did something happen today?"

Today wasn't something she could put into words yet. Rianth shook her head. "Master Bhren seems like he's waiting for something to happen and I'm tired of being the person he's most focused on. I don't know why he even works with me. I don't have any abilities." There. She'd said it. Voiced her biggest fear. "I've tried, Uja. I can't use magic. Probably never will be able to."

"You have a lot of strength in you, Sister. Maybe that's your magic. Not only regarding weapons, either. You have strength of character. I don't know anyone else here, save maybe Kaiden, who could have gotten us through those weeks of travel."

She nodded. Those had been dark times. "I noticed you weren't at weapons practice this morning."

"I like weapons training as much as you like working in the growing house."

She could almost see his smile through the darkness. Rianth had hoped Uja would follow in her footsteps. However, she was smart enough to recognize where her brother's talent lay. "We wouldn't be eating as well if it weren't for your magic touch."

"It's pretty amazing, watching things grow, nurturing what little we can affect. To know we're providing food for the entire village."

Pretty boring, in her mind. She'd rather be clashing swords with foes. There was a much more immediate rush in hunting and in training to keep the village safe. Not that there'd been any call to arms. Sequestered in the hills around Rushmore Mountain as they were, few ventured here with nefarious plans. Sure, she and Kaiden led most of the hunts, but Uja provided a much more vital role than she did in keeping the village alive and healthy.

"It's daunting, having the responsibility of feeding an entire village. You're one of the best at this. And very young to be shouldering the responsibility."

"I'm almost sixteen," Uja said, a hint of hurt in his voice.

"Don't get your hackles up. I know you're up to the task. This is me, Uja. Just checking in to make sure it's not too much for you."

"It's not. Really. I am so amazed at each new thing we coax from seed to plate. I've been trying new ways to fertilize that are showing promise. I hope eventually to have a self-sustaining system that will feed our people long after you and I are gone."

Rianth nudged him, and shoulder to shoulder they stepped inside the barn where Tevy lay sleeping, curled up as expected with the wolf pups and Sarsa. "As long as you're not overwhelmed."

"I'm not, Rianth. Not at all. There's lots of help. And Fraka has been—"

"Fraka?" It shocked Rianth to see Uja blush crimson

in the dim of the barn glow pot. Wasn't he too young to be interested in a girl? Her own interest in Kaiden had begun when she'd first come to New Hope. Based on that, maybe she needed to rethink Uja's feelings. His blush deepened as she watched him.

"Yes. Jonah and Raisa's daughter."

"I know that." Rianth knew Fraka well, with her light brown hair and pretty doe eyes. Kaiden had been raised as her brother.

"Fraka is now a gardener apprentice." Uja's face lit up as he spoke. "You should see her, Ri. She's better at this than I am, I think. Her ability to coax the seeds to grow is beyond anything I've ever witnessed."

"And she's pretty, too."

"She's beautiful!" As soon as he said it, Uja scrambled to pick Tevy up without disturbing the pups too much. "You know, in a kid sort of way," he mumbled.

Rianth grinned widely, then hid it when Uja stood with their brother in his arms. "I'm glad you have a…friend to help you in the fields," she said as they walked to their beds. "Just make sure you don't wear yourself out too much. You are gone before I get up in the mornings and you don't stop until well after the sun sets. I worry about you."

"We all do our part. You're busy all day, too, between weapons practice and Studies and hunting. And you have the added time with Bhren, too. He takes a special interest in you."

Dark shapes floated before Rianth as the day's memories hit her anew. She shook her head to dispel them. "It's only to prepare me for my True-Naming."

"Uh-uh. He hasn't done this with any other

candidate, and he's taught you privately for over two years." He settled Tevy in the bed they shared.

Rianth had tried hard to put her True-Naming and whether she could be the one to finally unlock the magic for all out of her mind. She hoped, though she refused to focus on it. "Sorry, Uja. I guess I'm trying not to think about it. To not get too nervous."

"Well," he said, imitating her earlier concern, "just don't overwhelm yourself."

Rianth swatted him. "Get some sleep. Tomorrow is another day of work."

"And I am tired. Goodnight, Sister."

"Goodnight, Uja." Worn out herself, she curled up in her own bed and pulled her blanket tight to her chin, wondering where Kaiden had gone off to. He hadn't been seen since he'd stalked off earlier, ignoring her calls. He hadn't even eaten supper.

Where was he?

~~~

He watched them carry the child until they were gone from sight. The fools never even saw him. His magic kept him cloaked. Safe from prying eyes. He walked out of the village with care. Masking his body was easy. Staying warm and hiding noise pulled more magic, and the power drained from him like blood from a gutted hog. He'd been gone from her too long. He only needed to find what she searched for, bring it to her, and she'd imbue him with unimaginable power. He could almost taste it, feel it lengthening his life. He was so close… When he'd come across the old man, Bhren, and New Hope, he'd thought for sure he'd found the right place. Something special resided here. He could feel it, so he'd settled in, demeaned himself to act like one of them.
~~~

And pinned all his hopes on the girl Bhren devoted so much time to.

Deep in the woods surrounding the village, he followed sounds to the messengers he must meet. *She* wanted to know how the search went. He shook his head, knowing she would not be pleased. Taegar angry was something he never wanted to see again. He rubbed his arm. The tattoo that had appeared along with his power burned like a molten omen.

He'd spent the last few years watching and searching. He was certain the girl, Rianth, was the one, yet the old druid hadn't found a drop of ability in the girl. What Taegar needed was here. He'd bet his soul on that. He just needed more time and more power to find it.

Letting his magic go, he showed himself to the two waiting men. Ruffians by their looks. Fringers who'd followed the golden road to Taegar with the same hopes as his. He sniffed. They would never equal him in any way. Taegar must see the truth. Only he could bring her what she wanted.

"You took long enough," the stockier of the two said. The other one nodded his head. There wasn't much to tell them apart. Same greasy, dark hair, same rotting teeth, same stench.

"I came once the village slept. She requires me to keep a low profile. You"—he sniffed again—"should know that."

"Well, *she* hasn't heard from you for a while, and she wants answers."

He refused to tell them that he'd not enough of the power left in him to conjure up a vision and speak to Taegar directly. "Relay this to my queen, that I am waiting and watchful. Something will happen soon. A sign, something. And I will bring her everything she has asked for."

"You can tell her yourself," Stocky said.

Before he had time to react, both arms had been pinned behind him.

While the partner tied his hands, Stocky got in his face and leered at him. "You're going to talk to her directly."

Desperation consumed him. He couldn't go to her. Not yet. He was so close. He knew her impatience had grown, but he needed more time. "Come now, my friends." He soothed. "There's no need to tie me up. I will go willingly to our queen." The false simper in his voice disgusted him as he tried to reason with the men.

"If I'm close," he continued, "then you have the opportunity to be with me when we carry our discovery to her. We will all be handsomely rewarded, I'm sure." The beatific look he plastered on his face was only half faked, for he knew he would be rewarded. Only him.

"We don't take orders from anyone 'cept her, so don't even try that. If you ain't found what she's looking for by now, you're outta luck."

"I can't leave. I'll be missed." The whine in his own voice disgusted him. He couldn't wait for the day when he'd have all he desired. No one would ever look down on him again. Until then, he had to find a way to stay, to keep searching.

He dare not go back. Not yet. Fury and desperation simmered to a boil and he began to struggle. He needed more time. He must have more—

The conk to his head caught him unawares and, with one final yelp of desperation, he gave himself up to unconsciousness.

The two men trussed him up, then threw him over one of their horses. "Go put that note in his room about him leaving for a bit. I'll wait here," the one said. Once all was in place, they moved off in the night, intent on fulfilling the charge they'd been given. The wind whistled at their backs, helping them on their way. A good omen.

After all, Taegar only rewarded those who were successful.

CHAPTER FIVE

Kaiden climbed the rocks with ease. He and Rianth had climbed them so many times together, he knew each crack and crevice. Once on top of the lakeside bluff, he settled against a lone oak tree on the rocky slope. Pine and spruce surrounded the oak, offering privacy and shelter and holding the wind at bay. The day's light had disappeared, leaving a midnight sky dotted with a myriad of stars, softened by the light of a waning moon that shone clearly on the lake below. The winter night air had a chill to it, but he didn't notice. Instead, he worked to make sense of what Bhren had told him. At first, he'd been shocked. He'd spent hours roaming the hills and forest with no plan except a desire to be anywhere but New Hope. Never had he been as torn as he was in this moment.

Runes never yet proven wrong had foretold that New Hope would be in ruins, burned to the ground. New

Hope! The only home Kaiden had ever known. He'd been raised by this village, much as little Tevy was being raised now. A rare traveler passing through New Hope had given him up for a few vegetables and a bit of meat. He'd been raised as Fraka's brother by Jonah and Raisa Darcy. While he loved them all like family, it galled him that the man who'd sold him for food had never even mentioned if Kaiden had been his son.

Kaiden owed everything to this town. Because of that, he must do anything and everything he could to keep New Hope safe. Today, he'd found out that the two things he loved the most would soon be separated, for not only had Bhren seen New Hope's fall, he'd also seen Rianth leaving and Kaiden forced to choose which to protect.

How could he be asked to make that choice? He loved both with everything he had. He knew Rianth felt something for him. He'd chosen to wait until they were both older and things were more settled to tell her his feelings. Now, he may have run out of time.

He sat up, unrolled the parchment Bhren had given him, and stared at the drawing of something akin to an upward arrow with a thorn in its side.

Beware of anyone carrying this tattoo, Kaiden, Bhren had said. *They are servants of one who brings the darkness.*

How could fate ask him to choose between Rianth and New Hope? There was no choice. He must find a way to protect them both. Somehow, he had to.

Quiet scratching whispered that he was not alone. Rianth climbed up and joined him cautiously. "Where have you been all day?"

Kaiden couldn't tell her any of what he knew, and

his silence would drive yet another wedge between them. Not the worst, if Bhren's foretelling was to be believed. Kaiden didn't want to talk. Instead, he opened his arms.

Rianth didn't question him. She snuggled into his side, pulled her cloak over them both, then held on as if it were their last night together.

Kaiden could not let that happen. He lay for long hours after she'd fallen asleep, holding her, toying with the hair he loved, keeping her warm and safe. That had been his entire purpose since she'd fallen into their village seven years ago. To keep her safe.

All that would soon change and so far, he hadn't come up with a single idea as to how to keep fate from intervening.

For the first time in his life, Kaiden was well and truly afraid.

~~~

"Let's go hunting," Kaiden said to Rianth over breakfast.

"I can't. I have Studies."

"They'll let you go. It's not as if anything new is being learned, especially since Deakon isn't here."

"That was odd, wasn't it?" Rianth said. "I mean, he just left."

Kaiden shrugged. "He's always been a little strange. Ask."

"Kaiden—"

"Please. Go hunting with me today."

The urgency in his voice surprised Rianth. They'd foraged in the woods many times, but usually on set hunting days. Not on a normal day like today. He stared at her so intently, Rianth nodded.

After their interim teacher released Rianth from the
~~~

day's studies and she checked on Tevy, Rianth walked out of New Hope with Kaiden.

"You're wearing gloves," Kaiden said.

"So?"

"You never wear gloves."

Rianth tried to keep her shrug casual. "It's winter, and I'm tired of having cold hands."

Kaiden looked at her for a long moment then, with a shrug of his own, kept walking.

The sun shone weakly through the trees from behind the hills and frost still coated the brush under their feet, adding a crunch to their footsteps that would make it harder to search for game. Rianth cocked her head as a thrush stopped chirping, warning the forest they were coming. This forest was as much home to her as New Hope was and peace filled her heart as they headed east, out past the Rushmore sculpture. Only a short hike from the lake their village had been built around, the Rushmore was an enigma, paying homage to a past civilization with no sense of the need for conservation of the world they lived in. The ancients had chipped away at the rock, molding it into their vision instead of preserving the natural beauty. Yet their vision had created a different beauty, that of man's oneness with the world he lived in.

Faces that time had covered in moss and vines, and the dark and light striations of weather and age, still held their original form. Chins, noses, even the granite cutouts that made the eyes follow you held strong.

Still, it seemed a frivolous endeavor, changing the very land that fed you into some sort of art. That would not be condoned in this day and age. As enigmatic as the carvings were, they also stood testament to a different life, where a lack of concern about the earth had led to society's end. Arrogance had been the downfall of their ancestors.

What remained of humanity now paid the price. Rianth and Kaiden wandered along old pathways more grass than man-made and down through woods that held half the trees they should, a pittance of life in a place that should be teeming with it.

The chill dissipated as they walked, morning giving way to midday and warming things enough that their footsteps were finally silent. She listened closely for signs of animals, watchful for winter berries or herbs to add to the kitchen coffers. Today, the silence seemed more pronounced.

They were below the Precipice of the Faces when Rianth decided she'd had enough silence. "Where were you yesterday and what had you so upset?" She'd planned to ease into the conversation, but forthright was really much more her way.

Kaiden didn't look at her. Didn't answer. Instead, he stopped suddenly. "Shhh. Did you hear that?"

"That's a bluff tactic. Answer my question."

With a heavy sigh, Kaiden turned to her. "I was in a bad mood yesterday. We all have those days."

"Right."

"You more than anyone ought to recognize what a bad mood day is like."

"Ouch."

"So I chose to be by myself and not take it out on you or anyone else."

"Like I do? Is that what you mean?"

"Well…"

"Cut it out, Kaiden. You were upset, not bad-mooding it. And it was because of something that happened when you met with Bhren, right?" Rianth stifled her own shudder, noticing the rigid stature Kaiden had adopted. Something, or some conversation with Bhren, *had* upset him. Really upset him.

"What happened yesterday?"

His stiff demeanor didn't budge. Rianth set her knapsack down and stood directly in front of him, inches from his face, then put her hands on his shoulders. For a moment, she wanted to forget everything and stay here, like this, with him. For a moment, she thought she saw the same sentiment in his eyes. Then he looked away, over her head, ending it.

"You're my best friend. I tell you everything." *Well, just about.* "You can tell me what's wrong."

"No," he said. "I can't. Not this."

Rianth stepped back like he'd slapped her. Kaiden had never before refused to tell her something. She'd always been able to pry secrets from him. This time, she saw the same rigidity in his mind that she saw in his back.

That scared her more than anything. What was going on? Did this have something to do with her? Why wouldn't he talk to her?

"You can't tell me anything?"

"No." His lips barely moved when he said the word. Wearing him down, like other times, wouldn't work. This time, it appeared he'd hold tight to this secret. Still, she had to make one more attempt.

"This doesn't have to do with my True-Naming, does it?"

The startled look on his face, even quickly covered up, unnerved her. It *did* have to do with her.

"You're scaring me."

He stepped closer, touched her cheek with the back of his finger. "I'm sorry. I wish I…" He froze as they stared at each other.

Rianth saw a world of secrets in the green of Kaiden's eyes. Eyes that swirled with torn loyalties and pain. Bitterness widened a small crevice of pain in her heart. She had to wonder if any of those loyalties were toward her.

CHAPTER SIX

"I wish things were different," Kaiden said. He desperately wished they were. He'd struggled all night to find a solution. He knew too much, the downside to being the highest-ranking apprentice. Damn Bhren anyhow. Damn the fates.

"Why can't they be?"

He glanced away, off toward the distant trees. "Because they can't."

The boar came out of nowhere, crashing through the brush, and heading straight toward them. Before Kaiden could fully unsheathe his sword, Rianth's sword had dealt the death blow, cleanly slicing through the animal's neck.

She stood over the boar, chest heaving, her dark hair waffling in the breeze, looking magnificent in the adrenaline-laced rush that infused her cheeks with color.

"How do you do that?" Kaiden said.

"What?" She cleaned her sword with a leaf.

"How do you react to danger before it is fully upon you? Even before me. If it weren't for that prescience of yours, I'd be besting you much sooner on the training fields."

"I don't know, but I'm glad for it. Maybe it's magic," Rianth said, wincing. "Sorry. All this special training with Bhren has me…hopeful."

"Maybe that magic is more of a curse than a blessing." Kaiden's voice was laced with the bitterness he felt.

"What do you mean?"

"Nothing. Nothing at all. Come on. Let's get this boar back to the kitchens."

Kaiden saw the look of puzzlement and hurt on her face. There wasn't a thing he could do to alleviate it. Nothing at all.

They sheathed their swords and Rianth knelt over the boar, laying her hand on it. "Thank you."

"Why do you do that?"

"It's Tevy. He says when an animal gives his life for our sustenance, we should thank it."

The boy did have an uncanny ability with animals. Kaiden made a mental note to talk to Bhren about that later, wondering if another of the Royan children had some innate power.

Both grew quiet while they gutted the boar and trussed it to a pole, then began the tedious journey back to the village.

The entire way Kaiden wished things were different. He prayed that Rianth might understand, eventually, and maybe even accept him as more than a friend, once she reached the right age. That she might accept his love.

He also prayed that Bhren's premonitions were

wrong.

Somehow, deep inside, Kaiden knew that they were not.

~~~

Look at me.

Ponte tried to straighten, tried to obey. His body refused to listen. Joints were locked in place by paralyzing fear. Confusion liquefied his brain. How had he gotten here?

Look at me.

He closed his eyes tight, hoping to purge the voice in his head. That voice, more insistent now, held nothing of the siren's song that had brought him to this point. Magic, it had said. Heady power beyond your wildest imaginings. He had listened. He only had to find some lost talisman. The task was one he'd been born for. His tracking instincts were unmatched, though with no description and no place to begin, he'd been doomed from the start. It had been an impossible request, even more so when his power had disappeared.

A bony finger lifted his chin and Ponte shuddered. When he opened his eyes, he stared into golden orbs in an ethereal mask. It had to be a mask. Otherwise, the woman who had offered him the world was without substance.

You have not found the trinket I desire.

"No—" He cleared a throat thick with mucous. "No. I could not find the trail." The whine that filled his words felt foreign to him. "With nothing to go on, I had no place to begin."

"You said you were the best," the shrouded figure said. "That you could find anything. That is why I brought you into my fold." She straightened to a height taller than most men. "That is why I endowed you with
~~~

my power.”

“I-I don’t know how to do what you ask. If you reinforced my powers, give me a bit more…”

His voice weakened as she leaned closer, the smell of decay flaring his nostrils.

“You have displeased me greatly. I do not give second chances often.” Her cloaked face cocked to the side. “I think you are not to be the exception to that rule.”

Ponte gulped, filling his lungs with air. He couldn’t breathe. Couldn’t speak. Could do nothing but plead with his eyes until red light shot from her hands toward his neck. At first, he felt nothing.

Then his head canted and fell, his body crumpling beside it, sightless eyes going dim.

Ponte had become the prey he’d tracked his entire life. He had succumbed.

“And you,” Taegar said, turning to the man still trussed and held by two of her acolytes. “You have displeased me, also.” She pointed a bony finger at him.

“Wait!” Deakon searched for anything to give him enough leverage to not end up like… He glanced at the dead man. His inert body had fallen several feet from his head. Gulping, he dared to look directly into Taegar’s golden ire-filled eyes. “I’m close. I know I am. I just need more time.”

“Close to what? Where?” She drew closer and only the bonds holding him stayed his flight.

With a throat-clearing breath, he worked hard to find the argument that would save his life. “I sensed something. A change in the wind. Someone who might be more than they are thought to be.” He chose not to tell her about the girl, and how strongly he believed she was the one. Not yet. He had no proof. If he was wrong, he’d be dead. Right now, he wasn't certain and needed more time.

Taegar lowered her hand, her eyes growing bright with interest.

With more confidence, he continued. "My magic waned before I could hone in on who, what, or where. But I caught a sliver of power. I need more time to follow this lead."

Taegar rubbed her hands together, the bone-crunching sound one that most men would squint and cover their ears to hide from. He stayed the course, keeping his eyes on her, letting an outward calm speak his argument for him. A calm that did not match the raging fear inside him.

A fear that escalated when she moved to within inches of him. "So you think, with more time, you can find this thread?"

"Y-yes," he said, gulping. "With more time and more power."

She stared at him for long moments, then turned and drifted across the cavern. "I could send someone else to your village. Someone with enough power."

"They aren't easily friendly to newcomers. I'm established there."

She turned back to him. "I think you are playing with me. I think you are begging for your life with reason." She wandered around the altar, then waved to the two men. "Release him. Let him return."

White light shot from her hands to him and he flinched until familiar power flowed into him, invigorating him, making him youthful again. He let out a long, slow, quiet breath.

"Understand me, slave," Taegar said, her voice

resounding through the cavern. "Do not cross me. If you do"—she pointed a finger at Ponte—"your fate will not be so easy, nor so quick."

He'd won. Soon, Taegar would realize that he was her equal. Deakon stood tall as he left the caverns and headed back toward New Hope. Soon, the talisman she desired would be in his hands, and all those who'd ever looked down on him would be destroyed.

CHAPTER SEVEN

Rianth lay in her bed, trembling with frustration. She slapped the bedding beneath her, wanting to hit something. A lot of somethings. She got up and paced the tiny room, kicked a stool, then lay back down with an arm over her eyes. Nothing felt right anymore. Kaiden had all but disappeared. He hadn't been there to wake her from her nightmares the past few nights. She'd even nearly frozen to death once sleeping by herself on their hill overlooking the lake. He hadn't joined her.

Rianth jumped up again. That worried her, especially now, on the eve of her True-Naming. This morning she'd chosen to avoid Studies, and their new teacher had tracked her down to call her out afterward. Who cared? She'd no longer be in class after today anyhow. Those who successfully passed their True-Naming were considered adults and expected to take up their new role in the village.

She hadn't eaten dinner, either. Food would not have sat well in her churning stomach. Now, with the soft light of the glow pots illuminating the way, Rianth left her room and wandered out of the village with no real plan, not at all surprised that her feet took her to the one place where she'd always felt at peace. The lake—a peaceful respite in the sparsely treed forest that surrounded New Hope—had always been her secret place when life got too crazy. Well, *their* secret place. Kaiden had found her here shortly after she'd arrived in the village and ever since then they'd spent a lot of time here together.

When she reached the top of the rock ledge, she didn't know whether to be relieved or upset. Kaiden huddled against their tree, looking exactly like she'd found him so many other times.

She didn't really want to talk to him right now, so she turned to leave before he noticed her.

"Join me?" His quiet words echoed across the short distance between them.

Rianth hesitated.

"Please."

Letting out a long breath, Rianth turned back and settled beside him. "I should have known you'd be here."

"I needed to think."

"Same here."

They lay like that for a long time, silent, cloaks drawn tight, viewing the crisp, star-filled sky. Rianth had always liked to draw imaginary lines from star to star, envisioning lions and bears and all sorts of drawings against the black sky.

Entwined in their own thoughts, neither moved for what seemed like hours. When Kaiden rolled toward her, Rianth held her breath, aware of how close he was, the way his hair seemed darker than the night sky, the scent of trees that always surrounded a man who spent hours in the forest.

Kaiden picked up a lock of her hair and twined it around his finger. "I love your hair." She could hear the smile in his voice. He'd always loved her hair, even used to brush it for her at night. She'd thought that meant…

No sense going there. Lately, he hadn't wanted anything to do with her.

"All set for tomorrow?" Kaiden's voice was almost as quiet as the forest.

"As ready as I guess I can be. I don't know what to expect. Can you tell me anything?" She knew his answer before he gave it. The only certainty about tomorrow was that the True-Naming ceremony was different for each person who underwent it.

"No."

"Not even what it entails? Like, is it a physical test or some sort of mental thing?"

"No one will know what their naming will be like until they are inside the tower."

"I've memorized that so many times in Studies. It's weird to think that tomorrow, my name will forever change. Are you happy now, to be Kaiden instead of Aiden?"

The first genuine smile she'd seen in weeks lit Kaiden's face. "I am proud to be called Kaiden. Proud to be named *thurisaz*. Proud of my ability."

She nodded. "That's what I want. I wonder what my name will become. Brianth, maybe?" She pulled grass from the ground and rolled it in the palm of her gloved hand.

He cocked an eyebrow.

"I know. I probably won't end up with a letter added to the beginning of my name. I haven't shown an iota of magical ability." *Not much, at least.* "Why do our names have to change anyhow?"

"From what I understand, it's a way of clearly identifying the hierarchy of magical power. If the runes foretell a change to the beginning of your name, like when mine became Kaiden, your ability is strong. If the change comes at the end…" His voice trailed off and his new, usual scowl wiped the smile off his face.

Rianth crumpled the grass she'd been holding and scattered it. For a minute there, they'd had a real conversation. "I wondered…well, what did your True-Naming feel like?"

"You know I can't tell you that."

Rianth sat up, pulling her hair out of his hand. "Not even if you felt some sort of…infusion of power?"

Kaiden sat up with her. "I'm sorry."

"For what? For not easing my worry about the ceremony? Or about the secrets you've been keeping? Or maybe because you've decided to no longer be a part of my life?" She couldn't help the note of anger that crept into her voice. This was the most important time in her life and her best friend had apparently chosen to not be a part of it.

"For all of it." He sat quiet for a moment, breathing in and out in concert with her own breaths. "Even if I tried to ease your worry, I'd probably only make it worse."

"Mysteries. I ask for answers and all you give me are mysteries. You and Bhren have barely spoken to me this past week. How am I supposed to prepare for tomorrow? How am I supposed to be ready when my teacher and my best friend have abandoned me?" She jumped up, shaking as she spoke.

"You've trained seven years for this day. Completed all the studies. Refined your abilities, especially with a sword. You can read runes better than anyone, outside of Bhren. You are ready. Trust yourself." Kaiden stood and settled his hands on her shoulders. "I admire you, know you. A lot. You have much strength in you, Rianth. Have faith in that strength. It will serve you well tomorrow."

She looked up at him, stared into eyes almost hidden by the moon's shadow, trying to discern something, anything about his thoughts. Kaiden turned his head, looking away, giving her no chance to figure him out. He'd given her not a single inclination that he'd be there to help her through the process. She was completely on her own now. A sadness she couldn't quite stamp out gave way to anger.

"It looks like I'll have to rely on that strength you say I have, because it's apparent my closest…friend…won't be there to help me at all." Rianth was done. She refused to wait for the apologies or excuses he'd never make.

She climbed down off the promontory in record time and ran back to the village, to her room, to the emptiness of her bed.

The man she'd loved for seven years had deserted her on the eve of her True-Naming. She shouldn't be a bit worried about tomorrow, because the worst that could ever happen to her had just happened.

CHAPTER EIGHT

Tevy pounced on Rianth's bed, rousting her from the sound sleep she'd only drifted into a short while earlier.

"Tevy, stop. I'm sleeping."

"You can't sleep. It's your True-Naming day *and* your birthday. Aren't you excited?" He laughed like the child he was, with not a worry in the world. A truth for their perennially happy Tevy, his laughter always infectious, like now.

Rianth's stomach lurched as she tried to keep him from jumping up and down on top of her. "Come on. You'll fall off and hurt yourself."

"Nah. That's not a far jump." With that, he leapt from the bed, landing like a cat on the floor. "See?"

Rianth laughed. "All right." She shooed Tevy off to the kitchens, promising to join him soon. Watching him leap his way out of her room, she wished everyone were as happy as her baby brother. Especially Kaiden. And

Bhren. They'd been more sullen and secretive lately than ever before.

Today was her eighteenth birthday. What she'd always thought would be a happy coming-of-age day now seemed more like an ordeal to endure. Well, to heck with them. She needed to calm herself. To be centered. This was her day. She'd waited many long years for this, and she didn't plan to let two grumpy men ruin it for her.

After a breakfast where Tevy would not be contained and she again couldn't eat, Rianth slipped off by herself for a cleansing in the warm, humid bathing house set over a small hot springs. Afterward, back in her room, she plaited her wet hair and slipped into the linen shift she must wear to her True-Naming. Boys and girls alike entered the druid's tower in this shift. She knew to wear only the shift, but Rianth slipped her father's bag of runes around her neck. They'd been her lucky charm this long. Maybe they'd help her through today. She'd reluctantly left her gloves on her bed. Not wearing them didn't feel right. She was vulnerable, naked.

Today would not be easy.

Uja surprised her, waiting outside. "Happy birthday, Sister." He held out a small packet for her. "Just…um…just some food. You know, in case you're in the…um…tower for a long time."

Moved to tears, Rianth blinked them back. She clutched the pack to her body. "Thank you. I needed this kindness more than anything today." She kissed him on the cheek, which made him redden even further.

"Have I ever told you how proud I am of you, Uja?"

He dipped his head as he shook it and mortification filled Rianth. "I should have." Tipping his head up with her finger, she looked him straight in the eye, wanting him to understand the truth in what she said. "You are the reason we are all alive."

He tried to shake his head more emphatically, but she held him. "You are. Believe that."

"I don't protect our home like you do."

Rianth laughed. "There's not much to protect around here. You know that. You protect also, though. You protect our fields, keep them safe and growing. Even in winter. That, little brother, is the lifeblood of our home. I am forever grateful for your talents and in awe of it at the same time."

Uja gulped. "Do you really think that?"

"Of course I do. I'm sorry I didn't tell you this sooner." Rianth hugged him long and hard.

When the bell tolled, signaling the time had come for her to appear before the druid's tower, Uja stepped back and nerves filled Rianth anew. She could jump out of her skin at any moment, she was so twitchy.

"Everything you do, you do well," Uja said, patting her on the shoulder. "This will be no different."

"Thanks, Uja. I love you."

"I love you, too. Go and find your future."

Even with Uja's fortification, Rianth walked to the tower shivering, as though she were walking to the gallows she'd heard had been used in ancient times. Wringing her hands together, it surprised her that she missed her gloves so much. Or maybe that was simply a metaphor for what she really missed. She shouldn't be alone on this walk. She'd asked Kaiden to accompany her as she went to find her fate. Each candidate could ask for a companion, but only to the doors of the druid's tower. Last night his answer had been apparent.

"Planning to go it alone, are you?" Kaiden stepped

into place beside her.

Rianth had to suppress her relief. There were too many unanswered questions between them. "I didn't think you wanted to be anywhere near me," Rianth said.

He stopped her, and turned her to face him. "Ri, I—"

"What?" She held her head up defiantly.

For a moment he looked like he would give her some real honesty. When she stared at him, he gripped her shoulders hard. "Remember what I said last night?"

"You didn't say much, if anything at all."

"About strength. You will be fine, as long as you remember how strong you are. You can weather this."

"Weather what? What is going to happen that I need to weather?"

Somehow, they'd made it to the wide circular common area with the druid's tower on one edge. True-Namings were an event here, and the entire village turned out for them. Rianth's day was no different. The area was filled to overflowing and the air of expectation felt palpable.

Jonah patted her shoulder, then a path opened up through the throng of people. A path that led to the door of the keep where Bhren stood waiting. Rianth's nerves hit their zenith. She wished she had her sword strapped to her side. That was her protection against almost anything. Her sword, her gloves, she'd had to leave everything behind for this ceremony. Almost everything. She could not leave the runes behind, no matter who said it must be so.

Rianth handed Uja's food packet to Kaiden. He'd gone pale and looked like he would be ill. She gulped as the bell tolled one final time.

"Remember, Rianth. Be strong. I'm sorry. I wish…"

Yet another incomplete piece of information. Rianth shook her head, shook off the hand that gripped her arm, and marched resolutely toward her future.

When the door closed behind her, she wanted to let her rigid shoulders relax. Somehow, she knew her conversation with Kaiden would not be the toughest thing she'd endure this day.

CHAPTER NINE

Not here. Anywhere but here. Rianth stood, not in the room at the bottom of the tower that she'd expected to stay in, but in Bhren's study on the second and top floor. In front of Bhren's dirt-filled table. Terror, and the memory of dark shapes surrounding her, rooted her to the spot. She clutched her hands behind her back, dearly wishing for the third time this day that she had her gloves.

Rianth stood straight and still and stared at the dirt with no idea how much time had passed. Finally, she turned to Bhren, who stood silent on the other side of the table. "What am I supposed to do?"

He cocked his head. "What do you think you are supposed to do?"

Was this the test? That she should be able to determine the next step? Rianth looked around the study. Nothing seemed different, nothing out of place. With only one window, glow pots lit the rock-walled room, adding soft light. She'd sat here many times, being taught, handed knowledge. Learning the hard way that she'd become susceptible to visions.

Bhren stood opposite her, still and watching. Her breath caught when it hit her. The table was her test. Rianth knew this would be the fire she must walk through to show her strength and unleash her ability to tap Earth's magic.

She must connect with the dirt so the magic could determine her fate.

Panic filled her as she tried to breathe. Clenching her fists, she shook her head.

Bhren continued to stand quietly, his face a mask, devoid of any emotion or attachment.

She couldn't do this again. He asked too much. Her True-Naming should be a test, not something that might mean her death. Was she required to step through the fires of hell? And if she survived, she'd become an adult?

How could they ask this? Rianth glared at Bhren. How could he ask?

He hadn't asked. Bhren had left it to her to decide what to do. This ritual had become the hope of humanity's future. The prophecy foretold that someone with the power to heal the earth would come along. In over one hundred years, not one soul had been found with that kind of power. Rianth hung her head. She'd been a fool to think her True-Naming would not be the most difficult thing she'd ever done. She tapped the edge of the table, trying to decide, yet already knowing what must happen.

So be it.

Her lungs filled with air as she took a deep, calming

breath and plunged both hands into the soil.

Dark shadows floated, just like before. Only this time, they floated around her. The fire, the light she'd seen streaking into each of them from the central hub, now came directly from her own chest, drawing her own energy.

Rianth felt the energy being drained out of her, like she'd become some sort of conduit. She grew weaker.

They grew stronger.

She must break the contact, but how?

One of the shadows stood apart from the rest. Eyes, deep pools of gold in a sea of black mist under a hooded cowl distracted her, called her.

"You are one of us. Be with us."

Evil radiated from those eyes. Rianth felt it like a blow to her body. Still, something in those golden eyes held her captive. She couldn't look away.

"Reach out to me. Let us find you so you can become one with us. Together, we can do anything. You can do anything."

A hand settled on her shoulder. Part of her recognized that Bhren had become one with her vision. Something to puzzle over later. Her complete focus must remain on the wraith in front of her.

The apparition glared at Bhren for a long moment before turning back to Rianth.

"Join us. Join with me. Come to me."

The voice beckoned, enticed. And all the while energy flowed out of Rianth. She knew the shadows would leave nothing. They'd destroy her if she didn't break the bond.

"Help me," Rianth cried.

I am trying, Bhren spoke in her mind. *But I cannot*

break you free from the soil. Something holds you tight. You must find a way. His voice was urgent. *Quickly. You must release yourself from this. The danger is grave.*

She knew that. She grew weaker with each passing minute. But how?

"Do not listen to this useless old man," the wraith said, loathing coated her voice with poison. *"He cannot help you, cannot guide you to the happiness I offer."*

The shadows focused all their attention on her. No, not on her. On the source of the energy. It came from her chest.

A bony hand reached toward her.

She looked down, recognized she was not the primary source of the power being drawn away. The bag around her neck seemed to be their focus. The runes, given to her by her father. Rianth reached for the bag, barely able to move, her arms seemed weighed down and heavy.

Inch by inch she edged her hand upward through an unseen barrier, as if digging through mud. Each time she closed in, the runes seemed further and further away.

"Come to me." The voice grew more urgent the closer she got to the runes.

"Join us in immortality."

Rianth touched the bag at the corner, fingertips brushing the soft suede. The power drain dipped. With a heroic effort, her fingers crawled over the bag. The power drain lessened more.

After an eternity passed, Rianth finally managed to close her hand around the bag. The energy flow stopped and the shadows jumped back as if slapped.

The malevolent golden eyes turned red with anger. "We will come for you. We will find you."

Someone—Bhren—yanked her hand out of the dirt and Rianth fell to the floor, exhausted and beyond caring about True-Namings or anything. She could barely move. She clasped the bag beneath her shift tightly as she gasped for breath. Pushing herself up, she fell back down, lacking enough energy to sit up. She tried again, her arms shaking as she forced herself to a sitting position. More time would have to pass before standing was possible. It was as if she'd just put in hours of hard practice on the training field.

Bhren lay beside her, his own chest heaving. His skin had turned ashen and he looked like he'd come through hell, and not unscathed.

"What just happened?" she whispered. "What were those…things?"

CHAPTER TEN

Shock filled Bhren as he sat up, trying to make sense of what he'd witnessed. The vision attempt had not been part of the True-Naming ceremony. He'd been desperate to see if the girl could repeat what had happened before. He knew now she could. No other in his long life had shown an ability for this type of vision. Rune foretelling, certainly. But to connect through some astral plane? Rianth was the first he had seen since the war.

She was special. And they needed to protect her, to give her time to come fully into her powers. He knew that now more than ever. The runes had foretold someone with great power was very close. She had to be the one he and the others had seen in the foretelling. The reason for the prophecy they'd written. All this time, he'd never known for certain if it were even possible. All these years, he'd waited.

The light outside brightened, probably a cloud leaving the sun behind. It was enough to lighten the room, along with Bhren's mood. For the first time in years, he felt like laughing, crying, running. The release of all his hopes in this one big rush overflowed within him.

Dismay quickly followed, along with a draining fear. What she'd just gone through, and he'd witnessed, had not been a vision. No, it had been quite real. She'd found her way to the *ehwaz*, the vision plane. A place between here and the afterlife, where what happened had real consequences. That person, that wraith they'd seen, had radiated malevolence. Who was it? He hadn't seen that much raw magic in a century or more. Yes, it had been the *awen*, Earth's magic he'd hoped to rekindle. Whoever it was had wielded more power than he'd seen in a generation. Could it be? No. That one had gone to the forever sleep at the end of the war.

What had stopped the power drain from Rianth? So far, she had shown little or no magical talent. Was that talent somehow blocked? Would she be able to find the key to her own power in time? So many years had passed, with the world's people buried under more strife than ever before. If she could not find a way soon, humanity might well be doomed.

Bhren needed time to think. For now, that would have to wait. He had a novitiate to walk through the steps of her True-Naming.

His own foretelling over the past weeks had shown him that danger was nearby. Until today, he hadn't realized how prevalent that danger was. Or how pivotal Rianth truly was to the struggle that was coming. He looked at the telltale bulge where the bag lay around her neck. He'd seen it, knew it might well be what the Guardian druids had created all those years ago. Since only the prophesied one could wield that talisman, Bhren had chosen to wait and watch. The fates had given it to Rianth for a reason, and only time would impart the reason she had been chosen as its guardian.

He admitted to a mighty curiosity about how she'd managed to break the bond the shadows had tried to forge with her, something that went beyond any ability he had. Until he had time to sort this all out, and until the day arrived when she must become the hope of mankind, he could do nothing except keep the danger at bay and try to protect her. For now, that was paramount. It meant she must not learn how important she was. Neither could anyone else, save Kaiden. Rianth must be hidden, which meant he must proceed with his original plan and pray that the earth would protect them all through the coming trials.

"No more questions. Stand, novitiate." He croaked the words out, cleared his throat, and repeated the command. "Stand."

He watched her struggle to do as he ordered. The power drain had been real. If she hadn't managed to break free... No, he would not consider what had not happened. He must stay in the present, complete what must be done.

Rianth Royan stood in front of him, shoulders back, stance proud, an aura of awareness surrounding her. She knew that whatever had happened, she had bested it. A part of Bhren wished he could acknowledge that. The girl had more strength than she recognized. In order to keep her safe, though, he must stay the course.

Bhren spread the white cloth of forecasting out on

the table and opened his rune bag. Runes that had foretold the strengths and futures of countless novitiates over the years. Runes that had always led him along the path he needed to tread, and that now, he must manipulate to walk a path he chose.

He stood before the table and beckoned Rianth to take a place opposite him. She watched the table, the soil within, with acute awareness.

Rianth had been well-schooled in the foretelling through runes. He'd made certain of that himself. Unfortunately, that made it even harder for him to do what he must now do.

Intoning the words of the True-Naming ceremony, Bhren tossed the runes, pulling every bit of power within him to turn them to his will. Turn they did, although sluggishly.

Rianth watched as they settled, read the runes with him, knew her determined place as well as he did.

She faltered, grabbing the edge of the table to steady herself.

"I thought—"

"The runes have spoken. Your training and strength have been foretold. You are *Rianthe*, no longer Rianth. You are *uruz*."

"No! It can't be," she said. "That can't be right."

Bhren almost broke at her anguished look. "Silence, student." He forged a tone of steel to keep her from questioning. "The runes cannot lie. Your fate is determined and you must announce."

He watched the play of emotions on her face. Knew how deeply he had wounded her, and wished beyond anything that he could explain.

Kaiden's words roared through Rianth's head, the memory of their last meeting filling eyes blurred by tears. *If the runes foretell a change to the beginning of your name, like when mine became Kaiden, your ability is strong. If the change comes at the end...*

It took every ounce of strength she had to remain standing. *Uruz*? She'd been True-Named animal handler? Bhren had led her to believe she had latent power. She'd hoped to enter this tower and feel the infusion, to become the savior of her people. How stupid of her. Because of her own arrogance, she'd made assumptions. Assumptions that were apparently very, very wrong. The fates had determined that she had only enough power to clean up after animals.

This couldn't be happening. "It has to be a mistake," she whispered.

"It shall be as the fates have decreed," Bhren said, staring not at her but at the wall behind her. "You must announce."

The red heat of anger consumed her, making her itch with the need for some action. This can't be her future. She was to become a protector. *Thurisaz.* She was meant to keep what happened to her parents from ever happening again. She must keep her brothers and her home safe. Her ability on the training fields had proven that. Animals? They were not her calling. It just couldn't. Even Bhren had given her the impression... "You did this," she said to Bhren. "You did something to change my True-Naming." She flung the accusation at him like the downward slice of a sword—quick, harsh, and true to its mark.

Bhren's face gave nothing away. He stood straight and tall, saying nothing.

Rianthe's scream of frustration never left her lips. It couldn't because then everyone waiting outside would hear and know her humiliation.

She hung her head. No matter what she'd thought or what Bhren had led her to believe, he hadn't manipulated the runes. That wasn't possible. The truth had been shown to her. She did not have the power. Would not be the one to provide a better life for her people.

Her True-Naming was completed. She was Rianthe. Animal handler. She wondered how she'd manage to walk outside. The entire village had turned out for her ceremony. Had they thought what she thought? How could she face their hope? Or her brothers?

Too soon, she was at the door. The commotion outside indicated the druid had lit the fire in his stove that told of the conclusion of another True-Naming. There was no way to delay the inevitable, so she opened the door and walked out to the landing, onto steps that chilled the bottoms of her bare feet and kept her only three steps above the throng of people that pressed close, hoping. Praying.

Bhren stepped out beside her. Rianthe couldn't bear to look at him, to be this close. She took a step to the side, away from the master she'd looked up to all these years.

Her friends and family waited with barely concealed impatience. Uja stood near Fraka, his expression hopeful. Tevy, for this rare moment, stood solemn and still.

Rianthe tried to apologize with her eyes. She would not be their salvation. That wound cut deep and made it difficult to speak the words. There was nothing she had to offer to the people of New Hope.

"I entered the druid's keep as Rianth, the child. I

leave as—" Her voice broke and she struggled for the strength to finish. Straightening, she stared at the steps in front of her, unable to look at her family and friends anymore. These people had taken her and her brothers into their homes in their hour of need and she could repay them with…nothing. All their faith had been for naught.

Kaiden. She needed Kaiden beside her to get through this. Rianthe raised her head and searched until she found him on the edge of the landing. She reached out her hand for him, then the abject look on his face sunk in.

He knew.

Had known before she'd even walked into that tower.

He'd given her as much to hope about as Bhren. He'd known, and hadn't told her. The days of absence, the secrets he wouldn't tell her, even his final pleas. It all made sense now. He'd known. And he'd betrayed her.

His look pleaded with her for understanding, but none would come. Her mortification was complete. She'd been used, led along for some game that he and Bhren had played.

The knife cut through her heart, sheaving off huge slices. Pieces devoted to him, to her love for him. Rianthe let the emotion fall, leaving only the ash of death in its wake. So be it. The only thing she had left was to refuse to be a pawn in whatever game they played.

Rianthe straightened and started over, masking her face, removing any emotion. She must do this. "I entered the druid's keep as Rianth, the child. I return to you now as Rianthe, *uruz*."

The gasp from the villagers proved her undoing, and Rianthe couldn't stand in front of them any longer. She ran. Off the landing, down the steps, all the way to her room.

CHAPTER ELEVEN

Once back in her room, Rianthe gave in to the mortification and grief that stabbed her soul. She tore the shift over her head, tossing it, with the bag of runes, into a heap on the floor, and yanked on her own clothes, knowing the cold wasn't the only thing making her shake.

Animal handler? What did everyone think? What would she do?

How could he do this to her? It was bad enough that she'd been found completely lacking of any magic, but Kaiden had known this would happen. He'd known and hadn't given her any warning. Apparently, his precious relationship with Bhren was more important to him than her. Had they planned this? Were they laughing in the tower over the prank they'd pulled on her?

Rianthe picked up her sword—forged more years ago than anyone knew—and ran her hands over the cool metal, automatically searching the smooth surface for flaws. It had been a gift from Bhren on her thirteenth birthday. This is what she excelled at. Fighting. Protection. Not taking care of animals. The whole village knew that. Rianthe's laugh was bitter as she strapped the sword sheath around her hips. She'd made quite sure they knew she wanted to be a fighter. How could she face them?

How could she face Kaiden? Day after day, knowing he had betrayed her like this? He'd been the only person she'd truly befriended after witnessing the ghastly death of her parents and realizing there was no one left to trust. That rang truer now than ever before.

Seeing him every day, knowing what he'd done… No. Living with that pain was not an option. Rianthe knew what she must do. She had to get away. New Hope would never again feel like home to her. It was time for her to forge her own way in the world.

She yanked her knapsack out and stuffed a change of clothes into it. She could forage for most of her food, but a stop by the kitchen for a few days' worth would help her gain the distance from New Hope she desperately needed.

Should she ask Uja and Tevy to join her? She's always been there to keep them safe. This was the only home Tevy had known. And Uja had forged a good life here, too. It wouldn't be fair to ask them to leave. Rianthe clutched her pack to her chest. How would she bear not being near them? To keep them safe, to love them, to see them grow into the possibilities she saw in each of them.

She paced back and forth in her small room, trying to think straight. Hunting had taught her well not to let emotion get in the way of planning. As she passed the mirror, she stopped to stare at her reflection. She looked like a wild woman. Dirty tears streaked her cheeks and her hair was a snarled mess. Had she looked like this when she'd come out of the druid's tower?

Rianthe stepped closer, running a cloth over her cheeks to remove any reminder of what had happened to her this day. Her entire life had changed in the blink of a moment, yet she didn't look different. Still the same shape, the same dark hair. Hair that Kaiden loved. She could remember with aching clarity each and every time he'd wrapped a strand around his finger. How she'd longed for him to show her the same reverence he showed her hair. She'd never once even felt his kiss.

Rianthe ran a finger across her lips. She never would now. And because of that, she needed a complete change. Rianthe reached for her knife and began cutting. She didn't stop until her hair lay in piles around her on the floor and what remained was less than an inch long.

"Nice," Tevy said behind her.

Rianthe stared at herself, at amber eyes that somehow seemed larger. Unshed tears illuminated them even more in the soft daylight. She didn't recognize herself.

Maybe that was a good thing. "You think so?"

He cocked his head from side to side. "Sure. It just got in the way, right?"

And held too many memories.

"You makin' any other changes?" he asked.

Rianthe sat on the side of her bed and beckoned Tevy to join her. Tevy, always full of joy. Always older than his years. How could she do this to him? "Yes," she said slowly. "I am."

"You're leaving." The turmoil in his eyes belied the matter-of-fact tone in his voice.

"I have to."

"How long will you be gone?"

"I don't know," she lied.

Tevy hung his head for a long moment before he spoke. "You're not planning to come home, are you?"

"I'm sorry, Tevy. I need to make a new life for myself. I am *not* an animal handler."

"That's pretty easy to figure out."

Her heart broke as she hugged him tight to her side. "I need to find out what…who I am. And I can't do it here. Not any longer."

Tevy climbed up on the bed, placed a hand on each of Rianthe's cheeks, and made sure she looked right at him before he spoke. "Don't blame Kaiden. There is a lot going on here, and we don't know very much of it."

"You always have an extra sense about this stuff, Tevy. This time, I think you're wrong. I saw the answer in his eyes. I may not understand, but he does. I—" Rianthe clamped her mouth shut. Anything she said would only slice the knife deeper into her heart and run the risk of making life difficult for Tevy here in New Hope.

Instead, she gripped Tevy's arms. "You and Uja will be okay, right?"

"We'll be fine."

"Be mindful. And don't spend too much time with the animals. You need human interaction too."

Tevy laughed. "Being an animal handler isn't so bad, you know."

"I do. It's perfect for you, little brother. Just not for me."

"Well, I will be *uruz* when my time comes, and proud of it. But yes, I will also listen and mind and do my studies.”

With nothing else to say, Rianthe kissed both of her brother’s cheeks and rose, pulled on her gloves and cape, then reached for her knapsack. “Tell Uja I’m sorry.”

“I will. Be safe, Sister.”

“I will do my best. I love you.”

“I love you, too. Don’t say goodbye. We will see each other again.”

“I hope so.” Her voice broke.

“And don’t forget this.”

Rianthe turned to see Tevy holding up the bag of runes she’d tossed to the floor with her True-Naming shift. She took them from him, hefting the sack. Better to leave them here.

Tevy closed her hand around the bag and stared at her with the wisdom of an elder. “You never know when this might come in handy. Take them with you.”

Rianthe nodded. “For you, Tevy.” She settled the bag once again around her neck. Hugging her brother one last time, tears that she’d tamed now flowed freely down Rianthe’s cheeks. Steeling herself, she turned away from the only life, the only family she’d known for the past seven years. Now, she would become a gypsy, moving as the need struck, never setting down roots. Like before they’d found New Hope. This was her new destiny, and the only tolerable existence for her.

~~~

Flames of raw, red magic arced through the cavern. Oblivious of the rumbling walls, Taegar threw bolt after bolt, sending rocks crashing into each other as they rained down onto the altar and floor. She’d had the talisman almost within her grasp. It had to be what the girl had clutched. Nothing else could have broken that trance. No
~~~

one else had the power Taegar controlled. This cavern was the only place that held magic. She'd made certain of that after those fool Guardian druids had thought to hide the magic and destroy her. No one would stop her, including some sniveling little girl-child.

Who was she? She'd come twice now in the vision world, something Taegar had never experienced before. Did that mean the girl had power? Where was she?

Weakness warned Taegar that she'd overused her power. She stilled, even though fury exploded within her. She refused to be forced into the deep sleep by a depletion of her power. The talisman that would forever bind Earth's magic to her had almost been hers. How many times must it fall from her grasp before she would wield its power?

Taegar moved slowly through the catacomb of caves, to the deepest, darkest place where she rested when she must. She warded the entrance against trespassers, then used one last bit of power to be certain each of her acolytes knew what this girl looked like and that she, and whatever she wore, must be brought to Taegar unharmed. She must have the talisman. She must.

Taegar closed her eyes, knowing that, until that time, she must save herself. Rest was necessary. For now.

CHAPTER TWELVE

He'd known she'd come here. She stood in their spot, looking out over the lake, still and silent except for clouds of breath she blew out and shoulders that heaved and fell in pain. He'd hurt her. There had been no choice. Duty had required it. That didn't make it any easier for him, and definitely not for her.

Kaiden approached with quiet care, knowing Rianthe sensed him, not wanting to spook her.

"I don't want to talk to you," she whispered, her hood falling to her shoulders.

Her hair! Kaiden barely held back his gasp. All that beautiful, silky, long hair just…gone. "You have to. I need to explain."

Before Kaiden had a chance to react, he was on the ground, Rianth's sword pressed into his neck. He didn't fight back. He saw the crimson fury in her face, in her eyes. A long time passed before she turned the sword broadside against his skin. She leaned down, her eyes following the blade of her sword until they met his.

"Now you want to explain?" Her voice sounded like the dark of a moonless night, quiet and devoid of any light. "After my life is ruined, with you fully aware that it would happen, you want me to listen to your why?"

He waited, almost hoping she'd cut him. Hurt him. Anything to assuage the pain he'd caused her. This quietness was unlike her and it scared him more than anything.

"I don't want to hear it, Kaiden." Her voice held little emotion as she straightened and sheathed her sword, only the sound of complete exhaustion, and the light in her eyes appeared almost nonexistent.

He'd helped to dim that light and could not think of a single thing to ease the pain he'd caused her. Pain that stung his heart like the wasps of summer, over and over again.

"You'll have to eventually. We can't live in New Hope and just ignore each other."

"No," she said, reaching for the knapsack he hadn't seen on the ground. "We can't."

Fear gripped him. "You're leaving?"

"Yes."

"You can't." He grasped her arms. "You won't be safe. I won't be able to keep you from harm."

"It's not your job to keep me safe."

"That has always been my job."

"Not anymore." Her eyes told the truth, even as the dried salt tracks on her face tried to deny it. He'd become dead to her.

Kaiden's heart broke into a thousand slivers of glass, each shattering into a thousand more. He almost doubled over as the pain sliced through him, expanding, freezing blood and sinew into immobility. He tried to breathe. It caught in his throat. Bile rose up and bubbled into the empty space. Kaiden let loose of her arms and clenched and unclenched his fists, trying to regain some control. He must convince Rianthe to stay, must reason with her. But how?

"Ri—" He winced when she shook her head at her nickname's use. "I know you're mad at me. Please, don't do something stupid because of that. I'll stay away. From New Hope. From you. Whatever you want. Just…stay."

"I can't. You and Bhren and your concocted animal handler selection make it impossible."

"It wasn't—"

"Wasn't what? Some ruse you two planned to ruin my life?"

"It wasn't like that. You need to understand, Ri. I—you have to stay. I can't protect you *and* New Hope if you leave. I can't keep you both safe."

Rianthe shook her head. "I'm not your job. Not anymore."

"You are. Look, I'll leave. I'll camp outside of New Hope. You'll never see me. Please. Stay!"

"It's too late. And don't do to Uja and Tevy what you've done to me, or I'll become your worst nightmare."

"I would never hurt them. I'd protect them with my life."

"You'd better. Goodbye, Kaiden." She looked almost like she wanted to reach out to him, but instead she clutched her bag tightly to her chest with her gloved hands. "I hope you find happiness in your secrets."

That was the last he heard of the voice that had invaded his dreams since she'd first stumbled into his life. He watched in despair as she walked steadily off, soon swallowed by the forest they'd mapped and hunted in together.

Despair rooted him to the spot and tore his heart from his chest. A week ago they'd been happy. And he'd been so close to proclaiming his true feelings. All these years of being by her side and still unable to tell her. She'd been too young. And now, when she'd come of age and he could finally profess how he felt, Bhren's visions had severed the tie between them as readily as Kaiden's own knife sliced through a blade of grass.

I love you.

What had he done?

ALLIANCE

CHAPTER THIRTEEN

The Fringes
Five years later

Rianthe always, always tried for peaceful resolutions. Sometimes, like now, she had to knock a few heads to bring everyone around to the right compromise. And sometimes she had to do worse.

"Let him go." Rianthe kept her words calm, her voice carefully modulated. No need to give Cordin any reason to escalate things. The man's mean streak gave peacekeepers a bad name. In five years she'd never seen anyone with a more misguided attitude about his trade. He was supposed to keep the peace, not badger inn and storekeepers until they paid him for services he hadn't even provided.

The face of the poor man currently being held upside down by his feet had turned the most unlikely shade of red. So much white showed in his round eyes, Rianthe would have laughed if she weren't busy keeping a peripheral eye on the three men moving to surround her.

Her primary focus was the man in front of her. Cordin Harm lived up to his name. He was dangerous and he liked hurting others. Too much. He'd gone too far here, requiring much more than the requisite room and board for keeping the peace.

"Let him go," she said again.

Cordin shook the man he still held up. His beefy arms didn't even look strained. "Make me."

Letting loose an exaggerated sigh, Rianthe gave in to the fact that diplomacy would not resolve this. She was getting so tired of always having to fight her way through to the right of things.

She took a step toward Cordin and he shook the man again. The three men who obviously worked for him tightened ranks around her as the rest of the small hamlet moved back. "So, you're going to let these losers fight your battles for you?"

"They are just the opening volley," he said with a hearty laugh. "I am the dessert, though, you will not make it to that point." His laughter rolled on as his men raised their swords.

A blur of gray and brown outside the circle of swords proved that she was ready. It was time. Rianthe drew her short knife and sword, felt the tingle of a coming battle flow from the sword, up her arms, and course through her body. "Last chance to give up and leave, Cordin," she said.

"Ah, *cheri*, I will miss sparring with you." He waved a hand at his men.

Rianthe caught the first sword as it barely started its

downward path. The second man's steel met her short knife. Metal clanged against metal. The third took a step toward her; he stopped short and got yanked backwards, his calf firmly in the strong jaw of a large wolf. His howl told Rianthe her partner had the edges well in hand. One down, two to go.

She side-stepped both swords, threw herself into reverse and stabbed, catching one man in the thigh. Still he came on, as did the other, both swords bearing down on her. Their eyes gleamed. They knew they had the upper hand. They could smell the win.

Instead of waiting for her doom, Rianthe laughed, adrenaline firing through every pore in her skin. She sizzled with energy, like she could take on the world. And she did.

She waited until they drew close, then dropped to her back and rolled. Her sword caught one man's leg, her knife sent a river of blood down the other's leg. Leaping back to her feet, she dove in, stabbing one in the shoulder. He screamed as he went down.

"Stay down or you die." She barely ground the words out before the whoosh of air sent her diving for the ground again, immediately rolling to the side as the same sword stabbed at her.

In a reverse back flip, Rianthe got back to her feet and turned to her adversary.

"Cordin. You decided to join the fight, I see." Where was the man she hadn't yet disabled? She couldn't see him.

"I don't dare let my men have all the fun," he said, circling, forcing her to move with him. He was drawing her off, hiding something behind her. Rianthe kept her eyes on Cordin, using her other senses to reach out.

She heard nothing behind her.

Felt no changes in the air around her.

No one screamed or gave any warning.

No. None of that happened. Yet, Cordin's smile widened, and the scent of sour mash reached her, grew stronger.

As Cordin's laughter renewed, Rianthe flipped her sword and drove it behind her, right into the gut of the third man. He would die an ugly death. Cordin charged, his massive body turning his sword into a battering ram through forward momentum.

Rianthe stepped aside, expecting him to roar past, unable to stop himself. Her one mistake.

He did not. Lighter on his feet than she expected, the bear of a man pivoted on one foot and came at her. Her sword, her arm, and a strong will to live—those were the only things that saved her.

Clang! Sword met sword. He pushed, she pushed back. And slowly, ever so slowly, he pushed her backward, down, toward the ground. His eyes sparkled with the promise of his win.

Her loss.

Rianthe's arm weakened under the onslaught. For the first time, she was afraid she might not win. This might be it. The end. Uja. Tevy. She'd never see them again.

No! That could not be. She must survive. She must see her brothers again. She would. She pushed against Cordin's sword, against him. He did not budge.

Suddenly, she knew what to do. Rianthe weakened further, bent her arm, showed her weakness.

"Aha!" Cordin yelled, pressing his challenge. It was his undoing, since he committed everything to the maneuver. Rianthe dropped at an angle to the ground, out of the way of his spearing sword. Before Cordin had even hit the dirt, she'd regained her feet. He turned, but too late, as she drove her sword through his black heart. She could hear its beat slowing, feel the vibration through her sword.

Ba-bumph. Ba-bumph. Ba-bumph. Slower and slower. Her sword still in Cordin's chest, she grieved as the light left his eyes. Death was so unnecessary. A tear fell. Her tear. It splashed gently on Cordin's face, his expression changing to one of peace as his eyes closed.

He drew his final breath as Rianthe drew in one more ragged one, straightening with an effort. Exhaustion barely suppressed, she stood tall and looked around her. The body of the other man she'd killed lay where she'd dealt the death blow. The other two had disappeared, probably to lick their wounds in some hole.

Pressure against her leg meant the danger had passed. Her partner, her faithful wolf friend, Taschia, grinned up at her with a lolling tongue. Rianthe petted her, tangling her hand in the wolf's fur in gratitude.

No one came near her. No one dared, until, finally, the innkeeper approached, nodding his head in gratitude. "Thank you, thank you, thank you, Peacekeeper Rianthe. You have saved us from an evil man."

Golden eyes hidden in the back of her mind came forward, staring at her with malevolent intent. Rianthe sheathed her sword. "Trust me. Evil is much worse than Cordin Harm."

"Well, at any rate, you've slayed our beast and we are grateful."

"I killed men because you could not solve your own problems."

He huffed, remaining silent. A part of Rianthe

wanted him to argue. She knew he stayed quiet, not because he agreed that loss of life was never good, but because she confused him. This hamlet's attitude would not be changed by today's events. Not like her, affected by each and every death at her hands. Thankfully, she'd found peaceful solutions more often than resolution by sword.

Rianthe walked to the edge of the fight area and picked up her cloak. Now that the adrenaline had left her, the chill of the fall season hit her. She needed to get out of here and beside a warm fire, alone with her thoughts.

"I'll take my payment and be on my way," she said.

He blustered, making Rianthe shake her head. She only ever asked for a few days' food. Rianthe placed a hand on her short sword and held her other one out. The innkeeper nodded and hobbled away, returning quickly with a sack of food.

A much smaller sack than his gratitude had indicated should be paid.

She turned around and walked away without a backward glance, Taschia at her side, wondering why she expected anything different from folks who lived in the Fringes.

~~~

Rianthe laid out her bedroll and sank down upon it, too tired to even remove her gloves to eat the bread loaf and cheese she'd been given. Meager offerings, considering she'd killed two men. She hated that she'd killed. Again. It happened, and the first time…that had been brutal. Her nightmares were now intermingled with visions of blood dripping from her sword. Yes, she killed. Because she had to. Rianthe preferred nonviolent methods to resolve issues. Unfortunately, others didn't
~~~

always see it that way.

She'd cleaned her sword in a nearby stream, but needed to give it a good polish tomorrow. Rianthe rubbed her arm. Her body had been used sorely this day and she would pay for it, having to lay low for a few days and recover her strength. It always bothered her that these fights seemed to drain her so badly.

No matter how much she'd wanted to find an easier life, that quest eluded her and everyone else. No one that she'd met in her travels had carved out anything beyond a meager existence. The Fringes were as depressed as New Hope had been. Food was scarce and any way to make a living was scarcer.

Taschia lay down next to her and the fire she'd built to ward off the autumn chill. Rianthe pulled her gloves off to scratch the wolf's ears, then broke off an end of the loaf and fed it to her.

The wolf had shown up at her side three years ago and never left. Had Tevy sent her? A qualm of homesickness washed over Rianthe as she wondered yet again how Tevy and Uja were doing. They'd be much older now. She probably wouldn't recognize the young man Uja had become. His True-Naming should have happened two years ago. Rianthe was quite certain he'd been named *fehu*. He would be a gardener–alchemist. He'd shown so much promise, his ceremony must have had a good outcome. Unlike hers. Rianthe shook the thought away. That kind of reminiscing didn't help her let go of the day's work and relax.

Tevy was about to turn twelve. Little Tevy, growing up without her. Was he doing his chores? Going to Studies? Or, as she usually pictured him, was he out running with his wolves?

and Taschia moved next to her, adding warmth to a night that now chilled her to the bone. The additional heat didn't help the cold that had sunk deep into her soul. Cold that did not come from the night, but from the runes and what she saw in them.

Reaching for her gloves to gather the runes up, Rianthe paused. In all these years, the old visions had continued to haunt her. Nightly terrors of her parents' deaths intermingled with an altar of shadows.

She'd been out here in the land of no magic for a long time. Maybe whatever had come at her in those visions couldn't reach her here. Deep inside, Rianthe knew different, and each dark night she was reminded that the horror could reach her anywhere.

Still, she was tempted to try, and out here, where no one would see, was the best place. She didn't need another fight tonight.

Rianthe rubbed her ice-cold hands together. Before, when she'd had the visions, Bhren had been there. He'd even saved her from who knew what in that last one. What if…what if they were real? What if she didn't find a way out? Would she be swallowed up into nothingness?

Those eyes, golden and deadly, still swirled in her mind like a cesspool. Yet something about them drew her. There was a powerful magic surrounding them. A magic she'd once thought she might have inside her. Still, at the point Bhren had thrown the runes to divine her abilities, she'd been found lacking.

The runes sat silent and unmoving in the soil. Rianthe reached out, her hand shaking so bad she pulled it tight against her chest. What was she? Some yearling with not a single bit of courage in her?

Rianthe closed both hands into fists, relaxed them,

took a deep calming breath, and reached out again, her hands poised above the runes. Before she could react, an intangible force grabbed her hand and yanked it to the earth—fingers, runes, and dirt intermingling.

The change happened immediately and powerfully. No longer did she lay with Taschia beside a warm fire in the woods of the Fringes. Pain sliced through her. Intense pain flowed through her entire body like a thousand tiny needles.

Golden eyes filled her vision, the same, but different somehow. It was almost as if they were surprised?

"I have waited long for you to show yourself. Too long. You have what I desire," the deep voice boomed, pounding through her head.

Rianthe bit back the scream but couldn't keep the whimper from escaping. The pain was so great.

"Bring the talisman to me and you will never know pain again."

She couldn't speak to answer, her voice muted by pain. Her body was on fire. Rianthe couldn't take it much longer. She would succumb.

She barely felt the nudge at her side. Reaching out blindly, her hands fisted around fur.

Another nudge.

"Bring it to me." The shrouded eyes moved toward her, hands reaching for her, pulling at her.

The hit came from nowhere and everywhere, knocking Rianthe to her back and sucking the breath from her lungs. The golden eyes disappeared, replaced by the sounds of night and the warmth of the nearby fire.

Rianthe lay there gasping, a heaviness in her chest she couldn't ease. She opened her eyes to two paws that stood squarely on her chest, and looked up. Eyes, one deep blue and one darkest brown, stared unblinking at her.

You are well?

Rianthe's mouth dropped open as shock replaced the pain and fear of the vision. "You can mind-speak?"

Of course.

"Why—Why haven't I heard…"

Taschia's head cocked. *You were closed to the possibility.*

Rianthe hadn't even known mind-speak was possible, unless you were someone like Tevy. She stared at her companion until Taschia stepped aside and sat docile and patient, waiting.

Rianthe sat up, careful to not touch the dirt around her bedroll, still working to slow her breathing and understand what had just happened. "How did you find me, Taschia?"

Tevy sent me.

Love gushed up in Rianthe at his mention. Tevy. Her Tevy. Years younger, yet still trying to protect his big sister. *Thank you, little brother.* She missed Tevy so much. Uja, too, but Tevy was special. What she wouldn't give to see his smiling face.

I miss him, too. I miss my brothers.

One of the best memories she had came from the day Tevy had so excitedly taken her to the barn to meet the pups. She'd met Taschia that day. Rianthe grinned. Somehow she'd known, staring into her odd-colored eyes, that they'd had a special connection. That sloppy kiss to her cheek had been more than a hello.

Taschia inclined her head, her lips curling in a wolf's version of a smile. *We bonded that day, sister. Our brother would not let me follow you until I was ready.*

The wolf sounded miffed as she picked up the nearby gloves in her mouth and waited patiently for Rianthe to tug them on before leaning into Rianthe's hug.

"Thank you, my friend."

You are very welcome.

Rianthe's grin ebbed. She couldn't sweep away the mountain of confusion that added to her discontent. Too much had happened to make sense of it all. That vision… No, that hadn't been a vision. They had never been visions, she realized. More like some sort of beyond-the-body experience. The pain had been real. Rianthe flinched and hugged herself to ward off any remaining needles of pain.

Taschia moved to her side, once again adding warmth and comfort. Rianthe felt lucky to have her companion. The day Taschia had shown up, she'd arrived at a skirmish just in time to bite a brigand's hand before he bore down on Rianthe with his sword, presumably to skewer her.

"All those times, all those battles, you never spoke to me."

Taschia rubbed her head against Rianthe. *There was no need.*

Rianthe scratched her ears. "I wish I could see Tevy." She picked up the runes, carefully wiping all dirt from them, and returned them to their bag. With it once again safely hidden around her neck, there was nothing to keep the memories at bay. Rianthe sought to understand what had happened. She swore the pain lingered, or was it simply the thought of pain?

And underneath that pain, she'd sensed something else. A sadness, a weakening, a plea. From the golden-eyed wraith? Rianthe found it hard to believe that one would show her any weakness. Had someone else been part of that vision? Or something else?

What is happening? The awareness of coming danger grew within Rianthe as she tried to reason out who and what she'd seen. Three times now the shadows and eyes had come to her. Each time more powerful. And this time…

Rianthe sifted dirt through her gloved hand, watched it fall like dark mist to the ground. Danger came for her. Danger would become her bedmate. She was certain of that now.

Someone comes, Taschia mind-spoke.

In a flash, Rianthe stood in a battle stance, her sword unsheathed. The awareness of danger hadn't just been from the vision. A more imminent cause invaded her mind, rushing through her body as alertness vibrated through her.

He comes.

"He?" But Rianthe didn't have to ask. She could already smell the forest of New Hope mingled with the woods of the Fringes. *Kaiden.* Even after all this time her gut roiled with acid emotion. Anger, hurt, frustration, and something else. Something she'd fought hard to suppress and refused to acknowledge now.

He stepped out slowly from behind a tree.

"Kaiden."

His lips curled up. "Almighty Kaiden to you."

Rianthe did not relax her stance. Rather, she reminded her heart and head of the truth she'd learned the hard way, that he was Kaiden the Betrayer. She narrowed her eyes, the only answer he deserved. She would not accept his baiting.

"You did not see me." His voice had changed,

become deeper, manlier. She still almost shivered as their nighttime and morning talks, when she'd loved to listen to his voice more than anything, filled her mind.

No. She couldn't think about those things. She must remember. Kaiden had become enemy, not friend. "I was waiting for you to make the first move."

He looked good. Better even than her imagination had guessed. Taller, if that were possible, and more muscled, more hardened. Her legs threatened to give way as she stared at him, shaking her head to break the spell. The flutter in Rianthe's chest must be an echo of a long-forgotten past. She did not have feelings for this man anymore.

Small lines at the edges of his eyes showed that he had laughed much in her absence. Rianthe clenched her teeth, wondering if that silly girl, Anniah, had put the signs of contentment on Kaiden's face. Then she reminded herself again she did not have feelings for this man.

He took a step forward, stopping to eye Taschia, who bared her teeth and growled.

"Close enough," Rianthe said.

A pained expression crossed Kaiden's face before he hid it. He held his arms out to each side. "My weapon is sheathed, Ri. I did not come here to fight you."

"Why did you come?" She hadn't planned on asking. Rianthe didn't want to know. Something in the growing urgency of his voice compelled her.

"It's time, Ri. Earth—" He closed his eyes. "New Hope needs you. The taint is growing. A storm is coming."

The first genuine laugh Rianthe had felt in years bubbled up within her as she sheathed her sword, replaced by a bitter taste when she answered. "New Hope doesn't need another animal handler."

Unless they didn't have one. Rianthe took a step toward Kaiden. "Tevy! Is Tevy all right?"

"He spends more time with the animals than with the people of New Hope, but other than that, Tevy was fine when I left."

"And Uja?"

Kaiden's expression softened, if that were possible. "Also fine. He and Fraka have married and are in charge of the growing fields."

Her heart swelled with the smile her lips couldn't show. "He's too young to be married."

"He's almost twenty-one. His True-Naming happened two years hence. Besides, this life ages us all beyond our years. Fraka is the same age. They married right after Uja's True-Naming, and the entire village blessed their union."

She'd hoped for all this time that Uja might find someone to share his passion with. Relief flooded her. If anything happened to Tevy or Uja, she'd never forgive herself.

So why was Kaiden really here? "Did Bhren send you?"

Kaiden's nostrils flared, giving her the answer she already knew.

"Still the druid's puppet, are you? Well, you can tell Bhren you found me, and that I am content where I am. I will not be returning at his beckoning."

"I can't tell him that. Something has happened."

"What?"

"I don't know. I… I sense an increase in the darkness and a danger I can't decipher. Bhren sent me for a reason, to tell you—"

The rustling of leaves and underbrush froze their conversation. Taschia's ears perked forward. Rianthe turned to face whatever came at them only scant seconds before Kaiden. They stood side by side, just as they had so many times on the practice field. It galled Rianthe that she allied with Kaiden so easily after everything that had happened. As soon as they dealt with this new threat, she'd force him to leave so she could get back to her life.

"She's this way. I saw her entranced and using rune magic."

Dram. Someone must have seen her during her vision. This wasn't good. The Fringes maintained a strict code about no magic and harsh punishments were meted out to anyone suspected of magicking.

"You told us back in camp that she was all twitchy and unaware you were even there. Ain't a one of us that can match her skills if she's aware."

Double dram. More people knew about it than just this group. It seemed her life in the Fringes had come to an end. If she didn't know better, she'd suspect Bhren and Kaiden of manufacturing this whole event on purpose to get her back to New Hope.

"She was enthralled, I tell you," the first man said. "Besides, we aren't one. They's four of us. Now shut up. We gotta hope she's still in the magic so she doesn't see us comin'. We'll take care of her right quick, then claim her things for ourselves. That sword of hers is all mine, though. You mind that."

"Looks like your secret's out, Ri."

"Shut up," she spat back quietly, knowing in her sinking heart that Kaiden's words were very, very right.

The brigands, four of them, burst through the brush

wielding swords they waved back and forth in crazy patterns. It was a wonder they didn't stab each other in their excitement. They stopped short when they saw a very ready Rianthe. Their eyes widened when they noticed she wasn't alone. The one who'd been speaking as they approached stepped forward, puffing out his chest and waving his sword.

"You have harnessed magic in the Fringes. By order of the closest camp leader, you are to be put to death."

Rianthe laughed. "And who is it that plans to carry out that order?" She ran a hand along her sword, watching the firelight play along its length.

"We do." He gulped.

"Just the four of you?"

"We don't need no others." He glanced at Kaiden, worry creasing the ridges on his forehead.

"You sure you don't want to go back for more help?" Rianthe's hope lay in the fervent belief that they would do exactly that, giving her time to vacate before they returned.

The men looked at each other, and she saw they wanted to. The leader barked at them all. "She'll be long gone if we go back for reinforcements. It's us or nothing. Get her, boys."

He charged, sword pointed out in front of him. The familiar rush of coming battle spread through her body. She easily side-stepped the man and slapped him on the back of the head with the broad side of her weapon. She didn't want to kill these buffoons if she didn't have to.

Kaiden appeared to understand her choice. He ducked under the slash of a sword and kicked the man's feet out from under him when he could have easily dealt a death blow.

The two that had held back joined the fray, splitting themselves two-on-one. Since they weren't skilled swordsmen, it wasn't hard for Rianthe to hold them off, but this would go on forever if she didn't end it. With the leader's next parry, Taschia nipped at his heel as Rianthe ducked, then sliced the tip of her sword along his arm. The cut wasn't a killing injury. It was long and he'd need quick tending to ensure infection didn't change that outcome.

Rianthe smiled. He'd have a good story to tell the rest of his life.

The man hollered as she struck him. The other three all stopped mid-swing, backing away as they looked to him for guidance.

"I think," he said with a gulp, "we need more help. No one expected her to have this man helping her."

They all nodded their heads, looking decidedly relieved.

The leader pointed his sword at her. "Don't you move, missy. We'll be back with more men, and I know you love a good fight. You need to pay for bringing that magic here."

As one, they all four backed away. Right after they left the clearing, they turned and ran as if their lives depended on it, if the noise of their departure gave any indication.

Rianthe laughed as she sheathed her sword. That had been fun. Then she caught sight of Kaiden and her laughter died.

"If that's the kind of battles you have here, I understand why you are still alive."

"And how many battles have you managed to entangle yourself in?"

The deep scowl on his face told Rianthe she'd hit home. There wasn't much to defend back in New Hope.

Kaiden, as always, did not bait easily. "At least I've been there if protection was needed."

Unlike her? Rianthe scowled, refusing again to answer his jab. Grabbing her knapsack, she started shoving her things into it, tying her bedroll on top. Once again, a single event had changed the course of her life. And also once again, Kaiden had become directly involved.

She tossed the rest of her water on the fire and stomped it out. "We have to leave."

"Because of them? Even if they bring back more men, we can take them."

"Not because of them. Because they accused me of practicing magic, something that is forbidden in the Fringes." She spat the words out. Everything she'd spent the last five years accomplishing, everything she'd worked so hard to forget, had collided and brought her life once again to the brink of choice. She only knew two places. New Hope and the Fringes. Now that staying here was no longer an option, it appeared she had only one choice left.

She would be going back to New Hope. With Kaiden as traveling companion. Things couldn't get much worse.

Rianthe thought of the vision she'd had scant moments ago. Worse could happen. Easily.

Death would keep on coming until it found her.

CHAPTER FOURTEEN

Kaiden traveled beside Rianthe and the wolf, keeping his peace. He'd wanted to question her about many things, like how she'd survived so well in a place that catered to outlaws. Her skill with a sword had improved tenfold, which meant she'd been using it, exactly as he'd been told. It had taken him weeks to find her, following the trail of her reputation. She'd managed for five years to survive as a sword for hire?

For all his years on the training fields, today's skirmish had been his first battle test. There'd been no call for arms in New Hope, despite Bhren's ominous intuition. A part of him was jealous that Rianthe now performed like a seasoned fighter, even as he knew it had been what kept her alive all this time. Fighting had become Rianthe's norm. Life had taught her skills he hadn't had time to.

Not a day had passed that he hadn't worried about

her, wondered how she fared, prayed that she lived. It had been the hardest thing he'd ever done to let her go. Bhren had told him he must. It was the only way to keep her safe.

It had been hard to hold onto that belief when there had been no imminent need to protect New Hope. Dark, cold nights he'd spent lying in her bed, wishing she were there with him. Wishing he could have told her what duty had demanded he hold close.

Her gorgeous, flowing hair was still gone. He'd thought maybe she'd done that because of him, except she'd kept it that way. Short hair looked good on her, made her eyes seem larger, more focused; however, he missed her hair. Would it still be as soft if he touched it? He almost reached out. Sheer will kept his hand resting on his sword.

Her skin seemed more tanned than when she'd been at home, earned from a life lived outdoors most likely. Her body was well-honed, lithe and powerful at the same time.

"Stop staring at me," Rianthe said.

"I haven't seen you in quite a while. Forgive me for being curious about how much you've changed."

"I've changed a lot. More than you'll ever be privileged to know."

"Still carrying that pretty big rock on your shoulder, though."

"Well, you gave me a pretty big reason for it to be there."

"Look, Ri, I'd like to—"

"Be quiet. Please. These woods are not safe. We have another few hours of walking before we're out of them. Until then, be mindful, aware, and quiet."

She stomped on ahead, her heavy footfalls clearly maintaining that quiet she'd scolded him about. Well, they had weeks of travel ahead of them. There would be time to get his answers. Time to wear her down. Time to make her understand how pivotal her role in their future was.

The glumness that had settled over New Hope was one that had Bhren worried and close-mouthed. He'd barely spoken to Kaiden these past months, keeping to his tower except for the rare True-Naming ceremony. At each one, he'd seemed charged with hope. And each time, he'd come out of the tower with the candidate and a look of such despair on his face.

The only time he'd shown any hint of joy had been Uja's True-Naming. Everyone loved Uja as much as his little brother. Uja had not grown as tall as most boys his age. He still might come into that, if he'd eat more. Rail thin, he let others eat before him, even though his expertise is what put that food on their plates. The entire village had celebrated Uja's True-Naming and his wedding to Fraka well into the night. He'd left the druid's tower and proudly proclaimed himself gardener–alchemist. "I am *fehu!*" he'd shouted, forgoing the usual chant. Everyone had roared with happiness for him.

There had been two more True-Namings since Uja's, with the same glum attitude from Bhren each time. After this last one, Bhren beckoned Kaiden to his side. "Once again, the result is less than hoped for. No one shows the promise we need. No one has what she has," he'd said. He never called Rianthe by name, as if not mentioning it kept her safe.

"Is she all right, Bhren?" It had been a long time with no word.

"Everything I sense says no harm has come to her," he'd told Kaiden. "However, the time is nearing when it may not be so. Come see me in the morning. There is much to talk about."

What Bhren had told him that next day had chilled his soul through and through. If the old druid was right, Rianthe would soon be in grave danger. Bhren had foreseen an awakening in the darkness, a renewed vigor in the search for the prophesied one.

"It is time for Rianthe Royan to accept her destiny," Bhren had said. He only used her surname with Kaiden. He'd told Kaiden of her parentage early on. And Kaiden had, once again, been sworn to secrecy.

"I pray that it is not too late, but recent visions have proven there is a dire need. Danger is near. Bring her home, Kaiden. Only you will be able to do so."

Kaiden had packed and been gone within the hour. Tevy, who always seemed to know the village happenings before anyone else, had wished him good journeys and told him to tell *her* he loved her and he'd see her soon.

So far, the opportunity had not presented itself to pass that message along. Kaiden prayed that, at some point, Rianthe would be willing to listen. There was much he needed to prepare her for.

Rianthe pushed them hard, reaching midday before she felt they'd traversed enough land to make it safe to sleep.

"I'll take the first watch," Kaiden said.

"I can do that. You get some sleep."

He saw the exhaustion in Rianthe's eyes, even if she refused to look at him. He knew his own mirrored the same. He could be as stubborn as her, though. "I will take the first watch. If you choose not to sleep, that's on you. I will let you know when it's your turn."

Tight-lipped, Rianthe glared at him, then nodded. "No fire."

Kaiden returned her nod.

"Fine. Wake me before dark." She looked around, then with practiced ease rolled out her mat under an oak tree and curled up beneath her blanket, her back to him. Taschia snuggled next to her and quickly settled into sleep herself.

Kaiden sat under a nearby tree, feeling every step of the hours of walking they'd done. He listened to the even breathing that told him she slept, but knew that the smallest noise would have her alert and ready.

Sleep sounded good. All he had to do was close his eyes.

The need is dire, Kaiden. Bhren's voice came to him. *You must bring her safely back to New Hope.*

Kaiden's eyes popped open. Duty kept him awake. For this once, duty and desire meshed into one thought.

Keep her safe.

~~~

"Where is she?"

Deakon felt the power draining out of him as Taegar held him with golden eyes better than any chains of iron. She'd been quiet these past couple of years after he'd returned to New Hope. In fact, he'd worried that she'd disappeared and with her, the magic he craved. Then, suddenly, he'd heard her summons in his mind, flooding him with short-lived relief.

She could pull back the gift of magic as easily as she bestowed it. Panic scrambled his brain. Could she sense that? And his fear?
~~~

"She has been elusive," he said, and more magic slipped from his fingers. He pushed breath out through his mouth, forced difficult words to soothe her. "The girl left this village." He didn't dare tell her how long ago that had occurred. "Someone has been sent to bring her to me."

Golden eyes bored into his soul, searching for the truth. "This must happen faster. Force her to quicken her pace."

"I have a plan."

"You always have a plan." She moved closer until molten eyes filled his vision. "Make certain this one does not fail. Make certain she is soon mine. Or I will make certain your death is"—she flicked a bony finger at him—"agonizing beyond your worst imaginings."

He stifled the shudder that ripped through him as her voice and the vision faded. Huddled in the dark woods, his options were fast diminishing. This plan had to work. He must find her, and make these people, who'd stumped him at every turn, pay for holding him back. Oh, yes. They must pay.

Soon, she would be in his hands.

Soon, she would become his gift to Taegar.

Soon, he would show everyone. Very, very soon.

CHAPTER FIFTEEN

"Ri, wake up."

Rianthe roared to life with knife in hand.

Kaiden stood back with his hands in the air. "It's your turn for watch. I need some sleep."

Chest heaving with the adrenaline rush of leaping from deep sleep to full alert, Rianthe tried to still her breathing while she tucked her knife away and nodded. "Go ahead and take my bedroll."

"Thanks," Kaiden said. He laid down, pulled the blanket over himself and seemed to fall fast asleep.

Full dark had not quite fallen, which meant he'd given her four or so hours to sleep. More than he should have, but since Rianthe didn't sense danger nearby, she'd try to give him the same respite.

The air had grown chillier. Rianthe pulled her cloak around her shoulders and settled down in the same place Kaiden had been. Taschia appeared from between two trees and settled next to her, drifting right back to sleep. Rianthe knew, though, that if she warned her companion, Taschia would immediately be alert and ready to fight. The wolf had saved her many times. It was strange to be able to talk to her now. Rianthe realized how nice it would have been to know they could communicate that way during a fight. The advantage would have helped tremendously.

As if reading her thoughts, Taschia commented. *We fought well.*

"Yes, we did." She smiled and ran her gloved hand through Taschia's fur.

Rianthe felt rested and that surprised her. She'd slept hard, without a single nightmare, which was unusual for her. Was that because of Kaiden's presence? He'd promised to keep her safe all those years ago. Had her belief in that promise lulled her into a feeling of safety today?

Golden eyes loomed in her mind and Rianthe knew there was no such thing as safety. Not for her.

Though Kaiden had remained quiet during their travels, Rianthe was more on edge than ever. He'd said there were things he needed to tell her, yet he'd kept his own counsel. Did he wait for her to ask him? That would never happen. With the exception of Uja and Tevy, Rianthe did not want to know. Did not want to care. Especially about Bhren. Or Kaiden. Or that fawning Anniah. Rianthe spat to clear the bile in her throat.

Over the time she'd been gone, Rianthe had tried to squash thoughts of Kaiden moving on, finding someone to share his life with. She glared at him. His shoulders rose and fell in sleep, yet his hand was ever on the hilt of his sword, his arms flexing each time he moved. Unusual for someone not battle-tested, even though he trained more than anyone. Had he seen battles she didn't know about?

Rianthe remembered those arms around her during nights when she'd imagined much more between them, and it cut deep that he might have turned to someone else, having never given them a chance.

A yearning she hadn't suffered in a long time made her melancholy. She wanted that again. Wanted to not need to be so strong all the time, to have someone's arms around her keeping her safe. Kaiden's arms…

No. Rianthe raised her fists to the air. She would not think about that. Could not. Weakness had torn her life apart once already. She had vowed never to let someone get that close again. And that included Kaiden the Betrayer.

Rianthe let Kaiden sleep until her senses started to tingle. They ate hard tack and the rest of her cheese while walking through the dark forest, washing it down from water bags refilled at a stream they crossed.

The next several days followed the same pattern until the forests of the Fringes gave way to remnants of an ancient civilization. Small things at first. Rusted out metal shapes they could not fathom uses for. Remnants of wood covered in moss, or the ever-growing vines that must have been a building or structure at one point. Fences made of stone that had stood the test of time no matter how much grass grew through the crevices. She'd seen these before and didn't understand them. They were too low to corral an animal. Had they been some sort of property marker? Had humanity been so protective of what they owned that they had to mark their borders?

They made camp in a small copse of trees near one

of those fences. "We're beyond the Fringes now. No one from there will follow us this far. I think we can risk a fire tonight." Their bodies were depleted. They could both use some meat.

Kaiden didn't reply. He set to gathering wood and sparking material while Rianthe set a snare. Soon they had a rabbit roasting on a spit over a small fire. Kaiden had found some root vegetables and Rianthe snagged some late season berries. Tonight they would eat well.

They divided the feast into threes and Taschia gobbled hers up, then disappeared, most likely to search out food more to her liking.

"Tomorrow," Rianthe said, "we'll travel through what the ancients called a city."

"I went through something like that while searching for you. An old sign on the side of the road said 'Sturgis.'"

"That's the way I traveled here. Our route now is more southerly. And that place, Sturgis, is nothing like Minne Apples. I've only been there once. It spooked me enough that I haven't wanted to go back. Ever."

"So why are we going through there?"

"Because I didn't want to stay in the Fringes any longer than I had to. There's a price on my head by now. Plus, snow is coming. I can smell it. This route gives us a better chance of getting close to New Hope before we have to slog our way through bad weather."

Kaiden nodded.

"There are a lot of places to hide in Minne Apples. Dark places. Danger lurks there, so we'll have to be prepared for anything."

"We are."

Rianthe didn't think Kaiden took her premonition

seriously. Her warning was not something to ignore. She'd relied heavily on her sense of imminent danger and had survived this long because of it.

"That's the most you've said to me since we started this journey," Kaiden said.

"What else is there to say?"

"A lot. I'd like to explain what's been happening."

"I don't want to hear it."

Kaiden tightened his lips but held his silence, stirring the coals of the fire and adding more wood.

Later, Rianthe settled into her bedroll with Taschia beside her. On the other side of the fire, Kaiden laid down on his own mat and covered up against the cold of the evening.

Rianthe started to ask a question, then stopped herself. She wanted to know, but didn't want to open a conversation she absolutely did not want to hear. Finally, curiosity won out. "Kaiden?"

"Hmmm?" He'd already started to fall asleep.

"Are Uja and Tevy really doing well?"

"They are. I told you Uja is married now and that he and Fraka oversee the growing fields."

"I…like that idea."

"What I didn't get to explain is that Fraka is pregnant."

Rianthe clutched her blanket to her chest as a warming happiness filled her. She knew that Uja and Fraka would nurture their child the same way they tended their fields. With tender love and gentle hands. "That pleases me," she told Kaiden.

"I thought it might. It's funny. It almost seems like the growing fields became more fertile at the same time, as if the babe provided something that had been lacking.

At least, they were more fertile when I left."

She sensed a darkening of the discussion. She wasn't yet ready for that. "And Tevy?"

He nodded at Taschia. "You remember the day those pups were born and we barely got Tevy out of the barn?" She could hear the smile in Kaiden's voice.

Taschia bared her teeth in a wolf-smile. Rianthe scratched her ears. Yes, they definitely remembered.

"Yes."

"That hasn't changed. Uja and I regularly rout him out and make him go eat and socialize. More often than not, he sleeps out there too, or in the hayloft. Three of those pups refused to leave him. Where Tevy is found, so are they."

"What about the fourth?"

"Grog is where the food is. Always."

"And the mother?" Sarsa had kept a close eye on her brood when Rianthe had last been there.

"She's still around. Getting a bit slower, but she can still keep that wolf den of hers in line."

Rianthe could just about hear Taschia's laughter as she snuggled into her warmth. "I am glad Tevy is able to indulge in his passion."

Kaiden grew serious. "It's more than a passion, Ri. I believe he has true magical ability. He channels it through the animals. I…well, this may seem strange, but the way he looks sometimes, when he's sitting there with one of those wolves, he looks like they are somehow talking to each other."

They are, as you surmised long ago, Taschia mind-spoke.

Kaiden doesn't know that?

Only I and the other animals know. And now you.

That widened Rianthe's smile. If she hadn't known about this ability until a few short days ago, it pleased her that Kaiden did not even yet know.

She curled tighter against Taschia. "Thank you."

"You're very welcome, Ri."

Kaiden thought she was thanking him. Rianthe chose not to correct him. He hadn't earned the right to know about her relationship with Tevy's puppy.

CHAPTER SIXTEEN

Morning dawned gray, and the drizzle dripping from low clouds weighed down their cloaks as they walked. Taschia disappeared to hunt, returning quickly and with an empty stomach.

It wasn't only rain that bowed Rianthe's shoulders. Something dwelt in the city they were about to pass through. Something she hadn't sensed until now, except as a latent worry. Something dark and vicious.

All three of them would be put to the test this day.

We are ready. Taschia's ears were forward, alert and watchful.

Rianthe wasn't so sure, and Kaiden's mood shadowed her worry.

They walked silently through the outskirts of town, then crossed the river on an arched stone bridge from a far gone time that surprisingly still stood, albeit with gaps and a few precariously twisted pieces of iron. Once over the bridge, piles of rubble from fallen buildings seemed as tall as trees in some places. They went around them when they could and climbed over them when there was no other option. Ivy-covered buildings grew taller the further in they went, disappearing into the low clouds and giving the place a spooky, dusk-like look.

Rianthe's worry increased tenfold the deeper into the city they went. Both she and Kaiden held their swords ready, and she clutched her knife in her free hand like it was the only thing keeping her alive. A rumble behind them caused both Rianthe and Kaiden to whirl around. Chunks had fallen off a tower, clanking their way down to the pile at its base.

"This place is creepy," Kaiden whispered.

Rianthe nodded in agreement, signaling for silence.

Kaiden gave her a quick nod back.

The attack came from all sides. Rianthe reacted first as a man dressed all in black flew at her from behind one of the rubble piles. Another followed him, and another. Rianthe threw herself into a high circle, her sword slicing cleanly through the neck of the first attacker. The next was on her so quick she barely had time to pull up her sword to stop him from dealing a death blow.

Taschia leaped high into the air at another one, her jaws clamping onto his throat. Flesh and blood flew as she ripped the life out of the brigand and he crumpled to the ground.

Kaiden had two on him at once. Had he fought before? There'd been no reason to in New Hope. Rianthe wasn't able to help him as another three ran straight for her.

"Remember," she heard the first one yell. "Taegar wants any wanderers we find brought to her alive."

"You wouldn't be able to kill me anyhow," Rianthe spat as they advanced.

"Maybe not," the talker said. "But we can surely wound you into submission."

Come to me. The words from her vision flew through Rianthe's mind. There was no time to sort out why, so she tossed the thought aside and focused on the attack at hand.

Rianthe took the first man head on, her sword deflecting his as her knife drove deep into the man's gut. The next swung his sword directly at her head as she yanked her knife back. Rianthe barely got her sword up in time, the effort of holding him off dropping her to a knee. Always find the advantage, Kaiden had taught her. She stabbed at the man's knee and he howled, releasing the weight he'd put into bringing his sword down on her. Grasping the opportunity, Rianthe swiped her sword in a wide arc, using the momentum to slice clean through the man's neck. Shock remained on his face as his head fell to the ground, his body following close behind.

The strong prescience of danger turned Rianthe on her heel just in time to see Kaiden kill one who'd had a sword barreling toward her back.

A quick nod was all the acknowledgement she had time for as three more men flew out of a nearby window and attacked. On and on the battle went. Side by side and back-to-back, she and Kaiden fought off the attackers. As had worked in the past, Taschia stayed on the outskirts of the battle, leaping in to tear at a knee, an arm, or a neck where able.

Rianthe downed another brigand with a sword to the chest. As she turned to fend off another, the grounded man threw a handful of dirt in her face.

The change was immediate. Shrouded golden eyes attacked her, fierce and all-encompassing. The onslaught brought Rianthe to her knees. Pain. So much pain. All she could see, all she could hear was the thrum of malevolent power directed solely at her.

Swords clashed behind her. A voice, urgent, called to her. "Ri!"

Still she couldn't break from the eyes that held her immobile and in agony. Wind whistled as something bit into Rianthe's arm. Warmth trickled down. A sword whizzed by her, severing the arm from the man who sought to maim her.

"Ri! Get back in the fight."

Kaiden. It was Kaiden who yelled to her. Rianthe shook her head, pushed the golden eyes away and registered the brief look of surprise before they faded into nothingness. She pulled herself upright, swiping dirt from her eyes, trying to clear the vision.

Kaiden fought four men by himself. She joined him, pulled two men off, and they soon dealt with the rest. Finally, no more came at them. Rianthe and Kaiden leaned on their knees, gasping for breath and reaching for some last bit of energy to stand straight. Taschia's tongue lolled out the side of her mouth, validating that each of them were completely spent.

"Are you all right?" Kaiden asked her.

Rianthe glanced down at her blood-spattered clothing and red-tinted sword. "A minor slice to my arm. You?"

"None, but it's not just a minor slice. Let me have a look."

"Taschia?" Rianthe asked as Kaiden rolled up her sleeve.

I am fine. She came across one of the piles of rock. *I scent no others except these that we have killed.*

Good, she mind-spoke back.

"Nice tattoo you have on this arm," Kaiden said.

She shrugged, unwilling to tell him why she'd gotten it.

"Looks an awful lot like the trees of home."

Rianthe wanted to wipe that smile off his face. "It's not," she glared. "It's just a forest."

Kaiden chuckled.

Rianthe tried not to look at him. She didn't want to see the way that smile changed him, made him more handsome than ever. Instead, she stared at the carnage around them, amazed that they'd survived. There were twelve dead men here. Twelve. Thank the runes that she and Kaiden were as skilled as they were. Very few could have lived through a battle like this.

Rianthe handed him the wound kit she always carried with her as exhaustion claimed any remaining energy she had. He cleaned her arm efficiently, while she found it hard not to lean in and sniff hair she still wanted to wind her hands through. Did he still smell like girl's soap? She smiled.

"What?' Kaiden said.

"Umm, I was just thinking you were pretty good in that battle."

"I have trained, you know."

Something in the tone of his voice made her pause. "You've been in battle before, haven't you?"

"Sure."

Rianthe sighed with relief, then stopped when Kaiden's ducked head indicated there was more to this story.

"Few days ago. In that place you tried to call home for a while."

He'd just proven himself a worthy battle mate, but that didn't stop Rianthe from gulping down her surprise.

"You mean that was the first you've ever been in a sword fight?"

He glanced up from tending to her arm, a fierce grimace on his face. "Turned out there wasn't much need in New Hope." His frown deepened. "At least, not to date."

"Wow. The Almighty Kaiden has finally had his first battle test."

He tied the last knot on her bandage a little too tight.

"Ouch."

"You've hurt worse. And in case you don't remember, I did save your life."

Rianthe gulped. "Yes, I know. You did. Thank you."

Kaiden inclined his head in acknowledgement.

"And, yes, I have," she admitted.

"Have what?"

"Been hurt worse."

Kaiden looked at her then. Really looked at her, and Rianthe stared back. She had scars, a normal thing in this business. None of them showed, though. And there were none that she would give him the satisfaction of seeing. He hadn't earned that right.

His nostrils flared and he quickly backed up, picking up his sword and looking over the carnage. Kaiden bent over one of the men and froze.

"What?" Rianthe asked.

He didn't answer, instead, he went from man to man, looking at the hands of each. Rianthe followed him. Each and every one of them had a tattoo on their palms, like an upward pointing arrow with a thorn in its side.

The chill that shivered down Rianthe's spine had nothing to do with the cold. Kaiden looked like he'd seen hell. He'd gone as pale as a newborn lamb's skin.

"What does that mean?" she demanded.

"The answer to that will take longer than I think we should spend in this place. Let's get out of this Minne Apples and then, once we think we're safe for the night, I'll tell you what I can. What I've been trying to explain ever since I found you."

Had she endangered them more by her stubborn refusal to listen to Kaiden? It seemed so, and that had been a very foolhardy decision on Rianthe's part. She looked around one more time before they cleaned their swords, picked up their packs, and headed west, both ready to put the remains of this city behind them.

In hindsight, Rianthe knew her choice had been a bad one.

Almost a deadly one.

CHAPTER SEVENTEEN

While Taschia went off to hunt, Kaiden and Rianthe hunkered down for the night under a tree that had grown in the middle of a hollowed-out, single floor building near the far edge of town. With no fire, the cool night meant an uncomfortable sleep.

"I'll take first watch," Rianthe said, stretching muscles that were most likely as sore as his were. Kaiden knew she was more battle-hardened than him, but she had to feel the same pain afterward. He nodded to her, unwilling to argue. He was too worried. That attack and those men identified by that tattoo had been waiting for them. Did they know about Rianthe? Did they know who she was? How far and wide was this search? The idea that this would follow them all the way back to New Hope concerned him greatly.

More than a little tired, he'd expected to fall into an immediate, exhausted sleep. He couldn't. He kept replaying the day. He still reeled from the enormity of his first real battle test. The combination of shock and euphoria thrummed in him like a knife's screech on the sharpening stone. All the years spent practicing had coalesced into his first battle reaction. He'd killed. For the first time. A darker emotion overshadowed the proof of his True-Named ability.

He couldn't see Rianthe, but knew she sat leaning against the tree next to him.

"Have you ever killed someone before today, Ri?"

Taschia whimpered as she joined them.

A long time passed before Rianthe answered, her voice a mere whisper that still shattered the quiet night. "Yes."

Another long pause came before she added, "Never by choice."

"Does it…get easier?"

"Never."

"Good," he said. An internal struggle kept him from sleep. He'd killed. He, True-Named *thurisaz*, had dealt death blows for protection's sake. Though the reason was valid, it did not make it any easier to come to terms with what he'd done. He'd reminded himself so many times today that when evil attacked, sometimes, death was the only answer.

Sleep continued to elude him, held at bay by fears he couldn't set aside. He could have lost her this day. The world could have lost her. Panic had filled his soul when he'd seen her immobile on the ground. Kaiden knew he would kill as many as he must to keep her safe. At all costs, Bhren had said, and he agreed. He'd give up anything to keep her safe, including his own heart.

Kaiden tried to block it out, to forget at least for a

while so sleep would come, but it kept replaying over and over as he stared into the darkness of night.

"Who's Taegar?" Rianthe asked quietly.

All the breath whooshed from his lungs at the unexpected question. Kaiden sat up and leaned against the tree, now shoulder to shoulder with Rianthe. Bhren had warned him to tell her only enough to convince her to come home, that she was needed. That order went against everything he believed. Rianthe deserved to know all of it. Once again, duty and love collided and he must make a choice. Kaiden hated it, but saw no other options. Bhren knew more than he did and Kaiden must defer.

"Taegar," he said, "was once a Guardian druid."

"From the Great Magic War? That was over one hundred years ago. I thought all the druids perished with the magic."

"Most of them did. You know that when the magic was released a struggle began between those who could tap that magic and those who couldn't but wanted to harness it for their own uses. These fractured ideals also touched the druids. You know of the Guardian druids who tried to guide mankind through this new evolution?"

"Yes."

"Well, a splinter group broke from the guardians, choosing to use the magic for their own dark needs. These became the Dark druids and were led by one of the greatest druids of all time…Taegar."

Rianthe's shiver vibrated through their touching shoulders and into him. He wanted to put his arm around her, to tell her he'd keep her safe. But she wasn't ready to hear that. She didn't trust him. Plus, he didn't know if he'd be able to keep that promise.

"The magic died because of the battle between the

Guardian and Dark druids."

"Pretty much," he said. "After that, mankind's struggle turned real and it became harder and harder for Earth to sustain humanity." He didn't want to tell her the rest. That should fall on Bhren's shoulders.

"That man called us wanderers. He said they were to bring any wanderers to Taegar. What do you think she's looking for?"

Kaiden did not want to lie to Rianthe, to explain that Bhren had sensed a renewed vigor in Taegar's search, and that her focus was on Rianthe. Instead, he hedged. "It's hard to know for certain."

He could almost hear her mind working and he begged her mentally not to pursue this.

"Bhren taught you much more than he taught me."

"You didn't stick around to learn. And he taught me so I could protect you." *And guide you in your choices.*

"How does Bhren know all this? I don't remember hearing this at all in Studies."

"You know that ring he always wears?" Kaiden said.

Rianthe nodded.

"That's the signet of his circle. Bhren is the last of the Guardian druids."

Rianthe recoiled like she'd been slapped. Thought fled as shock filled her. Bhren was a Guardian druid? That made him well over one hundred years old. Only magic could keep him alive that long, yet she'd seen no more than small amounts used to help New Hope. Anger flared up in Rianthe.

His magic is hampered, just as yours is, Taschia mind-spoke.

If that were the case... "How has he managed to live this long?" she asked Kaiden.

"You know some magic still exists. You have found bits and pieces of it. So have I, and Uja. Tevy too, I think, along with others. We've seen some uncanny abilities, especially in New Hope. Bhren still has the ability to tap a bit of magic. He used that. He also used the druid's sleep, a meditative sleep, until he was needed."

"If he woke up, then things must truly be getting dire." Rianthe didn't know what to think about that. He'd betrayed her so readily, it was hard to believe that he had mankind's best interests at heart.

There is no darkness in the dark man. Rianthe swore she heard a smile as Taschia mind-spoke, nudging her way in to settle between them, offering her warmth to each.

He'd have to prove that to Rianthe. So far, she hadn't seen anything except self-serving action from the old druid.

It is time to hear him. You will listen.

Too much had happened to make sense of. Bhren and Taegar and an epic battle from the past seemed to be invading their present. The outcome was cloudy. How would mankind survive it all? And what did this have to do with the shadows of her visions? With those glowing golden eyes, calling to her. Taegar. It seemed Rianthe would be thrust into the middle of this battle, and with no more magic to assist her than an animal handler. Rianthe shook her head, trying to clear it. "I need to think, Kaiden, and you need to sleep."

"I do," he said. She heard him settle deeper into the base of the tree. Had she heard relief in his voice? Did Kaiden know more than he'd told her? Once again, distrust flared in Rianthe. Only time would tell.

CHAPTER EIGHTEEN

Rianthe, Kaiden, and Taschia left the remnants of Minne Apples and its gray shroud of doom behind them as quickly as possible. Setting a harsh pace, they planned to spend as little time in the plains as possible. Here, with nothing to deflect the wind, a chill invaded their bones, and Rianthe and Kaiden hugged their cloaks close as they walked against it. It seemed winter was poised to come early.

The next several days offered little chance for rest. There were few places to shelter, hidden from searching eyes, as neither Rianthe nor Kaiden wanted a repeat of their last battle. Food was scarce and limited to wild corn, some berries, and the jerky they'd portioned out. Taschia disappeared at times, returning with the satisfied grin of a wolf who'd found a rodent or something to feed on, while the traps Rianthe set each night remained empty.

When signs of humankind's prior life began showing

up again, Rianthe figured they were close to the big river. She'd crossed this river further north five years ago, and it had been the first true test of her ability to keep herself alive. She'd barely made it and had rested for days afterward to regain her strength. She wasn't looking forward to crossing it again.

"We are getting close to the river. Where did you cross?" she asked Kaiden.

"North of here, I think. I was tracking you, so probably near where you did originally. The waters were treacherous."

"Very treacherous. Let's hope it's easier here."

By the time they reached the shore, daylight had faded. They camped in a copse of trees near a road that had two metal lines running along it. Rianthe had seen these before, along with the rusted out great machines that must have ridden along them. The bridge here seemed to be mostly intact. They would scout it better tomorrow.

Snares finally harvested two rabbits. They replenished their energy with a good meal, daring a small fire to cook it, then settled in to sleep. Sometime during the night, rain doused their fire, forcing them to huddle underneath a tree to try to stay dry. By morning it was clear that a storm had caught up to them. The sky remained dark, rains pounded them, and occasional bursts of lightning lit the area. There was no way they could check out the bridge in this weather.

"We can't see if the bridge is safe enough to cross," Kaiden hollered above the booming thunder. "We'll have to wait out this storm."

Rianthe had been watching the direction they'd come from for some time. A strange light bobbed up and down, growing steadily brighter. What made a light move like that in a storm like this?

Lightning turned the area into daylight for a long, crackling moment, thunder clapping right after it so loudly it shook the trees.

"Look," Rianthe yelled at Kaiden. "What is that?"

Kaiden moved to her side, and squinted as he peered in the direction she pointed. "I can't tell."

"It can't be fire. No fire could survive this rain."

"If it's not fire, then it can only be—"

"A glow pot!" they said together. And it was getting closer to them. Fast.

Glows were impervious to rain or water, providing a constant source of light in any situation. Glows were touched by magic. They didn't travel by themselves, though. They had to be carried.

"We need to leave," Kaiden said next to her ear.

"We don't have time to scout the bridge. They will be upon us soon. We have to cross now."

"We don't even know if the bridge crosses the entire river. It might end five feet off shore."

"It doesn't matter. If we stay here, we risk another battle. Who knows how many there are this time. Better to take our chances with the bridge."

She watched Kaiden's face as the water dripped off his hood. His tight lips and furrowed brow showed how foolhardy he thought this plan was.

"Can you come up with another plan?"

"No. Dram it all. I can't."

"Then let's get going. That glow is still moving toward us and it's getting closer all the time."

"Fine." Kaiden grabbed her arms. "I'll go first. You follow exactly in my footsteps."

Rianthe nodded. *Taschia?*

I have four feet to balance on. I will follow.

Hoisting packs made heavier by the drenching rain, they moved out onto the iron bridge, hugging sides that still had tall railings. Inch by inch, they made their way across. Rianthe glanced behind her. The glows were closer still.

"We must hurry."

"We can't. I have to test each step before I add weight. I can't see where the planks are rotted out or the iron is weak."

"They're getting close. We'll have to take our chances."

Rianthe ran smack into Kaiden's back when he stopped suddenly.

"The bridge floor is wiped out. I can't see the other side, so we can't jump. We'll have to turn around."

"We can't. They're almost to the bridge."

"Argghhh!" Kaiden hit the railing in frustration.

Follow me, Taschia mind-spoke.

Rianthe didn't hesitate. "Kaiden, watch Taschia. I'll follow her. You follow me."

She didn't wait to see if he followed. She knew he'd be right behind her. Taschia stepped carefully along the iron rail, balancing with each paw she set down. Rianthe did the same thing. It wasn't easy. Wind buffeted them from the north, rain pelted them, and the iron beneath their feet grew slippery. The road bed disappeared suddenly and only the rail they balanced on kept them from plummeting into the river to be swept away.

Step by careful step, they inched across the chasm. Rianthe's pack felt as though it weighed a ton, but she kept her balance and moved one foot at a time, making certain to balance before shifting the next foot. Forever passed slowly, and the voices behind them became more and more intelligible.

They had to find the other side soon or whoever chased them would be upon them. Time was running out.

Suddenly, Taschia leapt to the side, causing Rianthe's heart to stop.

I am across.

"She's across," Rianthe yelled to Kaiden. "We're almost there."

The ground rose beneath Rianthe. There was a gap where the rails were broken and twisted, but she took Taschia's leap of faith and jumped, landing on both feet on the far bank of the big river. Kaiden was quickly beside her, his chest heaving with the exertion.

They turned in unison to see where their followers were. Lightning struck the bridge, lighting up the black figures that chased them. "There!" one of them yelled as Rianthe, Kaiden, and Taschia were also illuminated.

Rianthe stared at their pursuers, wishing she could drum up some of that magic Bhren used to believe she had. They needed help and they needed it now.

The storm grew in intensity. Thunder roared and shook the bridge, and another bolt of energy struck directly on the iron lines. An explosion of sparks and light and fire blinded Rianthe for long moments. She froze, trying to keep her rising panic at bay.

When the smoke and fire cleared, one end of the bridge had disappeared, swallowed up by the mighty river, along with the men upon it.

Stumbling into a nearby building with a roof that was still mostly intact, Rianthe and Kaiden fell to the floor next to a panting Taschia. They lay there for a while regaining their strength. Rianthe gave thanks to the fates that they'd survived this day.

When she finally spoke, her voice was raw and hoarse from yelling. Kaiden handed her a water bag and she sipped from it until the thickness in her throat eased.

"I can't believe we survived that," she said.

Kaiden shook his head. "We shouldn't have." He turned to hug the wolf, who nuzzled his face. "Thank you, Taschia. You saved our lives."

Yes, Rianthe thought. *Thank you so much.*

You are very welcome, Rianthe and Kai-den.

Kaiden's eyes widened. "You…you spoke to me."

Taschia's version of a wolf smile appeared on her face as she thrust her nose under his hand, searching for more pets.

"She can mind-speak," Rianthe explained.

"And you're just telling me this now?"

Rianthe shrugged, laughing. "I only found out about it when you joined me on this ill-advised quest. She and I have been friends for three years. I never knew." In spite of the wet fur, Rianthe scrubbed Taschia's back with both hands, causing the dog to yodel with pleasure. "I've decided to forgive her. Completely."

A fair trade, Taschia mind-spoke, the irony apparent.

Kaiden laughed.

"Apparently, she's decided to let you hear her now also."

Another bolt of lightning lit the outside, closely followed by thunder. The storm was right on top of them.

Kaiden went to the doorway and looked out. "I'd sure like to get more distance between us and that bridge, or what's left of it. I don't think we'll be able to until this storm lets up a bit."

"Agreed." Rianthe pulled off her soaked cloak and hung it over a wood beam. She swiped water off her head, then dug in her pack for the scrap she used as a towel. Instead of drying herself further, she used it to remove excess water from Taschia's coat. Kaiden dug for his and helped. It was the least they could do to thank the wolf.

I will always save you. You are my friends.

It humbled Rianthe to the point of tears to hear her best friend of the past three years mind-speak those words. Tears threatened to spill from her eyes as she hugged Taschia tightly, not caring that Kaiden saw this weakness in her.

Together, they watched the storm rage outside. Friend to friend, paw to hand. Kaiden knelt beside Rianthe and put an arm around her shoulders, resting his hand on Taschia's back.

For this one bit of time, Rianthe felt a peace she'd missed. She sighed, knowing that tomorrow would bring a new set of problems to solve. For tonight, though, she planned to be with Taschia.

Be with Kaiden.

Be with herself.

~~~

Full darkness fell before the storm spent itself and the rains reduced to a light drizzle. Kaiden decided it was worth the risk to light a small fire and dry out more. Catching a chill did none of them any good.

Rianthe lay entwined in her blanket by the fire. Kaiden sat opposite her, also wrapped up. Their clothes hung from rafters and he hoped they'd be dry by the morn.

For the first time since that fateful day at the druid's
~~~

tower, Rianthe appeared content. Tired. Dram, they were all bone-weary. The look on her face, though, was peaceful. None of the perennial furrowed brow, the ever-watchful demeanor. He wished more than anything that they could go back to before her True-Naming. That he could soothe her from the ravages of her nightmares and tell her what he'd been bound to hold silent. Right now, he wanted nothing more than to hold her the way he used to.

"Kaiden?"

"Hmmm?" He was so lost in thought he almost missed her soft whisper.

"Would you hold me?"

Her blush showed, even in the low light.

"I mean, just hold me. Like…before."

This might well be the hardest thing he'd ever done. To have his arms around her. To be this close and be unable to tell her the words he'd wanted to for such a long time. But Kaiden didn't hesitate. Whatever fragile truce had been forged between them, he wanted to hold onto it for as long as possible. Forever would be nice.

He lay next to her, careful to keep them both wrapped in their own blankets, and pulled her into his arms. Rianthe curled into him and Kaiden bit back a groan. It took very little time for her breathing to even out. She slept. He reached up and smoothed a hand across her hair. Even short it remained as soft as he remembered it.

This was heaven for Kaiden. And hell. He knew for certain he would not be sleeping at all this night, and he didn't mind one single bit.

CHAPTER NINETEEN

Rianthe woke still wrapped in Kaiden's comfortable arms. She couldn't forget what he'd done to her. Not anytime soon. But for one night it had been nice to put it behind them and be with him like this.

Now, in the light of early dawn, this idyll seemed more foolhardy than not. She'd missed this, missed him in spite of what had happened between them. That yearning would be harder to bury now, though bury it she must. There were too many issues between them. Too many questions that needed answers. And too many answers she probably wouldn't like if she ever got them.

Rianthe slipped out of their makeshift bed, moved to a dark corner with her dry clothes, and dressed.

She turned to see Kaiden up and pulling on his own clothes. The way the light shifted over the muscles of his back as he moved was mesmerizing. She wanted to sit and stare at him all day. Run her hands over that lean torso for a lifetime.

Rianthe blinked and found Kaiden had turned. He watched her with that sideways smile she'd always loved. "See something you like?"

"Something I used to like," she said quietly, organizing her knapsack for the day's journey. Kaiden's scowl signaled the end to their momentary truce. Rianthe knew she'd caused it. She also knew it was just as well. There were too many secrets, too many hurts between them.

After the intensity of what happened on the bridge, their days fell into an almost comfortable pattern. Rise early, break camp, eat breakfast on the trail, walk all day, foraging as they went, then set up the night's camp. Each night Kaiden started a fire, Taschia went to hunt her own food, and Rianthe set the snares. More often than not, some small animal provided the sustenance they needed to walk another day.

It seemed comfortable, and that made Rianthe nervous.

The ground began to rise and fall as they crossed the hills that led back to the forests of the Rushmore. Nostalgia tugged at Rianthe like the warmth of tonight's fire, lulling her into a sense of security that she knew was false. The last five years, and especially these last days, had taught her that danger lurked around every corner.

Kaiden sat making repairs to their snare for tomorrow night's dinner. He'd always been introspective. These days, he seemed even quieter than he used to be. He'd said hardly anything to her in the past few days beyond the discussions about trail tasks. Days where he led or she led as they followed the sun west.

Nights he found some minor task to busy himself

with, like tonight with the snare. He might be silent, but his mind was active enough, if the furrowed brow he wore like a medal was any indication.

Rianthe had had about enough of the jangle her nerves seemed permanently stuck in. The time for answers had come, though she might not like them. "Are you delivering me to my doom?" she asked.

Kaiden startled. "Dram, Ri, you really know how to catch a man off guard."

"There are things you aren't telling me."

"You didn't want to hear any of it."

"Well, I'm asking now. I need to know what I'm walking into." She scratched Taschia's ears as she watched Kaiden, looking closely for the signs that he would once again lie to her. His shoulders dipped an infinitesimal amount, then he straightened.

"Come on," she said. "Are you really going to withhold information from me, *again*? That worked so well for us all the last time, didn't it?" The dig of pain still hit her out of nowhere. Rianthe resisted putting a hand to her chest to stem the flow of trust from her heart.

Kaiden's face remained an emotionless mask for seconds longer, then finally, he relaxed. "I don't know much more, Ri. There are a lot of holes in my knowledge. Bhren withheld information from me also."

"What *do* you know?"

"I know that Bhren said it was time to bring you home. For the most part, I think you should wait to talk to him. I may only confuse you further because I honestly do not know much more than I've told you."

"Except?" Rianthe prodded.

"Except that he thinks Taegar is actively searching for something or someone and he's worried it is you she searches for."

Rianthe laid a hand on her chest, over the bag hidden under her tunic. The visions. Taegar had seen her, seen the bag.

"Those tattoos we saw? They denote followers of Taegar's Dark circle. The danger is escalating and I am to protect you with every breath I take." He glanced at her with a small smile. "Not an easy thing to do."

She nodded. "And?"

"And I must protect you because...Bhren believes...strongly...that you are in fact, the one who *will* unlock the magic for all time."

Stunned into silence, Rianthe struggled to make sense of what Kaiden had said. Her words, when they came out, were slow, measured, and deadly. She had to keep a tight rein on her anger or she'd probably do something that she'd regret for a long, long time. "He named me animal handler. The runes named me animal handler. There is little power associated with that...job."

"He altered your True-Naming. Bhren used his powers to manipulate the runes. He did it to protect you."

Rianthe stared into the fire. She'd been right about Bhren's treachery, not that it eased any of the pain. "Why? I have no powers or ability to work the magic."

"I don't know, Ri. Honestly, I don't."

Rianthe's head whipped up. "You knew, didn't you? Almost a week before. I saw you leaving the druid's tower. You were upset. And you barely spoke to me between that moment and my True-Naming. You knew."

He didn't answer, only stared at her.

"You knew I'd be named animal handler."

Kaiden nodded. "Not specifically, but yes. I knew he would make it seem as if you had little power. To protect you."

"You knew what my True-Naming should have been." She repeated herself, she had to, in order to wrap her heart around the depth of Kaiden's treachery.

Kaiden nodded again, his face a mask devoid of emotion.

"You betrayed me," she screamed.

He remained still.

"Why?" The tears streamed down her face.

One word was all she got. "Duty."

The gaping wound in her heart opened wide and pain filled the hole contentment bled from. Rianthe stood and swiped at the tears. "Just so you know," she said, keeping her voice deadly calm in direct opposition to the turmoil inside her. "This"—Rianthe made a circle with her finger, indicating their temporary camp—"hurts even worse than that day did."

The suffering look on his face was too fleeting for her to care.

"I am done with you." Rianthe went to her bedroll, turned her back to him, and tried to let the night swallow her pain.

CHAPTER TWENTY

After a night spent thinking instead of sleeping, and knowing they still had some travel ahead of them, Rianthe rose, resolute in her decision to have it out with Bhren. The old druid had been right. The time had come for them to talk. She rolled her bedding, tied it to her pack, and continued their westward trek alone, leaving camp for Kaiden to deal with.

In less than an hour, he'd caught up to her. She thrust out a finger, telling him silently that he would not be walking beside her. Kaiden hung back, which in some ways was even worse. Now she truly felt like a prisoner being marched to an unknown fate.

Kaiden's scowl stayed firmly rooted on his face. Rianthe didn't care if he liked the situation or not. Kaiden was dead to her. Her entire focus lay ahead, on Bhren, and what she would say to him when she saw him.

Finally, with several silent days of journeying behind

them, including navigating another city which they negotiated very carefully, the woods of Rushmore loomed before them.

"Exactly like the trees on your arm," Kaiden said, breaking the silence.

"Once and for all, these are *not* this forest," Rianthe ground out. They made camp for the night underneath the awning of limbs that were special to these woods. Deep inside, Rianthe was pleased that she'd gotten them right, but Kaiden had lost the right to know that.

For her, this night was as sleepless as any. The pull of these woods was strong. *Home*, they called to her. *Tevy and Uja live here.*

You are home, Taschia mind-spoke.

"This is not my home!"

"This will always be your home, Ri." Kaiden had joined her and Taschia as they stared at the trees. "Whether you like it or not, you belong here."

"I wasn't even born here."

You were born to be here.

Had the whole world joined to fight against her? Rianthe stormed off. She needed to be alone. After all the years of it being her alone, then her and a wolf she thought wasn't able to understand her, this constant companionship made it hard to breathe. Hard to think. And Kaiden's solicitous manner made it enormously hard to maintain her righteous anger. Except toward Bhren. She would never forgive him for what he'd done to her.

They were less than a day from New Hope and still Rianthe didn't know how she would explain the depth of his treachery. Maybe she'd just run him through with her sword. No. That would be too fast for him.

She sat apart, watching the woods, running her hands

along her cloaked arms to ward off the chill. She'd designed the tattoo to remind her of these woods, exactly as Kaiden had said. This place had been a haven for her after her parents' deaths. A haven that had betrayed her when she'd needed it most.

Since then, she'd made her own way. She'd learned to fight better than Kaiden could have taught her had she stayed in New Hope. Rianthe had never lost a battle. Yes, that was unusual for a woman, but she was tall and strong and motivated. She intended to show them all that she could best each and every one of them, magic be drammed.

A part of her had always wondered if someone or something watched over her. Some of those battles had been pretty vicious. If it hadn't been for Taschia, she might never have made it.

You are strong.

The wolf came and sat beside her, leaning into her until Rianthe wrapped her arms around Taschia and buried her face in her fur.

"I'm not so sure," she whispered to herself, then berated herself for the weakness she'd shown.

"You *are* strong. One of the strongest I've seen." Kaiden joined them, keeping enough distance to show respect for her anger. "I've seen you battle, both in practice and for real. Your ability is uncanny. It might even be magically enhanced."

"I don't have the magic, Kaiden. I'm sorry you and Bhren think I am some savior. I'm not. I struggle and fight like everyone else."

"You took on the role of peacekeeper, and opponents that would have killed most others bowed to your sword."

"My will to live is strong, I guess." She smiled at

Taschia, who nuzzled her, asking for more attention.

"I believe you," Kaiden said thoughtfully. "And you have much skill to back that up. But you've survived skirmishes and out-and-out battles for years. Surely that speaks of some latent ability protecting you."

She didn't answer him. Rianthe wasn't ready to let all her buried hopes out again. She'd worked too hard to become Rianthe Royan, non-magical fighter for justice. To think that it had been aided all this time by the magic she'd disavowed was something she chose not to try to wrap her head around.

By the time morning rolled around, no answers had come to Rianthe. The air's chill had cooled further. A light, early snow had begun to fall, coating everything in a surreal dusty white. Rather than sleep under the cover of trees, Taschia had opted for wider spaces. She now lay curled in a tight ball, barely visible under her frosty blanket.

On any other morning, Rianthe would have taken the time to sit and enjoy the serene scene. Today, a restless and uneasy feeling in her gut told her it was time to finish the journey. She couldn't lay a finger on the reason, but something warned her of more trouble ahead. Were there more of Taegar's henchmen waiting for them so close to New Hope? And if they were close to New Hope, were they actually *in* the village? Could Tevy and Uja be in danger?

She sniffed the air. Whatever trouble headed Rianthe's way, it didn't seem close. Yet. Rianthe gazed at her gloved hands. She could try to find out, but at what cost? The shiver that ran through her had nothing to do with the snowy weather and everything to do with remembered pain and a deep, deep fear.

Kaiden walked off into the woods, presumably for his morning ablutions. There was no better time to try than now. Not giving herself time to think, Rianthe slipped off a glove and reached for earthen soil below the thin layer of snow.

The fear. The pain. They were immediate this time, and so completely different. No eyes appeared to twist the knife. Instead, Rianthe saw New Hope, but not the village she'd expected to find. This one was on fire.

She stood at the edge of the village circle, beside the crumbled remains of the druid's tower. Everywhere she turned, buildings burned. Bhren stood in the center of it all, blue fire shooting from his hands as he battled some unseen enemy. Golden fire attacked back, but she could not see from whence it came. Back and forth the streaks battled. Faster and faster.

Meanwhile, men with swords fought. In the square, in front of burning buildings...sword met sword. Men fell as shadows swung their blades. Shadows like she'd seen before.

Taegar was destroying their home.

Tevy! Uja!

A familiar warmth leaned against her, joining her in the vision. Taschia. It did nothing to assuage the panic that rumbled through Rianthe. With a roar, she drew her sword and swung to kill the shadow nearest her. Her sword passed through thin air. This was a vision. She had no substance, unlike the shadows that were killing everything she'd ever loved.

Tevy! *Rianthe reached out with her mind.*

Sister! *Rianthe didn't take time to wonder how he heard her, much less how he answered. Tevy's mind-*

speak was weak.

Are you all right? *she shouted.* Are you safe? Is Uja safe?

None of us are safe. We need help. We need you here. Now.

Rianthe swung her sword again, ineffective against anything. Her scream of angst was real.

She hit the ground hard. The fire, the village, Tevy all disappeared, replaced by a white background and a terrified Kaiden standing over her.

"What was that, Ri? What has happened?" His voice, still colored with panic, sounded like the roar of a bear.

Wet tears streaked her face. There was no time to waste on them. Rianthe leapt up, shoving her pack together. "We have to go. Now. New Hope is in trouble."

Taschia yodeled her own distress.

Kaiden grabbed her by the arm, spinning her around though she struggled to get away. "Not until you tell me what you were doing. You looked white as a sheet, like you were in some sort of trance. One hand on the ground, the other grappling for your sword as you screamed. And strong. Uncanny strong. I barely tossed you backwards and broke whatever waking nightmare you were having."

Rianthe pulled on her glove. "I have visions and New Hope is under attack and burning. We must hurry. Any more explanation will have to wait."

Kaiden looked at her for a long moment as she glared back at him. When he dropped his arm, he started throwing his own pack together. "All right. Let's go. The rest, we'll sort out later."

They ran for miles, yet even that didn't get them close enough to be of any help. Kaiden stopped them all for a rest.

"No." Rianthe fought against the arms holding her. "We have to get there. Now." She could barely say the words through the heaving breaths she took to get her wind back.

"We'll be of no use in a battle if we're wiped out. Let's just take a few minutes to rest and eat. Then I promise you, we'll redouble our efforts to get there as quickly as possible."

Rianthe knew he was right, even though her heart screamed to be there, to be helping, to know what had happened.

"I can try to see how things are there," she said.

Kaiden searched her face, looking into her soul to get answers. She opened to him, let him see all the pain in her heart. "How?" he finally said.

She pulled off her gloves. "By connecting with the earth. Taschia has been able to join me, to see. Bhren could, too."

Kaiden's eyes narrowed. It seemed Bhren hadn't told him everything.

"I'm not sure if you will be able to," Rianthe said. "But touch me once I'm in and we'll see."

She thought of home, touched the ground with both hands, and immediately saw New Hope. The fires burned everywhere. No building still stood. Even the druid's stone tower had been reduced to a rubble of ruins.

Kaiden joined her. She felt the strange but reassuring mind-link. He gasped at the devastation they saw.

Tevy? Rianthe reached out.

Hurry, Rianthe. We are...dying. Any reassurance at the touch of Tevy's mind disappeared with his mind-speak.

Hang on, Tevy. We're coming, Rianthe answered.

Hurry. Uja— Tevy screamed and disappeared from her mind.

The vision broke. Kaiden now knew the same horror and despair she did. It showed in the angst on his face. In the slump of his shoulders. In the fractured peace of his voice. "Come on. Let's go."

They ran for hours. There was no other choice. When they smelled the smoke, Rianthe knew they were close. And not in time. The fires were gone. Only ash and devastation remained.

Pain pierced her heart and Rianthe knew the truth in her soul.

They were too late.

CHAPTER TWENTY-ONE

New Hope had been leveled to the ground, smoke rising from holes in the earth where homes had stood. The snow did nothing to assuage the rotting smell of death and destruction. Rianthe, Kaiden, and Taschia ran through the rubble to the center of the village. So many bodies on the ground. So many dead. Tears streamed down Rianthe's face as she searched. For Tevy. For Uja.

Kaiden raced back and forth, turning as soon as he got to each person like he wanted to help everyone at once yet knew the futility of it all. His shoulders slumped when he finally slowed down enough to take a breath.

"Tevy!" Rianthe screamed.

"Over here."

She rushed to her baby brother, relief at hearing his voice destroyed when she realized he sat crying with Fraka beside the still body of their brother. Uja's hand still clutched the sword he must have picked up to fight with.

"Uja!" Rianthe wailed. "No, no, no. It can't be. Not Uja, no, no." Rianthe hugged him tight, willing him to breathe. Praying to anyone and everything. Not Uja. She couldn't bear it. Sweet, gentle Uja, who always wanted to be in the growing fields instead of training, must have fought to protect his home and died in the attempt. Tears streamed down Rianthe's face. She should have forced him to train. She'd protected him all those years ago, only to leave him completely unprotected in his hour of need. This was her fault. How could she have done this to him? To all of New Hope.

You did not do this, Taschia mind-spoke.

I left him.

This is not your doing.

Rianthe sat up, unable to fathom a world without her dear Uja in it. How would they go on? How could she, knowing that if she'd been here, things could have been different.

"You wouldn't have been able to change a thing," Kaiden said, choking on his own words.

Rianthe looked up, and saw the tears, the same guilt that scored deep lines of pain in her soul, on his face.

Tevy clung to her, crying silent tears of his own. She hugged him tight, afraid to ever let go again. When he grunted, Rianthe held him apart, felt his arms, legs, wiped the soot off his face, frantic to know he was unharmed.

"I'm all right," he said. "The wolves…" His voice broke.

My brothers hid him. Even Taschia's mind-speak was filled with sadness.

"I'm so glad," Rianthe said, hugging Tevy tight. "I'm so glad you're not hurt. So glad." Over and over she said the words, knowing she was crushing him to her, unable to stop herself.

Finally, Tevy managed to pull away from Rianthe. He stood, pulling her up. "We will take care of Uja in a while, dear sister. Right now, you are needed elsewhere." He pointed to what little remained of the druid's keep, a small outbuilding. Several people stood around outside.

"Bhren needs you," Tevy said.

"No. My place is here."

"There is nothing more you can do for our brother. Please. For me, go to Bhren. There is not much time."

Rianthe stared at him, saw the resolution in the twelve-year-old boy turned man that had replaced her baby brother, then caved to his wishes. She stood, her shoulders bowed from so many regrets and so much shame and grief.

They walked across the battle-strewn center of New Hope. Several more bodies lay where they'd fallen, their surviving families and friends surrounding them, grief spewing like the leftover trails of smoke that rose everywhere from lingering fires. The harsh smell of decay burned as she drew halting breaths, trying to quell her tears. Rianthe faltered and almost fell, overwhelmed at the losses. Kaiden held her arm, gave her strength she knew he didn't have. Together, they walked into the small room where Kaiden's parents, Jonah and Raisa, sat beside the druid.

Bhren lay on a blanket on the floor, ashen and obviously near death.

Rianthe didn't believe it. Bhren had the *awen*. He was *tiwaz*. According to Kaiden, he'd lived well over one hundred years. Didn't that make him immortal? He could not die.

He. Could. Not.

She knelt beside his still form, Jonah and Raisa moving away to hug their son and give her room. A new war raged inside of her. He'd been her mentor, her teacher, almost a father figure. He'd also betrayed her, stolen her most sacred wish. How did she not hate him? Not want him dead?

It took little time for Rianthe to realize she truly wanted Bhren to live, to be in her life, to help guide her through the strife she knew must come again, and keep coming until some ultimate battle ended it. She loved him. Loved Uja. Nothing else mattered now except holding on to whatever and whoever she had left.

Exhaustion consumed her as she collapsed beside the old druid.

"Student…" Bhren croaked.

Rianthe straightened, tried to show a peace on her face she did not feel. "Master."

"I must tell you—"

"Do not speak. Keep your strength for healing."

"No," Bhren said, reaching to clasp her hand. "There is no more time. You must know…" He gulped air, taking several rattling breaths. "Trust Kaiden. I'm…sorry. Your father…" Bhren's voice faded.

Rianthe had to lean down to hear his weak whisper.

"What? What about my father?"

"You're father"—Bhren gasped—"was…also *tiwaz*. Guardian druid…like…you. The magic…will come if…open…your…mind." His hand grew warm, then hers warmed as his grew cold, then colder.

When his hand fell from hers, the signet ring he'd always worn lay in her palm. "No. No, no, no. I can't— I'm not— I don't have your power, Master. I can't be…this."

"You must. New Hope knows. Earth…needs…you. You…only…hope." Bhren's whisper faded to nothing. He gasped one final time then, before there was even time to react, the forever breath left him.

Sorrow overrode shock as Rianthe bowed her head with Kaiden close beside her, mourning. Their losses were beyond recovery. The earth rumbled and the winds wailed their grief as the cries of such devastating loss filled the air around their home. An age had ended with Bhren's death. An age where the *awen* had awakened.

Magic that now ended with the death of the last remaining Guardian druid. For despite what Bhren had uttered in those final moments, Rianthe knew she could not tap even an iota of what Bhren had. Or her father. A Guardian druid? If magic was the savior of the earth, they had just lost an epic battle, one that they would not recover from.

His body began to glow, the long-ago memory adding to Rianthe's heartbreak. Soon, nothing but ash remained of the druid.

Rianthe stood and walked outside, Kaiden close on her heels. She looked over the village that had taken her in, now in ruins, death strewn about like hay in a manger. The village she'd deserted in their darkest hour.

Tevy joined her, sticking his hand in hers. "More might be gone if it weren't for Mokie. He got many of the women and children into hiding."

Faltering, Rianthe fell to the ground, pounding the dirt with her gloved fists. Uja. New Hope. Bhren. Despair weighed her down. These losses were unrecoverable. The last of the Guardian druids. Nothing would stop Taegar now. Rianthe knew, in her soul of souls, that Bhren had spent his life fighting this darkness. It had been the single reason he'd returned from the druid's sleep. To save the world. Earth. Humanity. Forever intertwined.

Earth would now perish. Humanity, also, and her own pride and lack of forethought had set this final downfall into motion. If she'd been here, things would be so vastly different. She had caused this. *Uja.* Pain raked her heart, shredded it until little remained. Nothing was left…except to exact revenge upon the person responsible.

"Who did this?" she yelled. "Who would do this to such a peaceful, small place?"

"Deakon," one of the men said.

"But he left New Hope long ago."

"He returned shortly after you left. He's been here these past few years, living among us. Then, this morning, he led mercenaries and these horrible cloaked shadows into New Hope. They tore the village apart as if looking for something." His voice broke.

"I don't think they found it," Tevy said, tears still not dried upon his face. "He was in such a rage. Ri, he had magic. No one knew until he started throwing fireballs in his anger. He burned everything. And…" Tevy's voice broke. "Deakon said something. Something I didn't understand." He lowered his voice, spoke words meant only for Rianthe to hear. "He said when *they* found the offspring of Damian Royan and killed them like they'd done the father, he would finally come into the magic he deserved. And we'd be enslaved to him forever."

Red rage boiled up and filled Rianthe as she stood. The man who'd helped kill her father had been part of their village all this time. He'd shown up within a year of her arrival and had been accepted just as she and her brothers had. He'd done his part to help the village and they had all worked beside him, shared meals with him, joked and celebrated with him.

She shook her head, unable to make any sense of it. It was too much. So much loss, and more would come if they didn't find shelter and food quickly. Winter already encroached upon them. Deakon had betrayed them, and Rianthe needed an outlet for the confusion and fury inside her. As well, she needed to make amends to the people around her. She must prove her sorrow and win their forgiveness. And allay her breaking heart. She vowed revenge for Uja. Bhren. New Hope. Deakon must pay for his treachery. And after him, Taegar. The man's comments about her father added to the proof that Taegar had been behind this.

"Where did they go when…when they were done?"

"Wait a minute, Ri," Kaiden said.

"No." Rianthe whirled on him. "Nothing you can say will stop me. I will exact revenge for his deceit. I. Will. Make. Him. Pay."

Kaiden tugged on her sleeve, and Rianthe yanked her arm away, glaring at him. He would not talk her out of this. Deakon needed to pay for the pain he'd brought down upon her home and the people she loved most.

"He will pay," Kaiden said. "But, Ri, look around you."

What remained of the village of New Hope surrounded them. Familiar faces, and some not so familiar. All covered in grime and soot and despair. All wide-eyed, searching for any bit of hope in this dismal turn to their lives. Searching for someone to give them that hope.

"We are needed here, Ri," Kaiden said quietly.

"And…" His voice broke. "We must take time to honor our dead."

Rianthe squatted and scooped up some dirt in her gloved hand, staring at it, clutching it like a lifeline. Bodies lay everywhere, causing her to choke back a sob. Taschia jostled Rianthe and she fell to the ground. Her sleeve rode up and momentarily, she was skin-to-soil.

Deakon, along with some other men, sat around a fire. He looked directly at her, unsurprised.

"Come and find me, girl. I know you want to."

The scene disappeared as fast as it came. Her rage did not leave so quickly, a struggle with her grief that left her shaking, both from her need to avenge her friends and family and her heart's need to have those that remained survive. They had to survive. If they could find the strength. If she could find it. She stared at the ring in her hand. Bhren had designated her as a Guardian. She had no idea why. She was no druid. She wanted only to hunt Deakon. To make him feel her pain tenfold. No. Not just hers. New Hope's pain. She wasn't alone in this.

She looked up. Would they even accept her in this role? What had Bhren said? New Hope knows? She'd deserted them in their hour of need. Deakon had destroyed them. Taegar had destroyed them. Because of her.

Revenge can wait, sister. New Hope needs you, Taschia mind-spoke.

Rianthe struggled to stand. It took every last vestige of her strength to stay upright and look around at the grimed faces staring back at her. None carried accusation or resentment. Anguish bowed their shoulders and despair dulled their eyes. Had they lost the will to survive? This couldn't happen. Not to New Hope. They had saved her, given her asylum in her time of need. She could not now desert them.

"She holds the signet ring," Jonah said to the people around them, coming up between her and Kaiden and placing a hand on each of their shoulders. "The vision that brought us all to this place has come to pass. A new Guardian druid has been chosen."

"I can't—"

Rianthe stopped when Jonah's hand tightened on her shoulder. "It is time for Rianthe, Kaiden, and those raised in this village to know. There would be no New Hope without the druid Bhren."

Everyone bowed their heads for a moment.

"We tell you now what Bhren told each of us in turn when we first met him. He searched the world for anyone with any minute ability to tap the *awen*, inviting us here to build a new home, gathering us to be part of the future of mankind."

Rianthe had never heard this. She glanced at Kaiden, noting the surprise on his face. He stared at the man who'd raised him like he didn't recognize him.

"Bhren knew a battle loomed. A battle to release and control the *awen*. A battle that would require all of us if the darkness was to be defeated. We have waited all these years for Bhren's indication that the *one* had been found." He reached for Rianthe's hand, held it out so all saw the ring she held. "Bhren's final act has shown us the way. He has told us that Rianthe is our future's hope. Our new hope." He turned to Rianthe, taking the ring from her palm, and cocked his head in her direction.

Stunned, Rianthe scanned the small crowd, a pittance of what New Hope had been. How could she be the one? Or guide a village that she'd deserted? As one, they all stared at the ring Jonah held. Hope began to supplant the despair in their eyes.

Bhren, whom she'd expected to live forever, hadn't. He was not infallible, and she believed he was wrong in placing his faith, and New Hope's, in her. Whether she thought she could do this or not, this was all she had left to give the people who'd opened their arms to her and her brothers. In truth, there was no choice to make. Rianthe closed her eyes and took a long breath. She clutched the bag of runes around her neck to fortify her resolve, then opened her eyes and peeled off her glove, nodding at Jonah. He slid the ring on her forefinger. It shimmered for a moment, then molded itself, now the perfect size for her.

"I believed in Bhren," Jonah said. "I believe in you, Rianthe."

A rumble of agreement from the group surrounding them bolstered her confidence. With another deep breath, Rianthe straightened, taking the first steps into a role she knew she wasn't fit for but accepting was the only choice she had.

"This has been a day of devastation," Jonah said.

New Hope's survivors nodded throughout the commons.

"Many sacrificed themselves to protect our home," he continued. "This is not the end of us." His voice strengthened. "We will survive because they gave their lives for us." He wound his arm through Rianthe's.

Tevy joined them, taking her other arm. Kaiden twined his with Jonah's.

"We will rebuild in their memory." His voice strengthened along with her determination.

One by one, the villagers joined arms until they

formed one big circle with no beginning and no end.

"We will grow more food in the ways that Uja taught us. Then"—Jonah gave her a nod—"and only then, we will avenge the deaths of our friends and our families."

Pain filled Rianthe's heart and renewed tears spilled from her eyes as she gulped. Dear, dear Uja. How could he be gone?

"We will build stronger shelters. Make it through the coming winter, then the next one, and the one after that. We will survive!" Jonah roared the last words and Rianthe sucked them in, letting them feed the aching maw in her soul.

A rumble started in the circle of people. At first, Rianthe feared it was a renewed effort by Taegar. But this rumble held a hopeful note. A note of faith. A chant began, quiet at first, then gaining in strength. "New Hope will survive! The earth will survive! We will survive!"

It continued, over and over. The village had decided. To live, and to support the plan that Bhren had apparently set in motion years before she'd even been born.

Rianthe joined her voice with theirs. She was to be Bhren's druid successor, even though she did not have his power and certainly didn't hold one iota of his wisdom or historical memory. Rianthe felt both humbled and overwhelmed. This was not what she'd come home for. She did not want to let go of the anger, the need to avenge Uja's death. For now, her thirst to retaliate had been replaced by a bigger need. New Hope was where she should be. Where she was needed. But not forever.

Taegar. Rianthe looked at the dirt beneath her feet. *We are not done. Know this. I will come for you.*

ORDEAL

CHAPTER TWENTY-TWO

On the eastern edge of the village, Rianthe stood at the edge of the Hallows, their now sorely used and overfull remembrance fields. So many stones, so many dead. Yesterday, all the departed had been carried to these grounds. Jonah had asked for volunteers to prepare pyres and set remembrance stones while the rest of the village searched for ways to survive the cold night. Every single villager, old and young alike, had raised their hands, herself, Tevy, and Kaiden included.

It had not mattered that all were exhausted. Around the clock, axes and shovels had sounded, while those that needed rest stood honor guard over their slain family and friends. Kaiden led the brigade and didn't stop until his hands were bleeding and he could no longer stand. Then he guarded, his hands bandaged, his head bowed in grief, while others dug.

In the village, Rianthe and the remainder of the

villagers began the long process of gathering anything usable for survival from the ruins. Jonah bent over one of the rudimentary fire pits, rubbing stick against stick. With some encouragement, a fire started. One of the talents that made Jonah an invaluable leader. They would have warmth and be able to cook.

Mokie led a group of men who worked to shore up crumbling walls as best as they were able, and Mokie's equally red-haired mother, Kathra, foraged enough food for a meager supper.

Now, in the cold gray of morning, with their breath puffing in the cold air, they said goodbye to their dead and honored them with the *kenaz*, the death rite. Jonah stood closest to the too long row of pyres, Kaiden straight and tall at his side. Rianthe stood stoically beside them, her arms tight around Tevy, with the wolves next to him, all still, all silent, all mourning.

If Rianthe's gaze strayed over and over again to the marker that would forever remind them of Uja's sacrifice, no one thought any worse of her. Everyone grieved their losses.

"We do not say goodbye," Jonah said at the end. "These family and friends will forever be with us in our memories, and in our continued existence. Instead of goodbye, let us make them a promise. That we will fight to honor their sacrifice. That we will survive."

"We promise!" everyone said. "We will survive." As one, the people of New Hope spoke. The wolves howled their agreement. Each person walked along the markers of glory, bowing their heads, whispering thoughts and words of love and sorrow. One by one, each left to return to the ruins and pick up the mantle of their existence, until only Kaiden, Tevy, Fraka, and Rianthe were left.

Fraka, heavy with the babe her husband would never know, leaned on Kaiden's arm, unable to stem the flow of tears she'd held in.

"I'm trying to be strong," she said with huge gulps. "I just...I'm going to miss him so much." She gripped her belly, holding tight to the only piece of Uja that remained.

Rianthe hugged her tightly. "I have no words, sister. I wish I could take away your pain. All our pain."

Fraka stared at Uja's stone. "I still can't believe he's gone."

"None of us can," Tevy said, standing in front of Fraka, placing his hand on her stomach. Fraka covered his. Rianthe and Kaiden added their hands, silence bonding their grief.

Fraka faltered.

"You need to rest," Rianthe said.

"There is too much to do," she said.

"Not for you." Rianthe turned Fraka away from the field of stones. "Your job is to keep this little one safe. Rest. There will be lots of time to help. We must all stay strong to endure what the next few months will bring."

Fraka nodded, letting Tevy and Kaiden walk her back to the village.

With no one to see except the dead, Rianthe finally let her tears fall. So much loss. Too much. She prayed for the souls of friends and family. Prayed for the strength and guidance to avenge these deaths. She wanted to question the villagers, to know more about how this had happened, then rush off into the wilderness to hunt down Deakon and force him to tell her Taegar's location while employing painful methods before she killed him very, very slowly. That wasn't her mission. At least, not yet.

Patience had never been her strong suit, but New Hope needed her. Not much remained and it would take the hard work of everyone in order to survive the hardships ahead.

Deakon had done his work too well.

Rianthe sank to the ground and ran her hand along the rough letters carved hastily into her brother's stone. Later, they would do more to honor him.

"Uja, Uja, Uja," she cried, laying her hands on the dirt. Hands she didn't dare to unglove to be nearer to his memory. "What will we ever do without your gentle guidance?"

She heard Kaiden returning, felt the nudge when he settled beside her. Without thought, she turned to him, let his strong arms console her as hers consoled him. Tears with no need for explanation wet their tunics as an alliance born of need cemented itself between them.

~~~

Burned out buildings smelled like putrid, blackened wood. And it wasn't a scent that wafted in and out. No, it hit like a tsunami and never stopped. Rianthe pulled the kerchief up over her nose, but the smell had already invaded her psyche. She'd never forget it. Never forget this defeat, all the sifting through ashes, and hoping to find some useful or heart-worthy items, only to have those hopes crushed again and again.

Lifting a board, she saw a scrap of linen. Thinking it might be a blanket, she uncovered it. At one time it had most likely been a cloak. Now, only a small, square piece of it remained. Still, she set it outside. If nothing else, it would fuel the fires they needed for warmth. The snow had not yet returned, but a chill still permeated the air, their skin, and their bones.
~~~

Fire destroyed everything. No, Rianthe corrected herself. Not fire. The Dark druid. Taegar. She'd sent Deakon, the traitor who'd caused this devastation. For the moment, Rianthe needed to be here, helping, the need to be gone in search of Deakon and Taegar barely suppressed. The winter would be harsh without this additional struggle. The growing fields had been the first thing lost in the fire.

"It's time for the gathering, Ri."

Kaiden waited outside while she shoveled more ash aside, searching for anything useful. Kaiden, who had barely slept since their arrival, had tirelessly worked to forage and prepare for another cold night. He hadn't spoken much and his face showed the ravages of his grief. Rianthe suspected he carried the same burden of guilt as she. They had no time to sort that out right now, and both knew it. They needed to help over one hundred people survive one more night. Then they must figure out tomorrow and the next day and the day after that.

Rianthe walked outside, brushing ash off her gloved hands, a totally useless endeavor. She only seemed dirtier for the attempt.

Kaiden followed her to the small building next to the druid's tower. This and the growing house, whose walls were mostly stone and mortar, were all that was left of the village, and neither had roofs or four solid walls. They'd all sheltered in these two places last night, away from the wind, and huddled close to ward off the cold of night as they sat awash in their grief.

Now, meeting with the most able-bodied of the village, they made plans.

"Two stone walls still partially stand in this outbuilding next to the druid's tower," Kaiden said.

"We can use tree limbs and branches to construct a roof over it. It might not hold everyone, but it's a start," Mokie added. It still amazed Rianthe that practical-joker Mokie had grown into such a fine, responsible man. And Anniah had turned into a lovely, conscientious young woman. That these two opposites were engaged also surprised Rianthe. A lot had changed in the time she'd been gone.

Jonah nodded at Mokie. "That's good, very good. Take charge and pull everyone you need to get this in place."

Rianthe glanced outside. "We have a few hours before darkness will be upon us."

Kaiden remained still and quiet beside Rianthe, watchful, but not joining the conversation. She turned to him. "We need to hunt."

He nodded.

Looking back at faces covered in grime and despair, Rianthe searched for Fraka, beckoning her forward. The woman's defeated, ungainly gait worried Rianthe. Fraka was far along in her pregnancy. Rianthe had rejoiced that a part of Uja would live, but the look of sadness on Fraka's face worried them all. Rianthe knew the feeling. For herself, she stifled that emotion. For now. Soon, she'd take time to steal away and have a moment. After they'd fed and found enough shelter for everyone to get through one more night.

Rianthe took her hand. "Can you organize the women and children and ask them to forage the growing fields?"

"There's nothing left," Fraka cried. "It all burned."

"There might be something. A leaf, some carrots or other root vegetables. Something."

Fraka nodded slowly, obvious in her belief that nothing would be found.

"What about Deakon?" Mokie asked, interrupting.

"What about him?"

"He needs to pay for what he's done."

"And he will." Rianthe's voice was cold steel. "Not now, though. Jonah is right. We need to survive first." She stood.

"We all have our duties," Jonah said. "We all know what must be done and how little light we have left to do it in today. Let's get to work."

Rianthe, Kaiden, and Taschia set out, laying several snares outside the village, then headed farther afield in search of animals. Kaiden carried his bow, something neither of them usually hunted with. Today, they must have meat, and lots of it, in a hurry.

Passing the Precipice of the Faces, they paused to rest on a man-made surface that sloped down to what must have been some sort of stage. Grass had cracked and broken most of the seats and vines covered most vertical surfaces. Rianthe wondered what this had been used for. Maybe to tell of the efforts needed to carve faces in stone? To her, it seemed an amazing undertaking.

Kaiden looked up from sighting in his arrows. "How long have you been having those visions, Ri? Have you had them all your life?"

She could sense the hurt in him. Could hear it in his voice. And she wanted to wipe the frown from his face so badly it hurt to look at him. They'd worked together closely of late. To return to their old ways, to be friends again… Rianthe wanted that more than just about anything. She needed her friend back. Too much had happened, though. Rianthe glanced away as she answered. "They started about a week before that ceremony you called my True-Naming."

His nostrils flared. "Well, at least that means you didn't hide it from me the whole time I knew you."

"I think," she said slowly, staring at him, "both of us have been harboring secrets."

Kaiden's mouth became a thin line. After several moments, he stood. "We'd better get to searching for some game." He helped her up.

Hours later they walked into camp with a boar trussed up on a pole, also dangling several rabbits they'd pulled from the snares as they'd walked back in. Setting the bounty down by the fires, they looked around.

The changes in camp were significant. The temporary shelter was larger than expected and might well keep the weather off most, if not all, of the village. Rianthe clapped Jonah on the back. "This will serve us well," she said, tugging on a stout limb. "For some time, I think. A lot has been accomplished today."

His smile, surrounded by the grime of a hard day's work, was bittersweet.

Tevy ran over and tugged at Rianthe's hand. "Look over here." She and Kaiden followed him to a roughly thrown together table, where some clay bowls and plates sat. "We found some dishes, and more are being carved out."

"I can't believe how much has been done in such a short time," Rianthe said.

A fire had been started in the village square. Women were already stripping and cutting up the boar and setting it to roast in pieces with the other game. Every bit would be used as something. Food, oil, and hides for warmth.

Fraka joined Rianthe and Kaiden, the first signs of

happiness on her face they'd seen all day. "You were right. We found turnips and carrots and potatoes. And some leafy spinach and greens further out. Several of the women scrubbed soot from the big cauldron." She pointed to a second fire where a tripod of limbs held up the large central cauldron they'd previously only used for melting snow in winter.

"We've got a vegetable stew thickening. We'll add some of the meat for flavoring. We'll eat tonight." Fraka grabbed Rianthe's arm. "We'll eat!"

Rianthe hugged her sister-by-marriage. "You've done much to make certain we survive, Fraka. I'm so grateful for you." She placed a hand on Fraka's stomach. "Have you been resting? You must take care of yourself and the babe."

Fraka nodded. "No one will let me lift anything. They treat me like a newling. I understand, but I do wish I could do more."

"You've done a lot. Be happy with that."

"I am." Fraka went off to help in the search for more useable items to help them eat. Even the wolves helped, dragging wood to the fires.

Rianthe felt the sting of tears in her eyes.

"Everyone is doing their part." Kaiden stood beside her.

She nodded. "I always knew they would, but this is beyond anything they've ever had to expect."

"New Hope is full of strong people. We will survive." He said it as a certainty, which reassured Rianthe.

"I am finally beginning to think you are right."

"I am. They work together well." Kaiden hesitated. "A lesson you could learn from."

Rianthe stared at him. "What does that mean?"

Kaiden shrugged, his face blank. "It means exactly what I meant it to. You have berate me for not telling you things, yet you don't think it's important to tell me about these visions you have until desperation forces you to. You don't give me enough basic information to keep you safe."

"Is that what this quiet thing of yours is all about? Because I didn't tell you about the visions?" She stepped in front of Kaiden, moved until she was as close as she could be to him. "Why would I tell something like that to someone when I have not been given any reason to trust them?"

Rianthe stalked off into the darkness, quite done with being around people. She needed some peace and quiet, a place to think.

She ended up in the rubble that had once been the rooms she'd shared with Uja and Tevy. This village had sheltered them in their direst need. Now it was in ruins, and her brother had died. Uja, so gentle and kind. Rianthe kicked at the soot. Why? Why had this happened? Hadn't enough happened to them? To everyone? Why must they suffer more?

She booted more ash with her toe, until she hit something hard and unmoving. Rianthe felt around in the dark with her gloved hands. A square corner, then another, and another, and another. A box? Digging, she unearthed the one-foot square box. How the wood had survived the fire, she had no clue. Settling on the ground outside where their hut had been, Rianthe found the clasp and opened the box. Inside, there appeared to be skins with indentations in them.

"You found my drawings," Tevy said, holding a

glow pot as he joined her.

"You draw?"

"Yes." He pulled them out, showing her one at a time. Village scenes were etched in the skins, then colored by some method she didn't know. There were animals in each scene.

One in particular, of a playful group of pups, made Rianthe smile. "Taschia."

Tevy grinned. "Yes."

"Thank you for her," Rianthe said.

"You needed a companion. And I needed to know you were all right."

"She has been much more than my companion. She is my friend, my sister, my protector."

I love you, too, Taschia mind-spoke, joining them, and settled beside Tevy, who grinned and scratched her ears.

"It's good to have you home, Tasch," Tevy said.

"Where have you been?" Rianthe asked.

Minding the young while the women work. Taschia made it very obvious by her tone just how beneath her the activity had been. *It has been nice to be reunited with my brothers, though.*

"I imagine, if you were all there, the children had very little chance to get into any mischief."

You are quite correct.

Tevy and Rianthe both laughed at the formality of Taschia's certainty. The next skin Rianthe picked up was of the three of them. Rianthe, Uja, and Tevy.

"I did that one from memory."

Rianthe held it closer to the glow. It was astoundingly detailed and accurate. She ran her hands over Uja's face, memorizing the lines, his smile, the eyes she would never see again.

"Do you think we'll forget what he looks like?" Tevy asked, a tear falling from overfull eyes. "I never knew what Mother and Father looked like at all. I don't want to lose the memory of Uja. It's all I have left, besides you." His sobs rent the air and Rianthe pulled him in tight, adding her tears to his. Taschia leaned into them both and the three of them stayed that way, drawing strength from each other, for a long time.

Rianthe turned him to see her face, see the resolution there. "You will never forget what Uja looks like. We will never forget," she whispered.

Tevy nodded and wiped his face with his hand.

Rianthe smiled, though tears still ran down her cheeks. All he'd managed to do was add dirty streaks to an already filthy face. She imagined hers looked as bad. "Come on," she said. "Let's go down to the lake and wash up." She sniffed the air. "We might actually be able to eat when we get back."

~~~

Kaiden watched them walk to the lake, followed them, making certain no harm came to them. He stayed back, unwilling to break into their moment, even though it was what he yearned for.

He missed her. He missed Bhren. What would he do without the mentor who'd practically raised him? Kaiden was thankful that his sister had survived, as had Jonah and Raisa, who'd raised him like their own. Still, he'd lost too much. Rianthe included. He missed the closeness they'd shared. Once, they'd talked about anything and everything. Kaiden hadn't known that with anyone else. He'd tried, after realizing she would not be coming back to New Hope. He'd tried to make closer friends. None of
~~~

them compared to Rianthe. He may not have been able to tell her everything, but he'd told her more than he had anyone. He'd shared his deepest fears.

When Bhren told him what must happen at Rianthe's True-Naming, Kaiden had known their relationship would be forever changed. Now, his home was in ruins, the love he'd waited years for had been destroyed, and there was no one to share his grief with. All he could do was to remain strong and carry on. Keep Rianthe and the village safe. This was all that was left to him.

But sometimes, like now, he wished more than anything that there were someone he could hug tight. Someone on whose shoulder he could shed these tears of grief he held so tight inside.

It was not to be. Rianthe didn't trust him and he wasn't certain he trusted her any longer either. So be it. He would be the loner the fates had decreed for him. That was the role of *thurisaz*. Bhren had told him that long ago, at his own True-Naming. He hadn't believed it to be truth, though, until tonight.

CHAPTER TWENTY-THREE

Several days later, Rianthe walked through the village with Tevy and Taschia at her side and Kaiden behind, always watchful, always protective. Rianthe knew well how to take care of herself, but Kaiden had taken his role as her protector to a whole new level. For now, she'd live with it. Eventually, she knew, they'd have to confront this thing between them. Everything in its own time.

It surprised her how much they'd accomplished in a few short days. Thankfully, after that first snow, more had held off, giving them precious time. The air still stank of fire and ash, but they'd managed to expand the shelter and add temporary walls inside allowing for some separation, as well as strengthening the structure. Things were coming along so well, it was easy to think there was some magic at work helping them. They planned to use this long-house style structure until things were more stabilized, maybe even through the winter. Then, in the spring, they could begin rebuilding the individual huts and expanding the village.

Enough of the kitchen longhouse had survived that they'd turned it into a makeshift greenhouse. A warming fire using rushes for a slow burn provided warmth. Already the seeds were showing signs of sprouting even though it was mid-fall. Uja's spirit probably helping to nurture them. The thought made Rianthe smile. That and Fraka's abilities. Uja had been right. Fraka was talented.

Kaiden had worked with several of the men on refining their hunting skills. Most of the hunters… It hurt too much to think of how many had given their lives for the hundred or so that had survived the attack. More hunters needed training. Because of everyone's hard work and the sacrifice of several boars and some elk, there would be game for sustenance, with more to come. Meat was being smoked in a makeshift oven, the hides tanned. Everyone worked at something, even the children, who fashioned replacement bowls and plates and cups out of clay. Just like before. Except it wasn't like before. A lump lodged in Rianthe's throat, thinking of Uja, of Bhren, and of so many others. Things would never return to the way they were. Not completely.

New Hope, though, was a village full of hardy, hard-working people and Rianthe knew that resilience would get them through this winter. They would survive and it made her heart glad.

With the village beginning to stabilize, she could now turn her thoughts to making the people who'd caused them so much pain and devastation pay for what they'd done. Deakon. Then Taegar.

"It's time," she told Kaiden later that day as they walked back from the lake with full water bags.

His lips thinned into almost nonexistent lines as they had many times since their arrival back in New Hope. He kept his counsel and only asked when they would be leaving.

Telling Kaiden would be the toughest part for Rianthe. This was her quest. She alone had decided not to put anyone else in danger. "This is my fight. It's personal."

"Why? Because Deakon was there when your father was killed? He also almost killed an entire village. Our village. These are my family, Ri. And whether you like it or not, you are too. I am duty bound to protect you, but even if I wasn't, I still would. When do we leave?"

He'd never give up. Rianthe knew him well enough to understand that he wouldn't let her go alone. "Fine," she ground out. We leave at first light."

"I'll be ready." Kaiden turned on his heel and strode ahead, spewing anger with every step.

Rianthe spent the afternoon talking to Jonah, making sure she'd done everything she could to help before she left.

"Will you keep an eye on Tevy while I'm gone?" This was the hardest part. Leaving her baby brother behind once more. If anything happened to Tevy…

"Don't worry," Jonah said.

Raisa joined them, hugging Rianthe. "Tevy's one of our own," she said. "We'll keep him safe. And if we don't, those wolves of his will.

Neither of them tried to talk her out of going. Everyone was torn between their new reality and going after the ones who'd created it. Jonah kissed her on the forehead and wished her well.

After dinner, Rianthe sat with Tevy as he fed the few food scraps he'd been able to pilfer to the wolves.

"I'll be leaving, Tevy," she said without preamble.

"I know."

Rianthe smiled and tried to ruffle his hair, but he batted her hand away.

Tevy ducked his head. "Don't do that. I'm twelve now, you know. Not a little kid."

Tevy had not grown as quickly as others his age and did not come close to being as tall as Rianthe. Maybe someday he might match her. Not yet. "You will always be my baby brother." She ruffled his hair again and he pushed her hand away.

"I…I just got you back. I don't want you to leave again." Tevy swiped an arm across his eyes.

Rianthe sighed. Leaving New Hope before, she'd been in a rage of hurt. Tevy had understood her reason. That didn't diminish what she'd put him through. This time, her own pain sliced almost deeper. His, too. She'd just begun to learn about twelve-year-old Tevy. Now she would leave him again for who knew how long. He'd be dealing with the aftermath without her or their brother to lean on. She would be abandoning the only brother she had left. Grief, never far, crashed into her again as she thought of Uja. Of how she should have been here. And now she was leaving Tevy behind, too.

Her lips trembled as she hugged him tightly. "I need you to be safe."

"The wolves will keep me safe."

Rianthe smiled at him through the sheen of tears in her eyes. "I believe they will, little brother." She drew in a deep breath, turning Tevy to face her. "You know I have to go."

Tevy hugged her back. "Just…come home sooner this time. This is your home, and you're the only family I have now."

"You have the village, and the animals."

"That's not the same."

"I know. I can't make any promises, Tevy. But when I'm done with what I need to do, I'll be back. All right?"

He nodded.

Taschia, who'd been playing with her siblings, strode over and nudged Rianthe.

"Thank you again for sending Taschia to me," Rianthe said, hugging the wolf. "She got me through some dark times."

"And helped keep you safe."

I will help keep her safe this time, also, Taschia mind-spoke.

Tevy hugged the wolf, too. *Thank you.*

Rianthe smiled.

"Both of you better come home. You hear me?"

His words and the demanding smile on his face would help Rianthe through these next days and weeks, she was certain.

Her life in the Fringes had taught Rianthe how to sneak into, or out of, an encampment. With night less than half gone, she stepped away from New Hope, pack in hand. Taschia trod silently beside her. Rianthe walked away from the village that had saved her, the village she'd walked away from once before and returned too late to stop from being burned to the ground. She would avenge them all—the village, her father, Uja.

"Going somewhere?"

Her knife was drawn in an instant. "Dram, Kaiden."

"I knew I couldn't trust you to wait."

"Look…" Rianthe put her knife away and set her hand on his arm. "It's better if I do this alone."

"Not going to happen."

Rianthe heard the steel in his voice. If they didn't go together, he'd follow. She knew that. In less than a fortnight, they'd gone from one uneasy alliance to another.

Once again, Kaiden would be in danger because of something she needed to do. Taschia, too. Maybe she should let this go. Chasing down Deakon wasn't worth their lives…or hers. Remorse fueled a rare indecision in Rianthe.

"Do you think this is foolhardy, Kaiden?"

Kaiden set down his pack and threaded both hands through his hair, clasping them behind his head for a long moment. "Yes."

Hackles rose on Rianthe's arms and neck.

"And no," he continued. "Where is Deakon going?"

"To Taegar. He must be. Which leaves us no choice." Foolhardy or not, they had to get to Deakon before he reported to Taegar.

Kaiden nodded, his face grim. "How do you know which direction to go? You didn't…"

His shudder mirrored her own. "No. I haven't tried to find him through the visions. Yet. My only thought was to get out of the village with my tracks covered so you couldn't follow me. Then…" She shrugged.

"Promise me you'll never do that alone again." He shook her by the shoulders when she didn't answer. "Promise me."

"I cannot promise," she said.

"Arghhh!" Kaiden threw his hands in the air, then

raked his hair again.

"However, if I need to seek something through the visions, I will always strive to do so in your presence," she finished.

"Well, I guess that's as close to a promise as I can ever get from you." He shook his head as he picked up his pack. "So, which direction?"

"In the past, the visions came to me. I've had no control over them until this last one, and I'm not sure I controlled that one. I thought about home and the vision became New Hope. I wondered if, maybe, I'd be able to focus, try to reach out for Deakon. See if I could get a hint of where he is. Get a direction to head in."

"Do the visions go both ways?"

Golden eyes speared her to immobility. "I'm worried that they can," she said honestly. "If they do, better to try while it's still dark and they can't determine where we are."

"They?"

"Deakon or…anyone." The night chilled further as she thought about the golden eyes of Taegar.

"How bad have these visions gotten?" he asked, his voice not quite masking concern for her.

"The worst one was…pretty bad. If Bhren hadn't been there to help…"

"When was that?"

"On the day of my True-Naming."

Even in the dark, she saw Kaiden close his eyes for a long moment. "I'm sorry, Ri. I'm so sorry."

"What are you sorry for? You didn't cause the vision."

"I couldn't be there to help you deal with the aftermath. I will forever regret that choice. Maybe, for a while at least, we could have a truce? I've…I've missed you, Ri."

A small piece of the ice chip in her heart broke off and dissolved as Rianthe nodded. They'd probably never return to what they were. Still, maybe something new could be forged. She'd held Kaiden in the highest respect once. Maybe, someday, she would again.

For now, they had a war to wage. Rianthe settled on the ground and pulled her gloves off. "Let's do this. Kaiden, if you see golden eyes, that's not good. We'll talk about that later, but know that this person is more dangerous than anything you've ever known."

The look in his eyes said they would definitely talk later as he gave her a curt nod.

Taschia sat in front of Rianthe, ready to break the vision if need be.

Rianthe drew a deep breath, took a long moment to focus on Deakon, and reached for the earth.

The change was immediate. Rianthe found herself in the common room of an inn. She looked around, feeling Kaiden's touch when he joined her in the vision. There was something familiar about this place. She'd stayed in one or two of these after she'd first left New Hope. It had not taken long for her to prefer the solitude of the woods. Too many folk thought they had a right to do with her what they pleased. She'd learned early on how to discourage them.

Searching for Deakon, she was disappointed when he did not appear in the common room. Her senses pulled her to the right, down a hallway. At the end, two shadowy figures whispered. Rianthe knew in her heart that one of them was the man she sought. He did not turn or even seem to recognize that she was there.

The other didn't seem real. The cloaked figure fluttered in and out, as if it were some sort of vision within a vision. It turned her way, nothing but shadow and deep, glowing golden eyes.

Taegar.

Rianthe gasped as fear drove deep, searching to turn her soul.

"Come to me," she said. "There is still time. Join me and you will become immortal."

The fear deepened. This time, though, Rianthe fought back. Struggled to lift the shroud that drew her to Taegar's will and muted her.

"I will never join you," she spat out finally. "And I will come for you. Beware, Taegar. You will pay at my hand for what you have done!" Rianthe screamed the words, for the first time able to have a voice in her vision.

It happened so fast, Rianthe almost believed she'd missed it. The faceless eyes widened in surprise, the look gone as quickly as it had come.

"Who are you?" Taegar asked.

"Your worst enemy," Rianthe promised. She looked down at her hands, wondered if she could will herself out of the vision. She closed her eyes and imagined brushing dirt off them, focusing on Kaiden and the woods.

When she opened them, the dark night woods surrounded her, the vision gone. Rianthe breathed the pine scent deep within, calming herself and righting her world. This time hadn't seemed as bad. It was almost as if she'd been able to be there in that hallway, beyond the vision. She'd found her voice for the first time and fear had not frozen her.

She had surprised Taegar, and that alone lifted her spirits.

Yanking her gloves on, Rianthe stood to see both Kaiden and Taschia staring at her.

You did well, Taschia mind-spoke.

"That was Taegar?" Kaiden whispered, looking Rianthe over from head to toe, then glancing from tree to tree in the darkness.

Rianthe nodded. "Yes," she said, since his eyes still swept the area as if looking for threats.

He turned back to her. "She's not even…she doesn't seem to have any…"

"Substance? I know."

"Is she alive, do you think?"

"I don't know what she is. I only know that she is dangerous." Rianthe watched as the full weight of her words settled on his shoulders.

"And most likely," he said, "the reason the world is in the state it's in." Kaiden took a long moment to stare off into the darkness, then straightened. "One fight at a time, right?"

"Right." She nodded. "I know the type of place that was, where people can pay to spend the night and get a meal, though I do not recognize that particular one. My senses tell me it's to the southwest."

Kaiden picked up both their packs, handing Rianthe hers. "Your instincts have gotten us through so far. Southwest it is."

CHAPTER TWENTY-FOUR

The first three days were uneventful. By morning of the fourth day, Rianthe knew the journey would be more than tough from here on. So much for the snow holding off. It had begun to fall in earnest. In a short time the wind joined the snow, turning the white world into a swirling, unbalanced frenzy of storm. Rianthe, Kaiden, and Taschia huddled close together.

"We need shelter," Kaiden said.

Rianthe nodded. The snow, wet and heavy, had soaked through her cloak. A chill she couldn't shake had settled deep in her bones. Kaiden looked just as bad. Even Taschia looked miserable.

"I've hunted this far," Kaiden said. "There is a homesteader a short way from here. He might let us hunker down in his barn for the night. Taschia, do you know where it is?"

The wolf yodeled her assent. Rianthe didn't dare

open her mouth or her teeth would start chattering, so she nodded again.

"Then you lead, Taschia. You can see better in this white." Kaiden tied a rope to Taschia, then around Rianthe's waist and, finally, to himself.

Taschia led them slowly through the blizzard. It seemed like hours before the faint outline of buildings appeared. They stopped for a moment to catch their breath, and Kaiden leaned close to Rianthe's ear.

"This one's a bit of a hermit, Ri. He won't take kindly to other humans invading his territory." Even with their close proximity, the whistle of the wind made it difficult to hear him. The storm was worsening.

"We have no other choice," she said. Would someone really turn travelers away in this kind of weather?

Kaiden reached for her hand as Taschia pulled on the rope. Leaning into the wind, which came directly at them, they put their heads down and moved slowly forward.

When they reached the door, the wind sloughed off suddenly. The door opened and their forward momentum carried them all straight into the cabin. Taschia righted herself easily, but Rianthe's and Kaiden's tumble didn't stop until they were perilously close to the large fire burning in the hearth. The door slammed shut behind them.

They stood and brushed themselves off, turning toward the now closed door. A large bear of a man stood there, an arrow nocked in his great bow and trained directly on Kaiden.

"Who dares step into my territory?"

"Roulf, it's me. Kaiden. We met once before. When I entered these woods not knowing they were yours."

He pulled the arrow back tighter. "Then you should have learned not to come this way again."

"We had no choice. That storm outside is raging." Kaiden waved toward the door. "I'd intended to skirt your property. Nature's fury forced us in another direction."

"Hmph." The bow dipped as Roulf released his grip on the string.

Rianthe let out the breath she'd been holding.

"Put your knife away, Ri," Kaiden said.

"How do we know this is not some ploy of his so he can disarm us both? That arrow can only take out one of us."

"Ha ha ha!" Roulf's laughter boomed through the cabin. "This one has much spirit in her," he said to Kaiden, leaning bow and arrow against the wall beside the door.

The big man rubbed his long, wiry beard as he waited for Rianthe to put her weapon away. She did so, but did not relax her stance until Roulf moved to the kitchen area of his one-room cabin.

Even with the large size of the open room, everything seemed small compared to the man as he moved around. Kaiden appeared relaxed, though that wasn't enough for Rianthe to ease off her readiness.

There was something about this man that confused her. He lived here in the middle of nowhere like a hermit, tried to scare off anyone who passed through, yet laughed at a moment's notice after pointing a weapon at strangers?

She didn't sense danger. It was more confusion than anything. This man was not who she saw, what she thought he was. The sooner this storm passed and they could get back on their way, the better.

Rianthe listened for the howling wind, surprised she heard none. She went to the door, intent on looking outside since there were no windows.

"I wouldn't do that," Roulf said.

Her hand on the doorknob, she turned to him. "Why not?"

"The storm rages whether you hear it or not. Opening that door will defeat the spell that keeps us safe and warm in this house."

"You have magical ability?" She pulled her hand back, intrigued.

"Indeed, I do." The air around him began to shimmer and the Roulf she'd met disappeared, slowly morphing into a small, thin, completely bald man. He stood no taller than Kaiden's waist. The only thing large about him were his blue eyes, which were round and seemed completely out of place in his pale face.

Rianthe stared at him, unable to contain her surprise. Kaiden chuckled.

"Did you know he could do this?"

"No, but I suspect you"—he pointed to Roulf—"always do the unexpected."

Roulf nodded. "It's a handy little trick for keeping snoopers and stealers away." He pointed to his chest. "No one would be afraid of me, so my alter ego keeps me alive."

"You do this with the *awen*," Rianthe said, wonder filling her voice.

Roulf nodded. "I can manipulate certain things, make them appear differently than they are. Like that storm outside."

"It's not real?"

"The storm is quite real, and you were fortunate to stumble upon my abode. I simply change the air surrounding my house, shaping it into a wall that keeps the storm at bay. Not far, though. Had you opened that door without me preparing for it, you would have broken my spell and brought the storm inside where I could not have contained it."

Rianthe glanced at the door and shivered, glad to be sheltered and not still outside. "So there are limits to what you can do."

He nodded, looking at her intently for a long moment. "I'm quite certain you sense limits in your own ability."

Rianthe shook her head. "I have little or none. Even if I did, very little magic remains since the war. Even Master Bhren struggled to find it."

"It is there if you choose to see it. So…" Roulf set a teapot and cups out, along with a plate piled high with bread and cheese, inviting them to sit with him. "You are students of Bhren the Guardian, are you?"

"Were," Kaiden said, his voice quieting to pass on the sorrowful news. "Bhren was killed in an attack against New Hope."

Hearing the words brought tears to her eyes still. Needing something to busy herself with, Rianthe took off her tunic and set it near the fire to dry, leaving her damp shirt on.

Roulf hung his head, shaking it back and forth. "I knew something was off." His sigh was filled with regret. Raising his head, there were tears in his large eyes. "He was a good man. A talented druid. The world is worse off without him." Roulf stared into the fire. "Much worse."

"You knew him?" Rianthe asked.

Roulf nodded. "I, too, was a student of Bhren the Guardian."

Kaiden frowned. "You've never lived in New Hope."

"No, I haven't. I trained under Bhren before New Hope. I knew him when he was in the place called New York."

"But that was before—"

"The Great Magic War," Roulf said, cutting her off. He laughed at her expression. "Yes, child, I am that old."

"How can that be?"

"Earth magic doesn't just give the earth new life. The *awen* also imbues its users with greater health and longevity."

"Are you immortal?"

Roulf laughed. "Hardly. I am living beyond my years, but I will perish at some point." He poured tea for each of them and handed around the plate. "There are limits to the power. More now than ever before. It's not like it was when the magic first appeared." He lifted his cup. "Now eat. Drink. Get warm. We can talk more afterward."

Rianthe bit into a seasoned bread that tasted better than anything she'd ever had before. "This is really good," she said. "Is it also an illusion?"

"No. It is real. I must eat just as you must."

"Yet the magic keeps you from aging."

"It slows the process." He cocked his head. "You will notice it at some point. I sense strong ability in you, child."

"Bhren thought so, too," Kaiden said.

"No. That can't be true. If I had this talent, I should have been able to save New Hope." Her voice broke. "I should have been able to save Uja."

Roulf glanced at Kaiden.

"Her brother," Kaiden answered the unspoken question.

"Ah." Roulf nodded. He came around the table and removed Rianthe's gloves, holding her hands palm up. "Your brother's blood is not here. His death is not your fault."

Tears blurred Rianthe's vision. It was as if Roulf saw straight into her soul. "I couldn't save him."

He let go of her hands, and cupped her face until she stared into his enormous eyes. "No, child, you couldn't. Even if you'd come into your magic. There is magic in you. Believe that. But it is not yet your time. You are not ready."

There was no dishonesty, no deceit in his eyes. He'd told her the truth as he knew it.

"How will I know when I am ready?"

Roulf laughed, wagging his finger. "That is the real question. One I am afraid I have no answer for." Roulf went to the mantle, and grabbed a gnarled old pipe and pouch. Once filled and tamped, he lit it with a stick from the fire and took a long draught. Pointing the long handle at Rianthe, he continued. "There is a dark cloak over the earth and it is said that only the prophesied one will be able to remove it. Until that time, I'm afraid darkness will continue to create chaos in everyone's life. Yours, Kaiden's, even mine," he said, the last bit whispered almost to himself.

"I guess I thought that, with all this talk of my having more magic than I believe I do, I might be that person."

"Only time will tell. Only time. Until then, you will most likely be tasked with keeping the darkness at bay."

"Taegar."

Roulf stared at her. "How do you know that name? I cannot believe that Bhren would have mentioned that one."

"He didn't. Not really. He probably should have, especially in light of the visions."

"What visions? Come, child, tell me." Roulf's insistence worried Rianthe. Did he have visions? Did he know the torture they could inflict?

Kaiden, who'd been sitting back and listening, leaned forward on the table. "I, too, want to hear more about these visions."

Rianthe took a deep breath. "I haven't had that many of them. Only five."

"I only know of the two, although you've promised to tell me about those first visions."

She shuddered.

"You're in a safe place here, child. Nothing can get to you. Believe me." The intensity of Roulf's gaze did not help Rianthe to relax.

"It's hard to talk about."

"When was the first vision?" Roulf prodded.

"At the end of Studies each day, Bhren called me to the druid's tower for extra work. One day I touched the dirt on his table. Bhren said that dirt went all the way through the tower to the earth." Rianthe wrung her hands together. "I didn't really have a vision then. More like an overwhelming fear. That time, I yanked my hands away before it got any worse."

"When did it next happen?"

"That same day. Bhren convinced me to see if I could do it again. After that, it next happened at my True-Naming."

Kaiden flinched, most likely stuck in his own memories of that day.

"I don't know if that was part of the True-Naming or if it happened coincidentally before the actual ceremony. When I touched the dirt, the change was immediate. I wasn't in the tower any longer. I was in some cave or dark place. There were shadows circling some central altar or…something. I couldn't see it clearly."

"Was that all?" Roulf asked.

"No. I was drawn to one shadow, taller than the others. They were all cloaked so I couldn't see bodies, only shadows, although they seemed almost…formless. When this one turned toward me, though, I didn't see a face under the cowl of the cloak. Only eyes. Golden, painful eyes."

Rianthe hugged herself so hard she thought she'd leave bruises. Kaiden pulled his chair behind her, scooted her back until she leaned against him, and she drew strength from an old comfort she'd missed more than she wanted to admit. For this moment, Rianthe let everything go and just tried to relax.

"It felt as if they wanted to drain all my energy." Their efforts had been focused on the runes around her neck. Rianthe withheld that information, not quite ready to share. At Bhren's insistence, she had spoken to no one about this. Not to Roulf, not to Kaiden, not to anyone. "I got weaker and weaker. If it hadn't been for Bhren, I think they might have drained all the life force from me."

"So not just a vision," Roulf said.

"No." Rianthe shook her head vehemently against Kaiden's chest and held on tight. The reliving was almost as painful as the event itself. "Pain. There was so much pain. I had no control. Always, the one with the golden eyes beckoned me to come. To join them. Live immortal with them.”

Both Kaiden and Roulf were silent, digesting what she'd told them.

“How did you pull out of the vision?”

“Bhren. When he touched me, he saw my vision. He tried to warn me. The next thing I knew, we were both on the floor in his tower. He'd pushed me away from the table.”

“Those were not just visions, then. You tapped into the *ehwaz*, the vision plane. Neither dream nor reality, yet both at the same time. And, I believe that shrouded figure was indeed Taegar,” Roulf said.

“Bhren whispered that name, too. I didn't know for sure until some men attacked us in the area called Minne Apples and they mentioned her. Kaiden told me more later about who Taegar was.”

“Is,” Roulf said. “I have always believed she did not perish in the final moments of the war. And I believe she is the reason the *awen* continues to elude both us and the earth, which remains barely able to sustain us. You were attacked?”

“Yes, and the men said Taegar wanted all wanderers brought to her.”

Roulf got up and paced back and forth, his hands clasped behind his back as he thought. He mumbled to himself over and over. “This is not good, this is not good. Guardian druids, Dark druids, the *ehwaz*. Not good at all. Don't get involved, Roulf. This is not your fight. Still, this is really not good.”

Rianthe tried to sit up, uncomfortable now that the vision-telling was done. Kaiden held her for an instance longer, then released her.

Roulf returned to the table. "Listen, child. You must understand some things. Whatever happened at the end of the war has stuck to this earth like potter's glue to terracotta. The magic all but disappeared. Only bits of it get through"—he waved his hand around—"or I couldn't do this. Bhren, also, would have been devoid of any magical ability. Latent magic can manifest in many ways. Strength with a sword, masking surroundings, the ability to bond to animals..."

Taschia whined.

"Yes, I know you can mind-speak, pup," Roulf said.

"Like Tevy, my brother, and his animals," Rianthe said.

"Or Uja," Kaiden interrupted. "And his successes in the growing fields. And you, Ri. You have an uncanny ability with a sword. And your prescience of danger is beyond a normal person's ability."

"Yes, yes, yes," Roulf said. "Exactly like that. But I have sensed for some time a...boldness to the storms that encroach upon us. Like a search is underway. I believe Taegar searches for you, child, and what you carry."

The bottom dropped out of Rianthe's world and she clasped the bag hanging around her neck, feeling as if the runes had been ripped from her.

Kaiden, who'd moved to stand by the fire, stared at her. "What do you carry?"

Slowly, Rianthe pulled the bag from beneath her tunic. "Just a bag of runes that my father gave me."

"Your father was...?" Roulf asked.

"Damian Royan."

All the breath whooshed from Roulf's lungs. "Guardian druid."

"Yes," Rianthe whispered. "I only found out that he

was a Guardian druid when Bhren lost his battle with life. What does this all mean, Roulf?"

"Damian Royan wasn't simply a Guardian druid."

The hair on Rianthe's arms tingled. "What do you mean?"

"Your father led the Guardian circle."

Leader? High mage of the most important circle of power when the magic awakened? How was this even possible? Flashes of memory hit her. Her father, regal and tall as he led his family on their journey. Always heading off into the woods at night, rarely sleeping, never aging, it seemed. Rianthe had followed him one night. She'd seen him huddled over something in the dirt, mumbling words she didn't understand. He'd seen her, but hadn't punished her. *Go back to sleep, dearest daughter. This is not something you need to know yet.*

At the end, he'd been a broken man, with the weight of the world in his eyes. Rianthe hugged herself, trying to dispel the melancholy of her thoughts. His fate…his fate could not be hers. Could it? If her father had passed on any power to his offspring, it had gone to Uja, or Tevy. Not to her.

"Both your father and mother were druids, child."

The impact of Roulf's softly spoken words hit Rianthe like a fierce blow. Her mother? She jumped up. Began to pace. Why hadn't she known? Why hadn't anyone—Bhren—told her? Rianthe fingered the bag around her neck. They'd died for this. Left her, Uja, and Tevy to fend for themselves because of this quest to heal the earth. She wanted to be angry with them. To tell them that their children were more important than anything. She hung her head, knowing she couldn't say that to them, even if they were here. Deep in her soul, Rianthe knew she wasn't meant to lead the meager life she did. No one was. The alliance between Earth and humanity had been severed and her parents had been charged with reigniting that bond's flame. Except they'd died before finishing that task. And Bhren, who'd known her parents, had thought she was the savior who would pick up the mantle of leadership and save the world. This was insane. She had little or no power. She knew that. Why couldn't she convince everyone else of her lack?

Roulf eyed her with an intensity that made Rianthe uncomfortable. "You know of the One Prophecy?"

Trying to focus, to set her own feelings aside, Rianthe nodded along with Kaiden.

"Recite it."

They glanced at each other before doing as they were told.

"Shattered by darkness the magic vanished. It lays in wait for one who's banished. Hidden power will blossom anew. Only by passing the darkness through."

"There is a second part to that prophecy," Roulf told them, then recited it for them.

"The runic key ignites the fire. That coupled with the conduit's power. Must send the magic to the white height. Defeating darkness, restoring light."

"Why were we not taught this in Studies?" Rianthe asked.

"It is not widely known. When Taegar split from the Guardian druids, what remained of the circle knew a crisis was coming and banded most of their magic into a talisman that would help defeat Taegar and the storms of darkness capable of overtaking the earth."

He sighed before continuing. "The war came to the Guardian druids too soon. Their magic was depleted after creating the talisman. Most of them were destroyed. Three escaped with the talisman you hold. You know now that they were Damian and Valena Royan, and Bhren."

Rianthe clutched the bag tightly. Even though her father's mission had been to heal the earth, his last thoughts had been to keep her, her brothers, and the talisman safe. He'd loved them. Grief rushed through her anew.

Roulf grasped her shoulders, pulled her down, bringing her attention back to him. She stared into eyes she knew told the truth, and saw that he was afraid. "You are in grave danger, Rianthe Royan. While she does not seem to know who you are, Taegar does indeed appear to be looking for you, and for the talisman you carry."

"Here," Rianthe said, pulling the bag from around her neck. "Take it. You keep it safe."

"I cannot," Roulf said, shaking his head. "I am at the end of my years and my magic is almost depleted."

Frustration bubbled up in her. "I don't have any magic," she shouted.

"You will when the need arises. You must believe in the magic, and in yourself. And you must stay safe until the time is right." He stepped back. "Who is it you search for?"

"A member of our village, Deakon. He's the one who caused its destruction," Rianthe said. "He is in league with Taegar and has probably joined her by now."

Roulf lowered his head for a few seconds, then raised it. "I sense that he is not yet with Taegar, but he will be. He is a pawn. Taegar sent many of these out years ago, I now believe, to search for the talisman. I have seen some moving through these woods at odd times in my life. Your quest is foolhardy, child. This Deakon is not who you want, and you are not yet prepared to take Taegar on. You need more training, more understanding."

Rianthe barely managed to keep from hitting something. Her family, and what they—she—carried, had been the reason behind New Hope's destruction. A white-hot fury consumed her along with a grief so profound she could not stand it. *Uja!* His death was her fault.

"Breathe, Rianthe, breathe," Kaiden said. "This is not your doing."

Roulf turned her face to him. "You cannot stop this danger. It would have come for New Hope no matter what, because Bhren was there. I am grateful that you were not on that fateful day." He paced to the fireplace and back, mumbling under his breath. "The earth has not called to her yet. It is not time. Bhren…woefully unprepared. We must keep her safe until…ready." He turned to Rianthe. "Will you not let go of this revenge?"

"No." Rianthe shook her head violently. "I need to see this through."

Roulf smacked his lips together, as if deciding. He laid both hands upon the low oak mantle of his fireplace, closed his eyes, and remained silent for some time. When he straightened, his voice held both resolve and defeat. "You must leave at first light. He has moved westward, toward the old city of Casper. You will find what you seek there." He sighed. "For now, much has been discussed here tonight and a good sleep will help you to make sense of it all. You two may have the bed." He waved toward the corner where a large four-poster bed sat. "I will sleep with my animals."

"But—"

Taschia reached out a paw. *The place his animals sleep is protected like this house. I will sleep there, too.*

Rianthe and Kaiden both stared at Roulf. "That's a pretty large area to protect. You have more magic in you than you say, old man," she said.

"Tricks," Roulf answered, waving his hand. "Just tricks."

CHAPTER TWENTY-FIVE

Rianthe curled into a tight ball against the wall, as far away on the bed from Kaiden as she could get. Misery washed over her in big, rolling waves of self-hatred. Roulf's words didn't help. In fact, they only added to the overwhelming knowledge that this was her fault. New Hope had been reduced to ashes because of her. Uja had died because of her. Sweet Uja, who only wanted to make things grow. If she weren't who everyone seemed to think she was, he would still be here.

It hurt so bad to know that she was to blame. Her hands curled around the bag that had always been her solace and the token whose rough leather had reminded her to slow down and reason things out. Trinkets, she'd thought, when her father gave them to her. A remembrance. Now, they seemed more of a sinister puppeteer, and the strings that held her up grew thin.

Not anymore. She tightened her grasp on the bag at

her neck, yanking it over her head. These runes were as culpable as her.

Rianthe climbed from the bed, strode to the fire, and pulled her hand back, fully intending to toss them into the fire. She stood frozen, indecisive, unsure of her direction for the first time in her life.

Sensing movement, she turned. Kaiden sat up in bed, watching her, not trying to stop her or talk her out of it. The steadfastness in his expression, the resolute belief that they must see this through, was more effective in staying her hand than if he'd lunged and tried to take it from her.

She wanted to be done more than anything. Nothing would bring her friends back. Nothing would give her one more chance to watch Uja tend his garden with a gentle hand.

It was too late for them. But not for the rest of humanity. In her heart, she did not believe she was man's redemption. Still, if she was meant to carry this trouble until the prophesied one came along, she had no choice.

Rianthe hung her head. "You knew I couldn't do it."

"Yes. If there was even a chance that it might help, you'd figure it out." He got up and joined her, putting a hand on her shoulder. "We'll figure this out together, Ri. I'll help any way I can."

Rianthe shrugged his hand off. This was her burden. Her responsibility. She brought this on New Hope. So be it. She settled the bag back around her neck and tucked it inside her shirt.

"I'm still going to make Deakon pay," she said, climbing back to the far side of the bed, turning her back to Kaiden. Everyone wanted her to put aside this quest to find Deakon. Was it so foolhardy to want him to pay for the death of her brother and everyone else?

"I know," he said quietly. "I want the same thing."

Hours later, Rianthe fell into an exhausted sleep, only to scream herself awake when her nightmares returned.

"Shh…shh…shh." Kaiden's low hum soothed her as he pulled her into his arms.

Rianthe didn't hesitate. She hugged him tight. She'd missed this so much. When, if ever, would this all end and give them some peace?

Morning dawned white but clear. After a hearty breakfast washed down with goat's milk, Rianthe and Kaiden made ready to head west.

"Be careful, child," Roulf said as he handed them food for the journey. "You are needed for greater things."

Rianthe raised her eyebrows. She still didn't believe Roulf, and no one would convince her otherwise. Not until something or someone forced her to believe.

Kaiden shook Roulf's hand, thanking the little man again for his hospitality. Roulf handed Kaiden a package and whispered something only he heard. Rianthe cocked her head, wondering what that was all about. Roulf looked tired, more so than the night before. Was age taking its toll on the last student of the Guardian druids? If that were the case, the world might have even more cause to grieve.

"Come on," Rianthe said after thanking Roulf. "Let's get going."

Rianthe pushed herself hard. Kaiden, too. She had to find Deakon. The blood coursing through her veins screamed for vengeance. Another, more elusive thread, pushed her just as hard. New Hope. Tevy, Fraka, and Uja's unborn child. She needed to be certain they were okay, needed to be back home.

It took another three days of slow, hard travel in makeshift snowshoes before they passed a sign with one end ripped off. CASP. Beyond the sign, remnants of the ancient civilization began sprouting up. It looked eerily like their trek into Minne Apples, except the crumbling buildings weren't as tall and it didn't seem as dreary and gray, probably due to the deep layer of snow that blanketed everything.

Still, Rianthe's sense of danger was heightened. They were close to their prey. They would find Deakon soon. She quickened her pace.

"Whoa." Kaiden held her back. "What do you think you're doing?"

"I'm going after the man who killed Uja."

"You are not rushing in there without a plan."

"Here's a plan for you." Rianthe yanked her arm out of his hands. "Deakon is going to die today, preferably at my hands."

"Ri, wait. Calm down for a moment and think. Revenge isn't the best reason to go after someone under normal circumstances. Anger only makes more fools."

Rianthe opened her mouth to refute that, but Kaiden held up his hand. "Let me finish."

It would be faster to let him say what he wanted to say, so she shut her mouth and waited, albeit not too patiently.

"What's one of the primary rules of combat?"

"To win."

"Other than that."

"You mean knowing your enemy?" Rianthe sighed.

"Also important. What I'm talking about is inciting anger. That will make your opponent misstep. And I'd rather our enemy make the wrong step than us. Revenge is never the best motivation. Red-hot, anger-filled revenge is nothing but foolhardy. I don't want to die today. I don't think you do either. We need to be calm and come up with a plan."

When he stood there quietly and waited, Rianthe capitulated. Dram it. She hated it, but he was right. "All right," she said. "What's the plan?"

"You haven't thought of one in all this time?"

"Well, um, no. I was focused on getting here."

It was Kaiden's turn to sigh. He squatted down on an old log and Rianthe joined him.

"All right," Kaiden said. "Unlike you, I have given this some thought. We sense that Deakon is here and we don't know if he's alone. In fact, I think we have to assume he's not. And that he's waiting for us."

Rianthe nodded. "He had help with him in New Hope. Some or all of them may have traveled here with him. And worse. There's every possibility that, despite what Roulf thought, Taegar may be here. Magic may be the only way to defeat them."

"We need to draw off as many of them as possible."

I can distract. I will go in, find them, and let them chase me. I will appear to be meat to them. Taschia shuddered. *I will lead them off, let you know how many remain.*

"No," Rianthe said. "It's too dangerous."

The journey itself is dangerous.

"Can you think of another way?" Kaiden asked.

"No. I don't like it, but no. I can't." Rianthe winced and hugged Taschia tight. "I guess that means we have our distraction. Kaiden and I will have to reconnoiter as we go. If there are guards, and we can get near them, we can try to deal with them quietly, bringing the numbers down even more and increasing our odds."

"I don't like it," Kaiden said. "It's not much of a plan."

"Got any other ideas?"

Dog and man shook their heads slowly.

"All right, then. That's our plan, such as it is. I think we should get closer, find a nearby outbuilding, and wait for Taschia to send us a message."

"Agreed."

They settled in to some ruins on the outskirts of town as dusk was falling. Perfect timing, Rianthe thought. Taschia would be seen, but she and Kaiden could move in under cover of darkness.

The only problem with this plan lay in her inability to let Taschia go. She sat petting her friend, not willing to put her in the way of such harm.

I am strong and fast. I will elude them.

Rianthe watched Taschia lope off with a heavy heart. Was she doing the right thing? Only time would answer that question. Deakon must be made to pay. It had become more than that, though. Whether she liked being involved or not, a larger problem loomed. Rianthe didn't exactly agree that the end of the world was coming at Taegar's hand. Still, it was obvious that the druid's actions intended harm to her brethren. And somehow, she'd been thrust right in the middle of whatever needed to be done to stop her.

She needed an indication of where Taegar lived. At the moment, Deakon was the only one who could give her that.

Which meant she must take her time killing him. Even that no longer sounded satisfying. This was dangerous. Crazy, even. They should have brought more men with them. Neither she nor Kaiden had wanted to leave New Hope unguarded. As well, if magic would indeed decide this battle, Rianthe knew of no one else who had that kind of magic. Bhren was not here to guide them or to use his magic anymore.

Rianthe sat in silent agony, waiting to hear from Taschia, praying that even if it was for the wrong reason, she'd done the right thing.

It is all right, Taschia mind-spoke. *I am well. Do not worry.*

Rianthe leaned against a sturdy oak, her thoughts a whirl of worry. She fingered the bag of runes, wished her father were here to give her some guidance. Or Bhren. She missed them both. Rianthe opened the bag and spilled the runes into her hand. Simple little squares with the markings of *Ansuz* and other signs on them. Markings that foretold of happiness or pain, and now were pivotal to the salvation of humanity. None of this seemed real. After staring at them for a long time, wishing them to give her some guidance, Rianthe tore open the bag and poured the stones back in. She withheld the final three, clutching them in her tight fist, praying on them that she had made the right choice. She put these three runes in the pocket of her tunic, unsure why but following some unheard instinct.

"Maybe I should hold onto the runes for you," Kaiden said.

She clutched the bag to her. No one except Tevy had held them since her father had first slipped them over her head. "Why?"

"Because of those visions you have that aren't really visions. Seems to me Taegar, and maybe Deakon, know a girl has this talisman. If something happens…if we get captured, these might go unnoticed if I'm wearing them."

It made sense. Still, it wasn't easy to hand them over. Her hand shook as she held the bag out to him.

"I'll guard them well, Ri."

"I know," she said. It still didn't feel right. She couldn't shake the feeling that something was missing. With a deep breath, Rianthe ran her gloved hand along her sword. She needed to let this go. She must be focused when the time came.

Kaiden hid the rune bag in his pocket, then crouched on his haunches, sifting dirt through his fingers. They each waited, buried in their own private hells.

There are voices ahead. I have not quite reached the town of man dens. There is a large, square box. The voices come from there.

How tall is the box? Rianthe asked.

Many times taller than I.

"So, some sort of large, square building," Rianthe said.

Kaiden nodded.

You come now. I will soon run like the wind.

Rianthe smiled, but it died quickly. *Be safe, sister,* she mind-spoke to Taschia.

Kaiden echoed the thought as he unsheathed his sword. They would leave their packs here to be retrieved later.

Hopefully.

CHAPTER TWENTY-SIX

Rianthe estimated they were about halfway to Taschia's man den when she heard from the wolf again.

I run. They chase. This is fun.

Be careful. With one last hopeful prayer sent for Taschia's safety, Rianthe's focus changed, praying that her instincts were right. Deakon had to be inside. He'd said he'd be waiting for her. She needed this to be over, so they'd need surprise on their side if they had any hope of surviving.

She heard small sounds, scented spicy food cooking, heard the muted crackle of a fire. Not too much movement and none in the perimeter around the building. It didn't seem like many were left. Maybe they'd get lucky. "Maybe eight or nine inside?" she whispered to Kaiden.

He nodded.

They neared the building, Rianthe's senses on high

alert. Taschia had done her work well. No one seemed to be on watch outside the structure.

Fumbling with something in his pocket, Kaiden motioned that he would go first and she should follow closely behind.

She raised her shoulders in question and Kaiden held out what looked like a rock. "Gift from Roulf," he whispered, then began muttering words Rianthe couldn't make out. She'd have to ask him later since he disappeared around a corner.

She followed quickly behind, and they inched their way along to an opening in the metal wall. Kaiden peeked inside, then held up four fingers to her. So there were four men from what he saw. She wanted to remind him that she thought there was twice that many, but they were too close for spoken words.

Before she could react, Kaiden had turned into the door. Was the man crazy? She followed him because she had no other choice, and they hugged the wall, remaining in shadow. True to Kaiden's raised fingers, four men sat at a table near the door. Guards? How the men did not see them enter, she did not know. She was, however, immensely grateful.

Off to the side, a big metal structure loomed, with wheels that looked like they'd been pulleys at some point. Any rubber or rope had long since disappeared and the structure was nothing but rust and holes. Right now, it would provide excellent cover, and they inched their way along until they could crouch behind it.

When Rianthe glanced around the other end, she saw more men sitting around a fire, eating whatever currently roasted above it. And there, on the far side…Deakon. Everything around her faded. Her ears pounded with the raging fire in her blood, her vision blurring. Except for him. The man who had killed her brother. He must pay. Every fiber in her body was consumed with only that one need.

Rianthe started to move, but Kaiden stopped her, placing a hand over her heart. She tore at it, needing to get to Deakon.

Kaiden wouldn't let go. Grabbed her tunic. Forced her to turn to him, to see his face, his eyes, the words he mouthed.

Be calm. Relax.

She knew that's what he was telling her. No anger. Only calm determination would win this battle. He was right, but it was so hard. Her whole body shook with the effort it took to calm herself. They lost time as she slowed her breathing, waited for the heat to be replaced by cold, calculating logic.

Finally, after too long a time, she nodded to Kaiden. She was ready.

He pointed that they should take on the guards, then the men around the campfire.

Rianthe nodded. They'd have a few seconds to deal with the guards before the others reacted.

They stepped out together, swords drawn, and managed to be almost upon the guards before they were noticed. Rianthe ran one through with her sword before he got his hand on the hilt of his. He dropped to the floor dead as the other leapt toward her.

Kaiden had not been as lucky. The second man had his sword drawn before Kaiden got to him, so he battled two at once. Pride flashed through Rianthe as she realized they were backing up, not him.

She had her own problems. The man fighting her

now was vicious and strong. He attacked again and again, pounding against her sword and her arm. Rianthe parried each hit, knowing she would not be able to do this much longer.

Searching for a weakness and finding none, she opted for the last trick Kaiden had taught her. She staged her own weakness, feinted when she should have attacked. The man's eyes gleamed as he thrust his sword at her. She came up underneath, sweeping his sword aside with hers, then driving her knife into his heart with all her might.

She barely had time to yank her knife free before the others were upon her. With her back to Kaiden, she could only hope he'd dispatched the two he fought.

Three swords went for her. The other one turned toward Kaiden. Deakon stood back, not engaging. The smirk on his face was a deadly grin. Rage opened the door and Rianthe had to work hard to close it, to keep her cool.

That distraction made things worse. One man's sword bit into the soft skin of her arm and Rianthe went to a knee, sweating with the effort to push the pain away. Blood flowed down her arm. Two swords swooped in. Rianthe fought back to standing, the effort costing her. She began to drive them back, no matter her pain. Swing after swing she kept at them, drawing on reserves she didn't know she had. By the sound of Kaiden's grunts, he was working just as hard.

She drew blood from one man's sword arm, and opened a deep gash in another's leg. Two down, one to go. As the last man advanced on her, she saw one of Kaiden's opponents fall to the ground.

Suddenly, something picked her up and threw her

against the wall. She hadn't seen anything coming. It was as if the air had thickened, wound its way around her, and tossed her like a ball.

Worse, she was stuck against the wall, her feet dangling. She could only watch helplessly as the man turned from attacking her and drove his sword through Kaiden's shoulder. "No!" Rianthe screamed, struggling to get free as Kaiden crumpled to the ground. She still held her sword, but it was useless. She could not move, could not help.

"I suggest you drop that sword, student Rianthe. You have lost. You will always lose," Deakon said.

Breathing heavily, wanting nothing more than to drive her sword through the man's black heart, Rianthe struggled against the unseen foe. She tried with everything she had to break the hold Deakon's magic had on her. She couldn't move. It had to be magic. What else could pin her like drying tunics to a clothesline.

Rianthe hung her head as blood dripped down her arm. She let go of the hilt of her sword, knowing she'd lost this fight. Kaiden lay unconscious on the floor. The only thing keeping the darkness at bay was that his chest rose and fell, albeit in jerky, irregular movements. He was alive. For now. She couldn't discern how bad his injury was, but it couldn't be good. She needed to be with him, to help him, now. Rianthe thrashed against the invisible bond that kept her against the wall, glaring at Deakon as she fought. The attempt was futile. She could not break free. Finally, unable to gain a single inch of movement, she stopped struggling.

Hold on, Kaiden. I'll find a way.

Suddenly, the air around her softened and she fell to the floor with a whoosh that stole her breath. Two swords were at the ready and kept her from rushing to Kaiden or attacking. Rianthe wanted to scream with frustration.

"Tie her up and bring them both to me," Deakon said.

She bit back a groan when they yanked her arms behind her and trussed them. Kaiden, still unconscious, moaned as they dragged him beside the fire. Rianthe was carried over one man's shoulder and thrown against the wall nearby, momentarily stunned. She struggled to a sitting position, but Kaiden lay crumpled where they threw him, worrying her greatly.

"Did you really think to best me, girl?" Deakon said, grabbing her tunic to pull her face close to his. "I can destroy you as easily as I destroyed your village."

"How—" Rianthe's voice shook with anger. She took a deep breath, then regretted it as Deakon's foul breath hit her. "How could you do that? It was your village, too. Your home."

"That place was never my home," he spat as he threw her back against the wall.

Her head hurt from the force of the hit. Dizziness threatened to swamp her and Rianthe concentrated hard to keep her focus. She wanted to shred Deakon's arrogance and make him pay for all the things he'd done. At the moment, anger was not helping. *Anger only makes more fools,* Kaiden's words reminded her. The only thing that would keep them alive until she found a way out of this mess was to feed Deakon's ego and keep him talking. "You lived there for so many years. Did you really hate New Hope that much?"

"I didn't hate it. To hate something, you have to actually consider it worthy." He began to pace back and forth. "I was indifferent. It, and all its people, are nothing.

You are nothing. You will never be as I am. I have great magic. I will live forever.”

He had magic? She'd never seen any sign that Deakon had any special talents. “The *awen* died with the Great Magic War, Deakon. You can't possibly be able to manifest it.”

He leapt back in front of her and grabbed her tunic again. “Do not speak to me in that tone, girl. Did you not just see one small sample of my power? Shall I show you more? I do have the magic. I have been gifted by Taegar. Look.” Deakon yanked her forward as he put his free arm out. The fire flared high with new life, growing dangerously close to Kaiden.

“I did that,” Deakon continued, letting her go and waving his hands like someone who'd gone mad. “My magic did that. And when I turn you over to her, all those who looked down on me will pay. And I will have immortality, as well. I will live forever!” He thrust his fist into the air, then looked at Rianthe again. “Unlike you and your friend here, who will not live until the morn.”

He kicked at Kaiden's still form. Rianthe winced at the weak groan that emanated from him.

“What's this?” Deakon said, picking up the bag that fell out of Kaiden's pocket. The bag he'd convinced Rianthe he should carry through this battle.

Rianthe closed her eyes, willed herself to not show the panic that consumed her. She could not let him know the runes' importance. If he took them to Taegar…

“They are simply the runes…he foretells with. Turn me over to whom?” she said, hoping to distract him.

“Never you mind, little girl.” Deakon opened the bag and spilled the runes out onto his hand. One fell to the floor and Rianthe hoped he wouldn't notice. Too soon, he reached down and picked up the wayward rune.

They were indeed in dire trouble if she didn't get that bag away from him.

Deakon moved to the fire, examining the runes. The markings on them flashed as the light caught them. Deakon smiled. "Murdo, come here."

One of the men stepped forward.

"We must get these to Taegar. She will want to see them as soon as possible."

"I will head out immediately," the man called Murdo said, reaching for the bag Deakon had put the runes back into.

Deakon laughed. "Do you think me that stupid? No, I will hand these to Taegar myself." He glanced at Rianthe. "I don't think Taegar will need these two," he said, hefting the bag. "This may well be the talisman she has searched so many years for. Make ready to leave at first light. We'll deal with them quickly and head to the caves."

Murdo's eyes brightened, but he nodded and gestured to his men to make the necessary preparations. Murdo went with them, leaving only one man behind with Deakon to guard Rianthe. Apparently, they thought rope would hold her.

Living in the Fringes, she'd always prepared for capture, even though it never happened. She'd had trusted allies tie her up over and over again just so she could practice escape.

It took a little longer to free herself from these ropes due to the need for stealth. Plus, her arm wound stung like crazy, slowing her down. Kaiden not moving, and with no word from Taschia worrying her further, Rianthe's attempts were sluggish at best. How would she ever pick up her sword and fight with so little energy?

Eventually, she freed herself. Her sword lay only feet from her, in front of the fire, but Deakon stood between. The only advantage she'd have was the element of surprise. And she must act quickly before the others came back. Thankfully, her sword arm wasn't the injured one. Still, she had a weakness that these men knew about. This would not be easy.

Rianthe's leap was true and her forward momentum into Deakon pushed him backward into the fire. The flames started to lick their way along his body. The bag of runes went flying beyond. Rianthe had no time to grab them. Deakon's man was upon her. She barely raised her sword in time to keep him from cleaving her in two.

The man, however, was not very skilled, and it took little time for Rianthe to dispose of him. She turned to Deakon, shocked to see him standing outside the fire, unscathed.

The rush of wind stole whatever air remained in Rianthe's lungs. Her body flew through the air, slapped against the wall as if she were a puppet.

"You cannot escape me," Deakon said, his laughter sending shivers through Rianthe's body. "You cannot defeat my magic. Shall I show you?"

The pain started in her feet, working up her calves and into the rest of her body. Rianthe screamed, her body on fire. Flames licked at her skin, burning it away until she was sinew and bone, her entire body consumed. She couldn't focus, couldn't concentrate. Agonizing pain shredded every movement, every thought. Except one. She would die this day.

No. No. No. She would not give in. Deakon would not win. He could not. Rianthe forced herself to look down. Slowly, her chin lowered until she saw… Nothing! No flames, no reason for the intense pain, which had not let up. Pain she knew might kill her. She must make it stop.

But how? Only magic stopped magic, and Rianthe had none.

You are the hope of the future, daughter. Do not be afraid to find your destiny. Her father's words swirled through the pain, along with Bhren's. *The awen will come if you open your mind.* The *awen* will come. She just needed to open her mind. Focus. On what? She'd been able to direct her visions when she'd focused on them. Could it be that simple?

Agony clouded Rianthe's thoughts. It was so hard to know, to think, to do… She gave herself up to the pain, focused on it, tried to see through it. When she pushed at it with her mind, it lessened. She heard screaming, knew it was hers. Instead of giving in, she willed the pain to diminish. Over and over again. A soothing began to fill her, like warmed liquid from the aloe plant washing away the pain.

Rianthe looked at Deakon, concentrated on sending that same pain back to him.

Slowly, ever so slowly, her pain lessened further. Deakon's look of surprise encouraged her. There was no noise other than the crackling of the fire. No wind blowing, no bright light. Just sensation, a power beginning to fill her, starting in her pocket with the rune pieces, and fanning out from there. Rianthe gathered it, let it consume her, used it to reflect the pain away, back toward the man who'd destroyed her home and helped to murder her father, her mother. Uja!

When the pain disappeared completely, Rianthe fell

to her knees with a thud, released from Deakon's hold. Deakon writhed on the floor, awash in the same misery he'd put her through.

Finally, he paid for his treachery. His pain could never equal hers. Could never replace Uja. Rianthe kept her attention on him, kept her power focused on his pain. He screamed over and over again, crying for mercy. "Taegar, help me," he pleaded. Rianthe strengthened his pain. "Stop, stop, please. Whatever you want…" Deakon moaned.

She watched him roll around like a snake with its head bit off, waiting for the satisfaction she had every right to. It never came. Only revulsion for what he'd done and disgust for what she was doing to him. This didn't feel right. Reacting like Deakon made her the same sort of person. She'd killed, but only after exhausting every other possibility first. She'd never purposely tortured someone.

She touched her cheek, felt the tears there. Tears of shame. This wasn't her. It wasn't who she wanted to be. Rianthe's focus waned. She took a deep breath and willed the power away, leaving Deakon gasping for air as the pain left him.

"You're not worth my soul," she said to him, drawing her own shaky breath.

Deakon pushed himself up, first to his knees, then to standing. He turned toward her, wavering back and forth in his own exhaustion. "That is why…" He gasped. "You will never be able to beat me. I *will* make you pay." He pointed to her, his hand beginning to glow with magic she knew would be used against her.

The smile on Deakon's face morphed to one of shock. His hand dropped and Rianthe watched the life drain out of his eyes. He fell forward to the ground, a knife sticking out of his back.

Murdo stood behind Deakon. "Think you can cut me out of what's my due, little man?" he spat, kicking Deakon's inert body. "Think again."

While he kicked Deakon again, Rianthe crawled around the fire. She had to get to the runes before Murdo thought of the… An unnatural exhaustion slowed her.

Murdo's sword came up. "Stop right there," he said.

Rianthe had no strength left to fight, therefore no choice but to freeze. She sat back on her knees, digging for the strength to fight one more battle.

He looked at her, a bemused expression on his face. "I'm not sure how you managed to defeat Deakon's magic. I suspect you don't even know yourself." He kept his sword pointed in her direction while he bowed down and dug in Deakon's pockets. When he stood, he hefted the bag of runes in his hand.

She could not let him leave with them. She had to stop him. Rianthe struggled to stand, pulling a knife from her boot and throwing it at Murdo. Her expert aim failed her and the knife sailed past him as she slumped back to the ground. Why was she so exhausted?

Murdo laughed at her. "You have no power left to stop me."

Power. Rianthe had used power to stop Deakon. She could use it now. She reached deep within her, searching for the magic, willing it to do her bidding.

Nothing happened. No matter how hard Rianthe concentrated, how much silent begging she did, the magic had disappeared. She pounded her hands in the dirt.

Murdo moved in front of her, tipping her chin up with the tip of his sword. "I think this magic thing is new to you, girl. Which means you probably can't give me the powers I want. So I must find someone who can." He stepped back, cocking his head. "I should probably kill you, but something tells me you'll be useful to me one of these days. So for now, it's your lucky day. All I want is this." He held up the bag in one hand, his sword, pointed directly at her, in the other as he slowly backed away. Rianthe slumped to the floor, no longer able to even stand. At the doorway, Murdo glanced back at her, hefting the bag and smiling. "It's my turn to taste the magic," he said before disappearing into the night.

Rianthe could not follow him because she couldn't even stand, much less walk. What was happening to her? She tried again to reach out to Murdo with whatever magic had helped her defeat Deakon. Nothing happened. The runes moved farther and farther from her grasp as she sat there struggling to even draw breath.

She turned at a noise behind her. Kaiden stood, sword in hand, wet, fresh blood covering his tunic as he wavered back and forth in the firelight.

Rianthe struggled to get to him. "It's all right, Kaiden. They're gone. We're out of danger." She helped him lay back down near the fire. He slipped back into unconsciousness as she peeled his shirt aside to better see the wound.

The stench of death lay all around them. None of that mattered until she staunched the flow of blood from Kaiden's shoulder and wrapped it. His head lolled back and forth as he drifted in and out of consciousness. Better to fix this now, before he was fully aware.

Rianthe dug for every scrap of remaining energy she had, searching on her hands and knees for her knife, finding it buried under a pack that must have belonged to

Deakon. She set the blade in the fire, then rummaged through a couple packs, grateful to find a clean shirt, which she tore up to use as a bandages. She glanced at Kaiden, who remained unconscious. The pain from what she was about to do would wake him up. Rianthe grabbed a small piece of rawhide and rolled it up.

"Kaiden," she said, taking his hand in hers. "I need to staunch the flow of blood. This is going to hurt. Here," she said, putting the rawhide in his mouth. "Bite down on this."

He didn't answer except to squeeze her hand, then he clenched his teeth around the scrap.

Rianthe cleared any cloth away from the wound and before she lost the nerve, set the red-hot knife to cauterize it.

His scream was muffled by the leather and then, mercifully, by oblivion as he passed out again. The bleeding had stopped, and Rianthe wrapped the wound with a poultice made from a small pack of herbs she carried in her tunic. She'd learned the hard way, after a nasty wound infection while in the Fringes, to always have herbs at the ready. After she'd placed the poultice on Kaiden's shoulder, she wrapped clean, dry cloth around his torso to apply pressure to the wound, rolling Kaiden with difficulty to wind the bandage around his chest.

She collapsed next to him, unable to move, her exhaustion from today's battle complete. Worse than she'd ever known before. She was tired and confused, unsure what had happened here. Had she used magic? And the runes…

Rianthe shook her still foggy head. She would have to sort this all out later.

You must wrap your own arm.

"Taschia!" Rianthe cried.

The dog limped in, favoring her hind leg.

"You're injured."

Not badly. I will live. You dress my wound, also.

Rianthe hugged her. "Of course, of course."

Taschia laid down beside Kaiden. Rianthe cleaned Taschia's wound, agreeing it was not life-threatening. She wrapped it with more of the cloth she'd torn into bandages. "What happened?"

I led them on a merry chase. They all stopped, except one. He showed great stamina.

Rianthe smiled at the respect she heard in Taschia's speech.

We fought. I won.

Rianthe scratched Taschia's ears. "I am very glad you won, sister."

It could not happen any other way.

"What happened to the ones who stopped?"

They went toward the sunset after another man joined them.

Murdo. Rianthe couldn't follow him, but at least she knew what direction he'd gone in. That battle must wait until they'd recovered. Glancing through the large doorway they'd entered the building through, she saw snow falling. Hoping the weather would finish Murdo off, she hugged Taschia again, burying her head in soft fur. "We did it, girl, didn't we?"

Of course we did.

Kaiden moaned.

Rianthe checked his wound, finding no new bleeding. His skin was warm and his brow even warmer. Beads of sweat were forming along his hairline.

It is the blood fever.

Fever? Infection? So quickly?

The wolf sniffed Kaiden's wound. *Poison. This is a mortal wound.*

"No!" Rianthe cradled Kaiden's face between her hands. "Wake up. Please, wake up." But all she got were more moans.

"We have to help him." Rianthe looked frantically around the ruins. The fire had dwindled. She rose with great effort, tiredness still consuming her. She added wood from a nearby pile then stumbled her way around the area, finding two more packs left behind by Murdo's men.

Dragging them back to Kaiden's side, she rummaged through them, finding no herbs or medicines. Nothing useful except a tin cup. "I don't know what to do," she said.

She had more herbs in her pack, except it was hidden in ruins outside of town. Night had fallen hours ago, and who knew what manner of man or animal lurked outside. Normally, Rianthe wouldn't hesitate, but her post-battle weakness had not yet abated, and she was not sure she could lift a sword right now, much less fight.

Kaiden began to thrash back and forth, giving Rianthe no choice. She must go for her medicines.

I will stay by his side.

Rianthe nodded and stood, picking up the sword she'd dropped when Murdo and his men ran off. She held it up. Even that small movement wore her out. She took precious moments to wrap her own wound and tuck her knife into her boot, then headed out.

She made it to the outbuilding and retrieved their packs, slinging one over each shoulder. Her knees almost buckled under the weight. Normally, this would be nothing to her. What had caused her to be this tired? Was this an after-effect of the magic, that it weakened one beyond anything?

The trek back to Kaiden and Taschia was slow and tortuous. She prayed the entire time that Kaiden would still be alive when she got back.

A growl behind her stopped Rianthe. Turning slowly, she saw the glow of eyes, heard the menace in that growl. The moon shed enough light that she could see an emaciated wolf standing there.

"I am not the answer to your hunger," she said softly.

The wolf's growl deepened. It backed her up a step, then its growl just stopped.

Rianthe watched it warily, moving her arm down her leg slowly to get at her knife.

Cocking his head to the side, the wolf seemed to be listening to something. Yet she heard nothing.

Just as she got her hand on her knife, the wolf whined. Staring at her for a long moment, it turned and ambled off. Just like that.

I told him you were not good to eat, Taschia mind-spoke.

Thank you. The words didn't do Rianthe's gratitude justice. She had not the strength to take on this wolf.

Hurry, sister.

Kaiden! Rianthe dug deep and found the strength to break into a jog. When she got there, Rianthe saw Taschia's worry immediately. Kaiden's skin had turned ashen, his pallor gray. She dug out her herbs and set them to steeping in water from her bag. The wait for the tea to cool was interminable.

Using a leaf, she dribbled the liquid into Kaiden's

mouth. Thankfully, he swallowed each sip. Next, she made another poultice, heated it with more of the tea, and placed it directly on the wound.

Kaiden thrashed, but Rianthe held him until he quieted, talking to him the entire time, chanting ancient druid words she had no memory of learning. Her own body grew warm as she prayed. For hours into the night, she fed him tea, changed the poultice when it cooled, and prayed.

You must sleep, Taschia mind-spoke.

"I know." Rianthe's voice croaked, as overworked and exhausted as the rest of her body was. Kaiden hadn't stirred in hours, so now it was time to let the medicine work. And continue to pray.

Rianthe could barely move a finger.

I will watch. You sleep.

Grateful beyond measure, Rianthe scratched Taschia's ear and curled up next to Kaiden. Taschia settled behind her, adding warmth to a night that held the chill of more snow in it.

Rianthe laid her hand across Kaiden's chest, needing the reassurance of his heartbeat, erratic as it was at the moment.

"I love you, Kaiden. I always have. Please don't die." She closed her eyes and gave herself up to the nightmares of the night.

CHAPTER TWENTY-SEVEN

Rianthe woke with a start from a dead, dreamless sleep.

All is well, Taschia mind-spoke. *You have slept long. That is good.*

Rianthe's thoughts were fogged by sleep, and the inside of her mouth tasted like she'd been drinking sludge. She stretched, glad to feel only a minor soreness from the arm wound. Her energy had returned too. She was much more like her old self this morning.

"Kaiden!" She placed her hand over his heart. Was it beating stronger? She prayed it was so. He was peaceful, not thrashing, and his pallor looked a little better.

He is better.

"I think so." Rianthe sniffed back her relief at seeing him alive. "Did we get more snow?"

No. More comes. We should go soon.

"We can't. Not until we can move Kaiden. And I

need time to build a sled."

It is so. Taschia stood and stretched. *I will hunt now.*

Rianthe nodded. "When you return, I'll go forage."

She banked the fire and set more herbs to steeping, stretching achy muscles while she waited. She definitely felt stronger today. That tiredness had seemed so unnatural yesterday, at least for her. And that thing with Deakon. What had happened? She'd tapped into some magic, but could she repeat it? Rianthe stared at the fire, tried to make it grow like Deakon had. If she found the magic that Bhren and Roulf said she had, maybe she could track Murdo, even in this weather, and get back the runes.

She narrowed her vision and thought, focused on the fire, and tried to see deep into the flames. Nothing happened. Whatever she'd done last night had been in the moment. Rianthe shook her head, despondent. Nothing had changed. Any ability she may or may not have still lay hidden, so no clear indication of Rianthe's place in this world had come from last night's battle.

This whole thing made no sense and she was tired of trying to understand it. Better to think of finite things, necessary tasks to keep them alive. Between Kaiden's sickness and the impending snow, she had enough to worry about.

Dribbling more tea into Kaiden's mouth and watching him swallow, she said the words again that, for some reason, she now knew so well. A healing incantation. Rianthe prayed it would work. That it would speed Kaiden's recovery.

This place still stank of death, so she dragged the bodies deserted by Murdo and his men outside and away from their camp, pulling Deakon on top. Covering the dead with tree limbs and brush, Rianthe decided to wait until they were ready to head home before firing the makeshift pyre. No matter who they were, everyone deserved to return to the earth from which they came. Ashes to ashes, dust to dust. Deakon's magic hadn't turned him to ash, like her parents and Bhren. Maybe because he hadn't come by it naturally, through a bond with the earth. This was yet another puzzle to solve.

Resting from the exertion, she drank some of the medicinal tea herself and ate the last of their hardtack. Like Taschia, she too would need to hunt today.

When Taschia returned, Rianthe set out to find food. She snared a squirrel, fattened for the coming winter. She also found some late berries, both edible and poisonous ones. Was this what the brigand's sword that ran Kaiden through had been tipped in?

The biggest find was more of the medicinal herb she'd just about run out of. For that, Rianthe was most grateful.

Back at camp, Kaiden still had not stirred. Through the rest of the day, Rianthe gathered wood and cut poles to make a sturdy sled. They couldn't stay here long and Kaiden, even if he woke, wouldn't be able to walk the distance back to New Hope.

That night, she sat beside the fire weaving strong grasses around the spruce poles she'd formed, making a sled for Kaiden to rest on. Sometime during the day, she'd realized that going after Murdo would have to wait. She could not do it alone, as much as she wanted to. And Kaiden would not be in any shape to fight, or even travel long distances, for days or weeks. They must go home. Recuperate. Then formulate a plan to get the runes back and deal with Taegar.

Kaiden would not like that he'd be riding home. Rianthe smiled. No, he wouldn't like that at all. There was no choice. Taschia had sensed it. More snow was coming. A lot of it, she feared. They'd need to move soon, even if Kaiden didn't wake up. A day, two at the most. Would he be able to withstand the journey? She glanced at him. His color was much closer to normal, but still he slept. Why didn't he wake up? Rianthe wished Raisa were here. She needed a healer's skill. His coma seemed unnatural to her. Had she gotten the poison out of his system or was he still in danger?

They slept, three bodies huddled together like the night before. Rianthe drifted off reassured by the much steadier beating of Kaiden's heart.

When she woke, it was to Kaiden's unfocused eyes. "You're awake."

"Yes," he croaked, and blinked. "Safe?"

"Yes, we're safe for the time being," she answered.

"How long?" Did his voice sound a little stronger or was it just Rianthe's hopeful imagination?

"The battle was two days ago. You've pretty much been out ever since then."

Taschia gave him a quick lick. *I am pleased you live, Kai-den.* She rarely spoke names. In fact, Rianthe did not remember her ever using her own name.

"What happened?"

It was too soon to go over that battle and all that had occurred. There would be time enough to sort it all out. For now, she kept it to a minimum.

"Deakon is dead." Rianthe had expected to feel happiness at the thought. Instead it seemed such a waste. She deeply regretted that she'd had no opportunity to question the man. "His men ran off, presumably returning to Taegar."

Holding off on the worst news, Rianthe picked up the cup. "You need more tea." Kaiden struggled to sit up, but Rianthe put a hand to his chest. "You probably shouldn't move yet. I'll help you."

After making tea, she fed him as before, using the leaf to help him drink. Awake, Kaiden drank much more. He also ate some of the berries she'd picked. It gladdened her spirit to see him alert. For the first time since New Hope had burned to the ground, Rianthe could breathe. Just for this moment, everything was stable in her world, and she thanked the good earth for that. There had been too much strife, too much danger. They all needed time to recoup.

Taschia had disappeared to find food. With only her and Kaiden here, and Kaiden awake, things were so different. Everything had changed. This felt intimate. Something had changed between them on this journey.

When she looked at Kaiden, he watched her closely through green eyes that seemed darker, almost as if he, too, sensed the difference. His eyes really were the most amazing color. Dark green, but with swirls of light in them. Set in such a handsome face. Kaiden hadn't shaved since they'd started this journey. She liked the look.

He reached up with his good hand, touched her cheek. "What are you thinking?"

"That your eyes are an extraordinary color."

Kaiden chuckled, then winced at the obvious pain that small movement cost him. The spell was broken and Rianthe sat up, surprised to find she'd been no more than inches from his face. It would have taken nothing to lean a little closer, snaring the kiss she'd dreamed about for so many years. Even when she'd hated him, she couldn't stop thinking about kissing him.

Kaiden cleared his throat. "How long do you think we can stay here?"

"Not much longer. More snow is coming. A day, maybe two."

He tried to move, to sit up, but the effort cost him and he grunted in pain. Rianthe reminded him to lay still with a hand on his chest. Kaiden covered her hand with his, then frantically patted his pockets, eyes wide, deep heaving breaths showing his urgent concern.

"The runes. Where are the runes?" Shrill panic strengthened his voice.

"The bag with the runes is gone," Rianthe said quietly, trying to take the sting out of the words with her voice.

"Gone?" He stared at her.

"Gone. Murdo, Deakon's man, took them." She paused. "Presumably to Taegar."

Kaiden struggled against her hand, trying to sit up. "We have to go. We have to get them back." He fell back.

"Stop, Kaiden," she said, her voice stern. "You're in no shape to go after Murdo. And if you don't take it easy on that shoulder, you'll never be well enough. Besides..." Rianthe reached into her pocket and pulled out the three runes she still had. "Some instinct made me separate these from the rest of the runes."

Kaiden's eyes narrowed. "You didn't trust me."

"I did this before you and I even had that conversation, based on instinct, not lack of trust. We can only pray that the talisman won't work without them. That's the only hope we have."

Kaiden lay silent. "Maybe," he finally said. "You're

right. It's our only hope right now."

He looked as miserable as she felt. "I'm sorry," she softened her voice and settled beside him, taking his hand. "This is my fault. I'm the one who had to have revenge."

"We both made this choice. And all of New Hope agreed."

Rianthe turned Kaiden's hand over and ran her fingers along the lines. This was so hard to say, but she needed to get it out. Needed to admit it. "If I hadn't been ready to tear out after Deakon, then kept talking about it through all the hard work, we'd still be there. Home. And…" Her voice dropped to a whisper. "The runes would be safe."

The raw, naked pain in Rianthe's face was more than Kaiden could take. He wasn't able to pull her into his arms and console her. All he had were his words. He pulled her hand to his chest, clutched it in both of his. "If this is your fault, then it is mine, too."

She shook her head, her eyes bright with unshed tears.

"Listen to me, Ri." He stroked her hand as he spoke, splayed their fingers together. "Do you think I couldn't have kept you in New Hope? Kept you from hunting Deakon down? I am still stronger than you, you know."

Her lips quirked up, encouraging Kaiden.

"Not by much," she said.

He chuckled. "That's a challenge I'll gladly take you up on when I'm healed. I came with you of my own free will. I wanted—needed—to make Deakon pay. When Roulf reminded us this was a foolhardy quest, we both knew we had to continue."

Rianthe nodded.

"What's happened has happened. Does it make our situation more dire? Probably. Do we have to try to keep the runes from Taegar? Definitely. Just not today. I think we need to regroup and heal. Be at our best, our strongest when we take on that challenge."

Rianthe laid her head on their entwined hands. Kaiden wanted to pull her even closer, to smell the sweetness that he loved. He settled for running his hands over her short hair, soothing both their souls with each stroke.

Rianthe sat up and he wanted to drown in the honesty that shone in her eyes. This was the Rianthe he remembered, the girl turned woman he never wanted to leave again. For a long while they sat like that, until Taschia broke the spell.

We go home?

Kaiden chuckled and Rianthe smiled. She extricated her hand and the cold around him grew. "We go home," they said in unison.

Good. I miss my brothers.

Rianthe stood. "We'll have to start out with you on the sled," Rianthe said, pointing to what she'd been working on. "I'm almost done."

Absolutely not. Kaiden shook his head. "I am not going to be dragged back to New Hope like some child unable to walk."

Rianthe held up her hands. "Look around you. There's not much here and if we wait too long, we'll be stuck here until spring."

"There's got to be a better way. Come here." He waved her closer. "Help me sit up."

It took a long time and a lot of pain and grunting, but

he managed to sit up against the wall with her help. Rianthe checked his wound.

"It hasn't started bleeding again, thankfully. In fact, I think it looks better than the last time I checked it." She pulled the bandage back further so he could see.

He inspected the ugly wound. He'd end up with significant scarring, but it wasn't red or angry. "This doesn't look too bad."

"Well, it was. The sword that skewered you had been tipped in poison. You went down and never really regained consciousness. Until this morning."

"I remember flashes, bits and pieces." Kaiden scratched his beard. "I could swear I saw you pinned against the wall."

"You did."

"Your feet, though. They weren't even touching the ground."

"Deakon called upon his magic. Magic endowed upon him by Taegar, or so he said."

"I didn't even know that was possible." Kaiden shifted his arm to a more comfortable position.

"Neither did I, but Deakon clearly had powers. He tossed me against that wall like it was child's play. Twice."

Kaiden looked around their makeshift camp. Daylight showed unmistakable flaws. They had only half a roof and three full walls. The fourth, a crumbled mess, was windward. If it got any colder, or the wind came up, they'd freeze to death.

"There's more to your tale than you're saying. For now, though, if I agree to the sled…" Kaiden rolled his eyes. "Do you think we can leave tomorrow?"

"Taschia is pretty well healed—"

"Taschia was injured?"

Only a minor hurt. She padded over to them, a self-satisfied grin on her face.

"You ate well," Rianthe said with a smile.

I ate very well. I am strong. She looked Kaiden in the eye. *I can pull you.*

"With my help. Yes, I think we can try to leave in the morning. It will be painful for you, at least at first. If we can make it back to Roulf's—and he lets us in—you can rest and heal further before the trek back to New Hope."

It wasn't how he wanted to return to New Hope. This felt like the worst defeat. They needed to get out of here, so there really was no choice. "Then we have a plan," he said, nodding. "As much as it galls me to be carried, I see no other alternative. We do not want to winter here."

"Agreed. We leave at first light."

Rianthe spent the rest of their daylight hours foraging for food they could carry with them and rushes to carry a smoldering cinder to restart their fire easier at night. That evening, by the light of the fire, she fortified the sled, testing its strength and used leather from the dead men's packs to fashion a harness to pull the sled with.

Kaiden watched her quietly, hating that he wasn't able to help. When she set the sled aside, proclaiming it ready, Rianthe made a new poultice. Settling it in place under his bandage, she chewed her lip, unusual for her.

"What is it you're not telling me?" Kaiden said.

"Um, well, we've been sleeping together, all of us."

Rianthe motioned to Taschia, which meant she didn't catch the grin on Kaiden's face. Thankfully.

"You know, for warmth," she finished.

Kaiden killed his smile before she saw it. They hadn't been close in so long, he'd thought anything between them had disappeared. Maybe, just maybe, there was still some hope.

Settling to the floor was an effort that proved to Kaiden the next few days would be brutal. His pain eased when Rianthe laid down beside him, giving him the fire side but sharing his warmth. Taschia settled on the outside.

It wasn't long before Rianthe drifted off to sleep, her hand on his chest, covering his heart. Kaiden lay for a long time, enjoying the moment, thinking about the day. She'd withheld something from him about that battle. Something she wasn't ready to talk about by the way she directed their conversation away from it. For now, he'd give her the time she appeared to want. When he was stronger, though, they'd have this out. She'd tell him the pieces she'd left out and explain to him how, in a dizzy, temperature-induced coma, he could have sworn he'd heard her whisper that she loved him.

CHAPTER TWENTY-EIGHT

They woke to a new coating of snow covering everything. Kaiden, foggy from strange dreams and still weak and in pain, struggled with settling onto the sled. He hated being this weak. Rianthe wore a pack filled with as much food and herbs as she could carry. Kaiden, on the sled, carried the cocooned rushes with embers in them for fire-starting. Rianthe harnessed Taschia, then slipped a simple loop harness over her own shoulder, and their trek home began.

Getting out of the structure went smoothly and Kaiden thought maybe today's travel wouldn't be so bad. Snow should have cushioned his ride, but instead, it only hid the bumps in the road. Rianthe and Taschia had little clue what lay beneath. Kaiden, however, knew every log and stick they'd traversed.

By evening, he'd had more than enough of the dratted sled, bumpy ground and all. He'd rather walk through hot coals than endure another day being pulled along like some newling. Plus, all the jostling made his shoulder ache like he'd been run through with another sword. The only benefit to the dry snow, it appeared, was that the sled glided easier, or at least, that's what both Taschia and Rianthe told him. Taschia bore most of the weight, but he'd seen sweat on Rianthe's brow each time they stopped. She was trying to take too much of the load off the wolf.

"Help me up," Kaiden asked Rianthe when they stopped for the night in a copse of woods that sheltered them from the weather, if not the cold.

"You should rest."

"I've done nothing except rest. I'm standing whether you help me or not."

Rianthe pressed her lips together, then moved to his side. She helped him sit up, then snugged herself under his shoulder. It took some work. Kaiden assisted as much as he could. Still, they were both damp with sweat by the time he stood. Not good in this cold.

The wave of dizziness hit him like hard clay. Kaiden bent over as what little there was in his stomach came up, jarring his shoulder in the process. The whole world tilted and wavered like the walls of Rushmore on a hot summer's day.

Rianthe steadied him and waited until he'd found his equilibrium. "I'm all right now," Kaiden said, leaning against a tree, hating how much this injury, or poison, or whatever it was, had taken out of him.

"You ready to lie back down?" she said, eyeing him.

"No. I will not endure another day on that sled." Even in the twilight, Kaiden saw the rush of anger color her face. He had to give her credit, she kept her mouth shut, about the sled at least.

"You all right here?"

"Yes. I just want to lean against this tree for a bit."

"Fine. I need to get a fire started or this cold weather will kill us faster than anything." She walked away slowly, as if giving him time to reconsider.

He would not. Kaiden leaned against the tree, frustrated beyond belief. He'd never felt weakness like this before. It was crazy, and it made his wound seem like much more than a simple sword bite.

He wanted to help Rianthe. He should be chopping wood, starting the fire. Kaiden pushed off the tree and took a step, but dizziness stopped him again.

What the hell was going on? It wasn't only the wound or the weakness. He'd been having dreams. Kaiden hadn't remembered anything from his delirium until last night. He'd woken up from a dream of golden eyes. A siren's eyes. Calling to him. Compelling him to join her, be one with her. This same dream had come to him while his body had been fighting the poison. He knew those eyes. Taegar. How had she found him? Troubled over a puzzle he could not sort out until he had more information, Kaiden pulled his focus back to the task at hand. If he was going to walk tomorrow, he must walk tonight and prove to himself and to Rianthe that he was capable. He *would* be capable.

~~~

Rianthe watched Kaiden slowly move around camp. He wobbled quite a bit, and twice she'd had to hold herself back from rushing to aid him when he'd shifted too far. Kaiden was prideful and would not take the help well. To be honest, she was proud of how he'd done thus far. When he'd first stood up, then threw up, she thought
~~~

he'd be back on the sled tomorrow. Now, well, it sure looked like he might be walking, at least the first part.

She threw a scrap of cooked rabbit to Taschia, who gobbled it up, then wandered off. She'd made a fire near a fallen log and sat on that log now. "Come and eat, Kaiden."

It took him a minute, but he made it to her side. When he didn't sit, she glanced up. The look on his face was priceless and she had to work very hard to keep her smile from busting out.

He stared at the log and his face turned crimson. Kaiden was…embarrassed. Embarrassed! Her strong man never showed mortification.

"All right. Just stop grinning and help me. I'm worried my legs will give out if I try to sit on my own. I'm as shaky as a feeble old man." His growl was as fake as his scowl.

Rianthe burst out laughing while she helped him. It wasn't often that she was in better shape than him. Even his smile held a shadow now. And there were still dark circles under his eyes. At night, he moaned in his sleep, something she'd never noticed before.

Kaiden had a long way to go before he'd be healed. Rianthe hoped the darkness she saw would disappear. This journey had been her idea. Kaiden had come because of some sense of responsibility. If he didn't recover…

"I hate this, you know," Kaiden said, finishing the bite of food he was chewing, staring into the fire, a dark, petulant look on his face. "I'm supposed to be protecting you, and you're taking care of me like I'm some newling."

Rainthe set her food down and stared at Kaiden until

he turned to her. She grasped both his hands. "You took care of me, protected me, kept me in line for many years."

"Yes, that worked out so well."

You ran away. That's what he wasn't saying. Rianthe refused to take the bait. Kaiden had always been better at deflecting conversations than having them.

"It may not have worked out how you wanted, but yes, it worked out. After I left, you kept an eye on my brothers. Tevy told me. And the time I was away from New Hope and away from you? I learned a lot, much of which I wouldn't have if I'd stayed. I learned enough to be able to take care of myself. And you. At least for a while."

She touched his cheek, her voice lowering. "You were gravely ill, Kaiden. I was so scared. This…" She waved at the sled. "This is nothing. I owe you a lot. Let me pay you back, at least this little bit."

Kaiden's eyes dipped to Rianthe's lips and she held her breath.

"I wish… I wish things had been different for us," Kaiden said.

"They still could be."

His gaze was so intense, so filled with turmoil. He looked away. "Not until we figure all this out. Until we give our people a better chance at survival."

Some things hadn't changed at all. Rianthe stood, tossing more wood into the fire. "We shouldn't have to wait. We shouldn't even have to fight this fight. It's too much. Who made us the saviors of the earth?"

"Fate did," he said quietly. "And there's no one I'd rather have as my partner, have my back up against in a battle, than you."

Just when she had a righteous anger going, Kaiden diffused it with one simple statement. Deflated, Rianthe poked at the fire. "It's not fair, you know."

"You're right. It's not. However, it is our duty."

Rianthe stared into the fire, completely forlorn. Their duty. His duty. Always more important to Kaiden than anything. Even her. Would she never come first? Not all the time, not when there were battles to fight or plans to make, but in these quiet moments, when it was just the two of them. Couldn't she have those few snatches of time?

"We'd better get some sleep," Kaiden said.

They curled up as they'd done before, and Rianthe lay there for a long time lost in bittersweet memories and wishes.

CHAPTER TWENTY-NINE

In the morning they started out slowly. Despite a pace that felt like crawling, by the noon meal, Kaiden was beyond exhausted.

"We could stop here," Rianthe said. "Or, if we use the sled, we might get a few more miles in today."

Kaiden groaned. "I spent the entire time in pain yesterday because of that thing." He shook his head. She was right. The sooner home, the sooner he could focus on healing and not as much on Rianthe. Holding her every night was tougher now than ever before. He could not tell her how he felt. Not until the coming storm was resolved. A darkness encroached further every day and now seemed to invade his mind at night. Not complete darkness. Kaiden shuddered. Darkness broken by golden eyes. Taegar. Why was he having these dreams?

After another two days of hard travel, the smoke of Roulf's cabin could be seen winding a loopy trail above the trees.

"Ahhh, it is very good to see you three." Roulf greeted them. "I did not mask myself or my home in the hopes that you would let me know you lived through the battle."

Kaiden, who'd been trying to walk again, stumbled, and had to lean against Rianthe to regain his balance. She shouldered the weight easily, but Kaiden knew they were all exhausted.

Roulf cocked his head. "You did not come through unscathed. Come, come, let's get inside. You can lie down and I will see how things are."

Roulf's feather bed felt like heaven and Kaiden sank into it gratefully. If he stayed right here for forever… He glanced at Rianthe. Maybe the world would stop turning for a little bit and give them all a chance to regroup.

"What happened?" Roulf asked as he pulled the bandages away from Kaiden's shoulder.

"A poison-tipped sword about a week ago," Rianthe answered.

"Ahh." Roulf prodded the shoulder.

Kaiden glared at the man and gritted his teeth against the increased pain.

"This is healing well. Much faster than I would have thought." He glanced at Rianthe, who had busied herself by the fire.

"Then why am I so weak?" Kaiden ground out the last word.

Roulf put a hand to Kaiden's forehead and stared long into Kaiden's eyes. "The poison is not all gone from your system. It will ebb, but slowly. You must give yourself time and rest or you will relapse."

"We have no time," Kaiden said.

"You have enough for this."

Rianthe joined them with a cup in her hands. "I made more tea."

Roulf propped Kaiden up and Rianthe sat on the bed beside him. He took the cup and sipped, grateful at least that she didn't have to feed him any longer. He wasn't certain how much more of that he could have stood.

As he drank the tea, Rianthe laid a hand on his shoulder, speaking words he'd never heard from her before. Words foreign to him. Some sort of spell?

Finishing his tea, Kaiden drifted off, trying to make sense of the words she'd spoken.

A dark void surrounded him. Kaiden reached out. Above, to the sides, nothing. Only floor beneath him. No light, no indication of anything being there other than complete and total darkness. Panic consumed him. He had to find a way out, to get clear of the darkness, find the light.

The golden eyes appeared. *I will help you. I am always here to help you. All you have to do is bring me the talisman.* Soothing, giving him a focus against the vertigo.

Kaiden woke with a start, disoriented. It took a while to remember he was in Roulf's cabin. The eyes stayed in his mind. The voice…it had been saying something to him. Kaiden tried to remember but the dream had already faded, the words lost with it.

He saw Roulf and Rianthe by the fire, their heads together in low conversation. Kaiden couldn't make out what they were saying. He tried to sit up, to go join them. It was hard. He was so weak. Kaiden's hand slipped on the side of the bed and he dropped to the floor, right onto his injured shoulder.

His grunt of pain was swallowed up by Rianthe's exclamation.

"Kaiden!" Rianthe rushed to him.

"Thought…join you," he mumbled.

"You need to rest, Kaiden," Rianthe said, trying to calm her racing heart. "Come on, let's get you back to bed."

It took some doing. Kaiden seemed to be slipping in and out of delirium. She and Roulf, with a little nudge from Taschia, got him back in bed. His forehead was warm again. They'd overdone it traveling here. He wasn't well enough to endure it all. She soothed his brow with her hand, continuing until he relaxed and drifted off, seeming to sleep quietly. And all the while praying that Kaiden would get better. He had to.

She rejoined Roulf by the fireside. "He seems to be slipping back into the fever."

Roulf shook his head. "I do not think so. I believe he is simply worn out. Rest will do him much good." Roulf sat back and removed his magnifiers, cleaning them with a corner of his robe. "You spoke words to him earlier."

"They came unbidden to me, back when he was so gravely ill. Is it some sort of incantation?" The sting of tears blurred her vision, and Rianthe tried to hold them at bay.

"That is a healing prayer you spoke."

"How do I know that? How did I know those words?"

Roulf did not answer. Instead, he leaned forward, grasping both of Rianthe's hands. "Look at me."

Rianthe did so. Roulf stared long and hard, almost into her soul. When he sat back, he seemed more troubled than ever.

"I sense an awakening in you. I do not know what holds it back or how it will manifest itself. Will it come in bits, like this prayer, or all in a rush when most needed? We do not know. Heed me, though, you have strong magic in you, child. Do not doubt it."

"I have doubted it my entire life." Yet, Deakon's end had…well, something had happened there. She'd managed to fend off his magic. Maybe…

Rianthe told Roulf what happened in that final battle, how she'd pushed back against Deakon's magic and how utterly and unnaturally tired she'd been afterward.

He nodded. "This should prove it. You do have the magic. It will come to you when it needs to. For now, you will have to be content with that."

"Why did I get so tired? I was more vulnerable afterward than ever before. I couldn't have lifted my sword."

"Druids believe that there is a balance to everything. When something is used, something else is used up. That is the balance of the *awen*, that it depletes you and you must have time to restore yourself afterward. You do get used to it…somewhat. Gah!" Roulf hit the arms of his chair. "I wish I had remained in training. I do not know enough. All I can do is warn you based on my intuitions. Be mindful when the magic comes to you. Do not let it use you up."

Rianthe turned to the fire, staring at the flames, wondering how magic could possibly use her up when she didn't even know how to manifest it. Every step of this journey had added questions instead of answers. She grew tired of the confusion. What would it take for her to get some answers?

CHAPTER THIRTY

It took another four days before Kaiden showed signs of improvement. Roulf slept with his animals each night. Rianthe had chosen to sleep with Taschia by the fire and give Kaiden room to recover.

Today, for the first time, they stepped outside and took a walk around Roulf's forest. White dusted the trees but they didn't need their cloaks for warmth. As they walked farther into the woods, the snow grew deeper, the air cooler, and the trees more laden with the white weight. Rianthe decided it must be Roulf's magic keeping the winter elements at bay.

"I think we may be able to travel tomorrow," Kaiden said.

"I'm not so sure. You got sick all over again just getting here. It will take more days than this to reach New Hope."

"Yes, but I feel the need to be home. We've been

gone too long. They need our help."

"New Hope was doing well when we left. They had food and increasingly more shelter. They will be fine for another few days."

"Still, I'm worried. Something seems…off."

Kaiden's intuition had always been trustworthy, so Rianthe took notice when he didn't like something. "What feels different?"

He sighed. "I'm honestly not sure. I just think things will be different."

"All right, then. Let's go home." Rianthe frowned. This kind of discussion, this getting along? She liked this. Too much.

The next morning, the weather outside was cold, but clear. Rianthe turned to Roulf.

"Not my doing," he said. "What you see is what you'll have as you walk away."

They'd packed the night before. Roulf had given them extra provisions so they wouldn't have to cook, as well as bushels of fruits and vegetables for New Hope.

"My magic is waning, child," Roulf told her. "I cannot keep the fruit from rotting and it will go to waste if you do not take it."

Rianthe wasn't certain she believed him, but New Hope would be grateful for the food. Kaiden piled the baskets on the sled she'd fortified over the past few days. If Kaiden needed to rest again, they'd figure that out when they had to.

After feeding them too much, Roulf followed them outside. He bowed down to the wolf, and whispered in her ear.

What did he say to you? Rianthe asked.

We spoke words between kindred spirits.

That is no answer.

It is the only answer I can give, Taschia mind-spoke. Her ears turned forward, toward home and her family. Rianthe would get no more from her friend.

She hugged Roulf as Kaiden cinched the sled harness to Taschia. "Thank you so much for everything you've done for us, Roulf. I don't know what we'd have done without your help."

"It wasn't only for you. Still, you are welcome." He glanced at Kaiden, who remained busy tightening the straps. "The poison does not seem completely gone from that one. Keep an eye on him. Watch for any sign that he might…relapse."

Rianthe looked worriedly at Kaiden. "Will he be all right?"

"Only time will tell. He is strong and his heart is in the right place. With you." Roulf smiled as heat filled Rianthe's cheeks.

"I wish," she mumbled under her breath.

"Be patient, child. Give him time. He will come around."

"I'm not so sure."

"In the meantime, go help your village. They need you. Just be watchful for changes all around you. They will come, and you must be ready."

Kaiden joined them. "It's time to go."

Rianthe nodded. "Will I ever see you again?" she asked Roulf.

"I am old, child. One of these days, my magic will fade, and so will I. But, the fates willing, we will share a meal again one day."

Roulf gave Kaiden's hand a hearty shake and, with a wave, returned to the warmth of his house.

After walking a ways, both Kaiden and Rianthe turned to see the cabin one last time.

It was not there. Nothing except snow and trees filled the glade. No puffs of smoke, nothing. The winter woods appeared completely fresh and undisturbed.

"He sure didn't wait long after we left to disguise himself again, did he?"

He is a strange man. But also very nice, Taschia mind-spoke.

Both Kaiden and Rianthe laughed as they agreed with Taschia.

It took them twice as long to return to New Hope on this final leg. Rianthe refused to listen when Kaiden wanted to push himself. They rested often and stopped early each night. She knew he was grateful, even if he wouldn't admit it. Stubborn, duty-bound man.

Near twilight a few nights later, they reached the shores of a large, deep green lake. A lake they both knew. They'd caught many fish in it. New Hope lay on the far side, only an hour or so walk. They could see smoke. Normal smoke this time. No burning village, just cook fires.

It lightened Rianthe's heart to be so close to home. This ordeal was about over. If there were other battles out there to be fought, she prayed that they would hold off. Kaiden, New Hope, even she herself, all needed time to recover.

As they arrived on the outskirts of New Hope, one of the main boughs holding the sled together broke. They unharnessed Taschia so she was free to run ahead while they ditched the well-used sled. Every part of it was close to breaking like the branch had. Others from the village could come gather the remaining supplies. Kaiden kicked the sled into a small coulee while Rianthe laughed.

"I never want to see a sled again as long as I live."

"It served us well," Rianthe said, still grinning.

Kaiden laughed too. Finally. His mood had lightened with each day closer to New Hope and that filled Rianthe with optimism. "Come on," he said, holding out his hand. "Let's go home."

Rianthe put her hand in his, her own heart gladdened by his smile. It was going to be all right. They were going to be fine.

They passed the Hallows. A monument of rocks had been added to the far end, standing as an additional reminder of those lost. Both bowed their heads, letting their sorrow wash over them one more time. So much loss.

They walked down familiar paths to the center of the village. Because winter snow had tamped down all the underbrush, Rianthe could see through the trees, see the flat, white-covered growing fields. Uja's fields. Remorse swelled her throat.

"Everything's all right, Ri." Kaiden's voice was uncharacteristically soft.

Rianthe hadn't realized she'd paused.

"What will we do without him? What will I do?"

"The same thing we'll all do. We'll survive in his honor." He put a hand on her shoulder.

That was all it took for Rianthe to turn straight into his arms. "We will, I know. I'll still miss him, though." *And I'll always carry this guilt. I should have been here.*

You could not have saved him. Taschia's mind-speak was echoed by her brothers.

I could have tried.

Do not be sad, sister. Uja is well-remembered and

loved. And more awaits you in camp.

Rianthe heard Taschia's pack howling their agreement. They were right. Uja would always be with them. Time alone would heal this wound.

Time heals all.

Nodding, Rianthe stepped back and swiped at her tears.

"That felt nice," Kaiden said, his voice cautious.

"Don't get used to it," Rianthe said, immediately regretting it when Kaiden stiffened. "I'm sorry. That was uncalled for." She ran her hands through hair that had grown a couple inches since she'd left the Fringes. Rianthe didn't remember deciding to grow it out, but maybe she'd give it a try. She could cut it at any time.

So much had happened in these past few weeks, including more emotional upheaval than she'd felt since her True-Naming. She'd been hardened in the Fringes, and falling back on the learned instinct to protect her heart was natural. She'd sworn never to let anyone in again, especially Kaiden. Still, it didn't seem right. Not anymore. Especially not after what they'd been through together.

Kaiden watched her with wary eyes.

Rianthe placed a hand on his chest. "Truly, I am sorry. Habits ingrained in me from the Fringes. Don't let anyone past the wall."

His eyes searched hers. Rianthe struggled to keep from looking away, not wanting him to see what lay buried deep in her heart. Finally, he broke the spell and sighed. "We both have a lot to learn. For now, let's enjoy being home."

CHAPTER THIRTY-ONE

Eager, Rianthe and Kaiden quickened their pace. They arrived at a village transformed in the weeks they'd been away. A few structures had been rebuilt. The long house shelter now looked like it had become the kitchens and communal eating area. Wood was stacked tall and long. Even the smell of the smudge pots, once distasteful to Rianthe, now meant that they were coaxing winter growth out of vegetable and fruit plants.

Raisa, Kaiden's foster-mother and Jonah's wife, saw them first and rushed to hug Kaiden, then Rianthe. By the time they'd separated themselves from her happy welcome, it seemed like the entire village had crowded around them. Laughter was everywhere as Rianthe and Kaiden were surrounded and jostled into the long house.

Tevy waited for them there, a wide grin on his face as Rianthe rushed up to him and pulled him into her arms. "Ah, come on, Sis. Let me go," he squealed as she hugged him tight.

"Never," she said, but she loosened her grip enough so he could pull away.

"Hey, kid," Kaiden said, ruffling Tevy's blond hair. "You look good."

Tevy hugged Kaiden just as tightly as Rianthe had hugged him. Then he stared at Kaiden for a long moment. "You're home now," Tevy said finally. "You can heal." He looked pointedly at Rianthe's arm, which still ached sometimes. "You can both heal."

"How could you possibly know—" Rianthe started, then stopped.

"Taschia!" they all three said together.

Tevy knew and therefore did not worry. I am with my brothers now. I am happy.

So are we, Rianthe mind-spoke back. *So are we.*

Arm in arm, she, Kaiden, and Tevy walked the village with Tevy excitedly showing them all the things that had been done since they left. Most importantly, the storage cellar, dug into the earth, was filled with winter wheat and vegetables and meat. Enough food to get them through several more weeks.

"Go inside the dining house. Someone's waiting for you," Raisa said, giving them both a nudge.

Rianthe looked at Raisa, confused. Then it hit her, Uja's babe! She ran the rest of the way and threw open the new doors.

Fraka sat near the rebuilt ovens, keeping warm.

Rianthe hurried down the long table aisle, Fraka's wide smile drawing her forward.

"Welcome home, sister. Would you like to meet your nephew?"

"More than anything," Rianthe said.

Fraka stood and settled the swaddled bundle of love in Rianthe's arms. She pulled the cloth back and stared into the dark eyes of her newest family member. "You're all right?" she asked Fraka, glancing up.

"I am more than all right. He was born two weeks ago. The birthing was not difficult. And he is such a good babe."

Staring into his eyes, Rianthe swore she could see Uja in the depths of them. His dark, fuzzy hair stood out in all directions. Rianthe laughed. "He has his father's hair."

Kaiden peeked over her shoulder at the newling. "He does," he said, approval in his smile and voice.

"I named him Ujami," Fraka said.

Baby Uja. Ujami. "I… I like that. A lot." Baby Ujami looked at her, his small hand wrapping itself around her thumb, and her heart. The sting of tears filled her eyes. Rianthe let them spill over. "He's so beautiful."

"Uja will always be with us in this babe," Fraka said, placing a hand on the blankets that surrounded her son. "I didn't think it was possible to love someone more than I loved your brother, but my heart overflows for this babe."

"Mine, too," Rianthe whispered, sitting down, unwilling to give Ujami up. "Mine, too."

They sat there talking for a long time, catching up. Villagers welcomed them one by one with hearty handshakes and not so careful pats on the back. Kaiden winced more than once at the enthusiasm of their welcomes.

A long while later, they stood before the beginnings of a stone structure. It was an incomplete shell with no roof or anything inside. Yet it already stood taller than the other buildings.

“What’s this going to be?” Rianthe asked.

“It’s the new druid’s tower,” Tevy said, pride evident in his voice. “It’s where you and Kaiden will live. Not together, of course. You know…” Tevy’s face burned crimson, and Rianthe was certain hers looked the same. Kaiden shuffled from foot to foot in obvious discomfort. “Not like *that*.”

“Not like anything, Tevy,” Rianthe said. “We can’t stay here. This place is not for us.”

“You have to.”

“Why?”

“Because you two, you’re the new druids of New Hope.”

“Oh, no, we’re not,” Rianthe said.

Kaiden stepped backwards, looking stunned at this new revelation.

“Yes, you are.”

Rianthe shook her head. “What makes you say this, Tevy?”

“Bhren told me.”

“Bhren!” both Kaiden and Rianthe exclaimed. “Bhren is dead.”

Tevy puffed up with stubbornness. “He told me you must have a druid’s keep and how to build it.”

“But…how…” Rianthe didn’t even know what to ask, she was so shocked.

“He came to me one day while I was in the remembrance fields.” Tevy had apparently decided he’d won this battle, because he pulled them inside to excitedly show them around. “See, two bedrooms,” he said. “And this doorway will go to a smaller building attached. That’ll be a bedroom for me. And it’s going to be two rooms tall, the same as Bhren’s!”

Rianthe wandered around the inside of the circular stone walls, running gloved hands over the rock. The floors were still dirt. Eventually, she knew, they would be covered in wood. In the center, a hollow post made of rocks cemented with mortar stood, halfway to the roof.

"That's my personal project."

"What is it?"

"It's an earth tower." He put his hands on either side of the column, running them up and down. "He told me how to build it and that it must be right here in this spot." He pointed to the ground. "He said it must go all the way to the tower room."

Rianthe's worry sense tingled. "What's an earth tower?" she asked quietly, afraid she already knew the answer. Kaiden stepped beside her, placing a hand on her shoulder.

"It will be full of dirt, tying your tower to the earth. He said it was part of your magic."

"No," she said, backing up into Kaiden. He squeezed her shoulder in reassurance, reminding her he was here, that he had her back. "No, no no," she said again, staring at the mini-tower. Bhren couldn't…wouldn't ask that of her.

Tevy looked decidedly worried now. "Did I do something wrong?"

Rianthe blew out a deep breath, trying to let the fear go. For Tevy's sake. "No, little brother, you did everything exactly as you were supposed to. And I'm grateful. It's just…"

"It's been a long journey," Kaiden said. "We're tired and could use some rest."

"Oh, oh, oh. Of course." Tevy smacked his leg. "I'm sorry. Yes, we've already made up beds for you." He blushed again. "Sis, you can sleep with me. Kaiden, there's single men's quarters on the far side of the village." Tevy shrugged. "Sorry, but it'll have to do until we can finish the tower."

"That will be fine," Kaiden said. His voice said more than his words. Rianthe was quite certain he planned to remain there even after the druid's keep was completed. Anything would be preferable to this tower. She completely agreed. Neither of them were old enough, wise enough, or hardened enough to lead like this. She wondered how the men would tolerate a warrior-woman joining them in their lodging. She absolutely did not want to live here. She was not, and would never be, Bhren.

The next morning, it seemed everyone in the village wanted to talk. It took a long time to tell their tale. It was well into the afternoon before Rianthe found some time to herself to think.

She wandered around, seeing all the changes to New Hope in the light of day. Eventually, she found herself in front of the druid's keep.

It didn't surprise her at all to find Kaiden standing there. Together, they stared at the stone wall.

"I don't feel like a druid," Kaiden finally said.

Rianthe shook her head. "Neither do I."

"We were both apprentices, sure. But isn't there some sort of ceremony or something that says 'All right, now you're a druid'?"

Rianthe shuddered. "No more ceremonies for me, thank you. As for this…well, I guess we'll just have to take it one day at a time."

"Together?" Kaiden reached for her hand.

His was warm, comfortable, like coming home. "Yes," Rianthe said, nodding as she squeezed back.

"Together."

EPILOGUE

"This is what you have searched for," Murdo said, hefting the bag of runes.

"You found this on the girl? Where is she?"

On the girl? "No. On a man. They'd been in his pocket."

"But always, I've seen…" Taegar's voice trailed off. "Bring them to me. I will question them."

"They are not with me."

"They are dead?"

"Yes," Murdo said. The winter must have taken care of them by now. He'd pushed his men to reach the caves quickly. Even then, it had still taken some time. And those two would not have been in any shape to travel anytime soon.

That fool Deakon had almost destroyed all his plans. Murdo had worked hard to get the distasteful man to trust him. In the end, Deakon's magic couldn't protect him from human greed.

Magic. Exactly what Murdo sought. Power beyond even his imaginings. She would give that to him. And he would not be some secondary consort to be toyed with. No, he wanted much more. He wanted it all. The only thing standing between him and his goal was the reward she must give him for what he'd found.

"Bring it to me," Taegar said, holding out an ethereal hand.

Murdo pulled back a bit, jangling the bag as he looked at it. "I think not."

The golden eyes narrowed. "You will give me this thing."

"I will."

She reached out again. Oh, yes, the Dark druid clearly desired what he held. A part of Murdo wondered what he might do with these baubles. Nothing until he could tap the powers that Taegar had. "Only once you've rewarded me," he continued.

Taegar's form grew taller, a full head above his own, and moved until she stood right in front of him, eyes glowing brightly. "I can take them from you."

"You won't." Murdo smiled. "Because you don't just want this bag. You want to know about the one who had them."

When her bright eyes became tinged with red, Murdo knew he had her where he wanted her. Was he playing with fire? Certainly. The reward would be worth it. Unlimited magic. Not the paltry amount Deakon had been given. He, Murdo, would share in Taegar's wealth of power. And live forever. He could almost feel the infusion already.

"My suggestion is this…" Murdo said. "You share

your power with me. Give me access to the wellspring you tap. Once I have tested its strength, I will give you the runes and tell you all I know.”

“I could convince you to tell me now,” she said, her voice low, menacing.

“But you won’t.” He changed his voice, made it more soothing. “Because deep down, you’ve wanted someone at your side. You don’t want to be lonely anymore. I am smart, and I am strong.”

Taegar floated away from Murdo, focusing on the white power welling up from the altar. Murdo gave her time to let his truth sink in. He glanced around, noticing for the first time that they were alone. There’d been several of Taegar’s cloaked acolytes in the cavern when he’d first arrived.

That she wanted to handle this negotiation in private encouraged him further. Never let others see your weakness, he thought, knowing he had become hers. He smiled. “What is your decision?”

Taegar turned to him slowly. “So be it,” she said in a voice dripping with an unnatural sweetness. “You want power, I’ll give you power.” Her arm shot out, power arcing toward him. His clothes disappeared and the runes fell to the floor. Murdo puffed up his chest and held out his hands, feeling the power fill him. Heady power, strength beyond imagining began to burn within him. It grew and grew until he could take no more. Still the power came, bringing intense pain with it.

“Who did you take these runes from?”

“Deakon,” he gasped as he fell to the floor.

Taegar stood over him, pulsing white light still pouring magic into him. “Who,” she said with slow precision, “did Deakon take the runes from?”

"From…a young man…New Hope. Stop. Can't…take…more. Must…stop."

Murdo stared into Taegar's eyes and saw the truth there. She would not stop. The last thing he saw before fire consumed him were her eyes, bright with fury and triumph.

Within moments, he was no more than ash on the floor of the cavern.

Taegar leaned on the altar, weaker than she'd ever imagined she could be. She'd gone too far with him and now paid the price. Soon, she would have unimaginable power. Unlike that fool Murdo, she knew how to manage it.

She opened the bag of runes and poured them out into her hand. Reached into the white magic, waiting for the dam to break and the power to bind to her, to pour in, hers to command for all time.

The tower of white flowing up from the altar sparked brighter than she'd ever seen, but only for a moment, then dimmed. Time that could not be measured passed with no change to the weakness that consumed Taegar. Finally, she pulled back, knowing something was amiss. She stared at the runes. Either they were not the talisman, or something else was needed.

Taegar screamed. She'd waited so long for this. Over one hundred years, and it had been almost in her grasp. Using power she should not expend, angry red bolts struck the walls of the cave over and over again. Rocks crumbled and fell all around her.

When she stopped, half the cave had been destroyed, including the altar. She knew what she must do. She pulled herself up, calling her faithful to join her. Five of them entered the cave, disregarding its ruined state in their stupor.

Find him for me, she told them each. *Bring him to me.*

As one, they turned and left, their mission the only thing of importance to them.

Taegar moved toward her crypt, setting protection wards as she went.

Again she must sleep. When would this end? When would she have what she desired?

She would revive, her power renewed. And soon, she would have the young man from New Hope in her grasp, and with him, the final piece of the puzzle.

Then he would die.

The End.

Thank you for reading **Survival**, the first book of the Earth Legacy series. If you liked Kaiden, you'll learn more about him in the second story, **Enlightenment**. If you enjoyed this book, please consider leaving a review on your preferred buying site, and know that it would be greatly appreciated.

For new release information and news about Laurie Ryan, please join her newsletter. Sign up available at www.laurieryanauthor.com

AUTHOR'S NOTE AND ACKNOWLEDGEMENTS

I hope you enjoyed the first story in what has, for me, been an epic adventure. Growing up reading authors like J.R.R. Tolkien, Anne McCaffrey, and Terry Brooks, I often had my head in otherworlds. The opportunity to create my own otherworld is a lifelong dream for me. And I couldn't have done it without a lot of support.

To my critique partners, Lavada and Faye, thank you, thank you, thank you. You let me cry and laugh and rage through this process without complaint, and you smoothed out well, everything. To my beta readers, Kathy and Alaina for helping me see the finishing touches needed. To Nadine, for being very patient with my ellipses and em dashes.

To Bethany, who's ability to drill down to what's visually important helped me find a title for this series. And for designing a cover that made me cry when I first saw it.

I strove to pay homage to druid beliefs in this story because of their unfailing love and respect for nature. While most of the terms in this story are runic in nature, I chose *awen* to represent Earth's magic. It translates as something like flowing spirit or inspiration. It felt completely right for this series, which is all about listening to the earth as it tries to help us all find a way to survive.

I believe we are near the point where drastic changes

will be needed to ensure the continued existence of future generations. This story, this series, comes out of that belief. I hope you enjoyed it.

Thank you.

BOOKLIST

Contemporary romance stories by Laurie Ryan

Fantasy by Laurie Ryan

Survival
Enlightenment
Birthright

Tropical Persuasions Series
Stolen Treasures
Pirate's Promise
Dare To Love

Standalone

Northern Lights
Healing Love
(also part of the Holiday Magic anthology)
Lost and Found

Women's Fiction by Laurie Ryan

Show Me

ABOUT THE AUTHOR

Laurie Ryan writes fantasy and contemporary romance. Growing up a devoted reader, Laurie Ryan immersed herself in the diverse works of authors like Tolkien and Woodiwiss. She is passionate about every aspect of a book: beginning, middle, and end. She can't arrive to a movie five minutes late, has never been able to read the end of a book before the beginning, and is a strong believer in reading the book before seeing the movie.

Laurie lives in the beautiful Pacific Northwest, in the shadow of Mt. Rainier and a short drive to beach-walking next to the Pacific Ocean, with her handsome, he-can-fix-anything husband and their gray, seventeen-pound cat, Dude.

www.laurieryanauthor.com